MW00629099

LONG LIVE THE BARON

INCONVENIENT SCANDALS
BOOK ONE

NINA JARRETT

ROGUE
PRESS

To Dee, the truest friend I have ever met.
Your honor knows no bounds.

DOWNLOAD TWO FREE BOOKS!

FREE GIFTS FOR SUBSCRIBERS:
Two captivating prequel novellas by Nina Jarrett full of
unrequited feelings and steamy romance.

**A writer for fighting for his muse. A captain returned
from war, searching for his wife.
Two delightful novellas about the power of true love.**

* * *

London, 1818. Dinah Honeyfield can't wait any longer. In
love with her family's long-term houseguest, she's
determined to get him to reveal his affections before her rich
industrialist father marries her off.
Lord John Pettigrew gave up his birthright to follow his
dreams. And with nothing to offer a potential wife, the
aspiring author despairs he'll never be able to win the hand
of the one who's been his muse.

Can they rewrite their future and plot a path to forever?

* * *

Mrs. Lydia Lewis has given up on broken promises.
Marrying her soulmate only to be attacked during his
heartbreaking absence, she finds refuge as an incognito ducal
housekeeper.
Captain Jacob Lewis is angry and hurt. Returning from
military service to discover his spouse has vanished into thin
air, he begins an almost hopeless search to bring her home.
Can this star-crossed pair reclaim newlywed bliss?

* * *

Interview With the Duke and *The Captain's Wife* are the
delightful prequels to the Inconvenient Brides Regency
romance series. If you like worthy heroes, fast-paced plots,
and enduring connections, then you'll adore Nina Jarrett's
charming collection.

Subscribe for instant access to these twin tales of passion:
NinaJarrett.com/free

PROLOGUE

"The rise of the birds in their flight is a sign of an ambush.
Frightened beasts indicate a sudden attack is coming."
Sun Tzu, L'Art de la Guerre (The Art of War)

* * *

JULY 20, 1821, JUST AFTER 6 A.M.

*T*he baron is dead.

Brendan Ridley staggered through the gloom of the study, slumping into an armchair to stare at the corpse lying on the study floor. A pool of blood framed Lord Josiah Ridley's head while his sightless eyes stared into the infinite abyss. The mahogany desk was in disarray, drawers hanging open and papers strewn to suggest that someone had searched its contents in haste. Candles flickered in the early morning light as if to punctuate the macabre scene with grotesque emphasis.

Brendan rubbed his temples in agitation, realizing with dread that he had just inherited the title of Baron of Filminster.

Long live the baron.

A heavy dose of irony accompanied the thought. How did he feel about this revelation? Pained? Numb? Relieved? Indifferent? The man had never been a true father to Brendan. And on Brendan's twenty-first birthday, he had found out why when he had been banished from the family home in Filminster.

Lord Josiah Ridley was not, in fact, his parent but his uncle, who had prevented a scandal by stepping into his brother's place as both baron and groom to Brendan's mother. His true father, Josiah's older brother, had been thrown from a horse just weeks before his wedding, and Brendan had entered the world a mere seven months later.

He and the baron had not spoken in years, Brendan living in this London townhouse while the baron remained far away at Baydon Hall in Somerset. Until, unexpectedly, the man had found the fortitude to make the journey to London for the much-anticipated coronation.

Whoever had killed his uncle-father had chosen the worst of weapons, considering the baron's mortal terror of all things equine. The lord had not left his country seat in two decades because of his deathly fear of horses, yet the murderer had apparently clubbed the older man to death with a heavy sculpture now lying near the body—a sculpture of a jolted horse rearing up. Evidence of blood on the muzzle proved that the baron's notion that he would die at the hand —hoof—of such a creature was not unfounded.

Brendan groaned, rubbing his temples once more at the realization that this situation was likely going to get worse ... much worse.

He would wager everything he possessed that later this morning he would be accused of patricide, and he strongly suspected that Lady Slight would not be coming forward to provide him with an alibi.

CHAPTER 1

"He will win whose army is animated by the same spirit throughout all its ranks."
Sun Tzu, L'Art de la Guerre (The Art of War)

* * *

JULY 19, 1821, ONE DAY EARLIER

"*L*ily!"

Her heart sank. Lily Abbott positioned her silver fork on her plate and, pinning a broad smile on her face, turned to face her mother. She did not miss her brother pressing his twitching lips together, his chocolate brown eyes dancing with humor as he lifted his cup of coffee for a sip.

It was Lily's third Season—a fact that was causing increasing panic in Mama, who wanted her to expediently make a match.

Lily had hoped that Aidan's recent return from his Grand

Tour would split Lady Moreland's relentless pursuit to wed her off. However, her brother's lack of matrimonial plans was apparently more acceptable than his unwed sister.

"Mama—" The cheerful tone of excitement was deliberate. Lily had always been exuberant, but she had been cultivating it as a shield to thwart her mother's efforts. She had found if she chattered for long enough, it made Mama quite lose her train of thought so that Lily could steer the conversation to safer topics and make her escape. "—you look lovely! Your gown is immaculate, and the beadwork is so intricate. You will quite distract everyone from the King's coronation robes with such a glorious ensemble!"

Aidan snorted quietly behind her as Lady Moreland stopped to preen for a moment, smoothing her hands over her skirts as she peered down at her coronation finery. Lily's flattery was not unfounded—her mother was exceptionally handsome with her sleek brown hair offset by the pearl-studded gold and red velvet coronet denoting her rank as viscountess.

But the distraction only worked for a moment before her mother remembered why she had been looking for her daughter.

"What happened with Lord Ashby?"

"We danced together. It was a waltz, and the music was sublime. I think the musicians were highly skilled and I could have danced all night—" Behind her, Aidan snorted quietly again, clearly muffling laughter as Lily babbled on. Her brother obviously knew what she was doing.

"Lily!" her mother interjected with a sharp tone.

She shut her mouth and smiled innocently. "Yes, Mama?"

Lady Moreland appeared unwilling to tolerate Lily's attempts to change the subject. The coronation had likely brought marital prospects to the forefront of her mind, and

Lily was afraid she could not divert the direction of the conversation.

Glancing over her shoulder, she threw a pleading look to her brother, who was watching while continuing to drink his coffee.

"Lord Ashby was quite taken with you, but after he danced with you, his mother informed me he had quite lost interest. What did you talk about while you were dancing?"

Lily lifted a hand to rub her earlobe as she sought an answer. Her ability to obfuscate with babble seemed to be waning today, which was not surprising considering how tired she was from returning home at dawn.

"I simply remarked on the talent of the musicians and how fine the servants' livery was. I may have mentioned how glorious the ballroom appeared, bedecked with hothouse flowers and—"

Her mother groaned. "Did you chatter the entire dance?"

"I suppose I might have."

"Oh, Lily! How will you ever make a match if you will not stop blabbering like a fool?"

"Mother, I think we should acknowledge that Lord Ashby and Lily are ill-suited."

Lily's heart leapt with relief when Aidan interrupted. Ever since her cousin, Sophia, had left their household to marry the Earl of Saunton the year before, Lily had had to contend with her mother's matchmaking unaided. Now that her brother had returned home, perhaps they could work together to thwart Lady Moreland's impatience so Lily could make the match she wished for. One founded in love and mutual admiration, such as the one her cousin enjoyed with the earl, rather than one based on suitability and her mother's expectations.

Not that Papa would require her to make a match she did

not wish for, but Mama's pressure was enough to make life distinctly uncomfortable.

Lady Moreland frowned at her son, clearly confused. "Whatever do you mean?"

"Lord Ashby, if I am not mistaken, is an utter bore who only speaks of horseflesh and hounds. Not to mention he is thirty years her senior and has several children from his previous marriages. Lily and he have no commonalities between them and would have nothing to discuss at the breakfast table."

"Matches have proved successful over less. And Lily's babbling must be reined in."

"I find Lily's conversation delightful and her optimism infectious. She amuses me during even the most melancholy of days. If Lord Ashby does not appreciate her for the jewel she is, and will cast her off after a single dance, then he does not deserve her."

Their mother relaxed, evidently disinclined to argue with her oldest child. "You could introduce more of your friends to her, Aidan."

"Perhaps I shall."

Lily had been casting looks back and forth from her mother to her brother over her shoulder and was quite relieved that the heat had left their little quarrel. She winked a thank you to her brother, who smiled in return before his eyes shifted to peer over her shoulder. His jaw dropped open in amazement.

Lily spun back to see what had captured his attention and clapped a hand over her mouth to hold back a giggle while her eyes widened in surprise.

Lady Moreland burst out laughing, clutching her midriff in an uncustomary display of emotion as she beheld her husband, who had entered the room.

The older version of Aidan, Lord Moreland was a handsome man in his fifties, with graying brown hair and a square jaw, who towered over most men. Which made his attire ever more unsuitable.

King George IV was known for his ostentatious fashion sense, which was the only explanation why, for his coronation, he had instructed the College of Arms to exhibit the strictly required dress for the lords attending.

Lord Moreland was garbed in antique dress hitherto only seen in portraits of lords long since deceased. He was wearing a tight-fitting doublet with shining buttons. His gold and white breeches formed a puffy skirt, which stopped at his upper thighs to reveal a long expanse of white-stockinged legs, and he wore heeled shoes. A red velvet cape lined with ermine and the ruff at his neck completed the humiliation of his costume.

"Good Lord! I have never been so happy that I am a mere heir and not the holder of the title!" blurted Aidan.

Lily lost her fight to hold back her reaction, shaking with glee as her father turned a ruddy shade and rolled his eyes at his family's blatant disrespect. "The other options were worse, in my estimation. My tailor insisted this would suit me best."

"That is hard to believe," gasped Lily as she struggled for air.

Lord Moreland looked over to his daughter and chuckled in response. "Perhaps he advised me for his own amusement."

When Mama finally calmed down enough to speak, their earlier discussion appeared to be forgotten. "Aidan, we will be out late, so you must stay in tonight and keep Lily company."

Aidan nodded. "I promise to keep an eye on my little sister and ensure no harm befalls her, Mother."

Lily smiled in joy. Since returning home, Aidan had been

so busy cavorting with his friends, they had barely spent any time together. She wanted to hear about his travels to the Continent and the adventures he had had in Florence and Rome, but he had been out almost every night.

Lily knew entertaining a younger sister was not the most appealing prospect for an energetic young buck such as Aidan, but she missed spending time with him as they had once done. The disparity of their sexes and the expectations on young ladies, compared to young men, had become more obvious now that they had both entered adulthood, and she yearned for the simpler time of their youth before he had left England.

"I expect you to keep that promise, young man!" Their mother's words were stern, but her expression was affectionate.

It thrilled the entire Abbott family to be reunited with Aidan after his extended travels abroad, and Lily was pleased to have a reprieve from her busy social schedule to enjoy the evening with her brother. She had been so lonely since Sophia had married, and an evening with Aidan was a wonderful prospect.

* * *

BRENDAN DREW A DEEP BREATH, then reached out and opened the door to his rooms. He could put it off no longer. Lord Filminster had arrived two days earlier, his first visit to London in as much as two decades, and demanded Brendan's presence downstairs today. The baron had sent word of his imminent arrival, but Brendan was certain he would cancel the trip, so he had been surprised despite the warning.

Most of Brendan's acquaintances would describe him as an affable young man who always had a friendly word for everyone he met. If he were honest, he caroused too frequently with his friends. Not to mention, his days were decidedly idle. But he took the time to lift the spirits of the people around him, and he enjoyed visiting his sister and brother-in-law, the Duke of Halmesbury, as well as his nephew, Jasper.

Yet seeing Lord Filminster for the first time in some years had reminded him of the wrenching anxiety that his uncle raised in the region of his gut, which was currently twisting and writhing in his belly as he began his reluctant walk down the hall.

Fortunately, he had not seen the baron much, but today he was to meet with him in his study. The baron's study.

Dammit, it is my study!

Brendan had been working out of it since leaving Filminster on his twenty-first birthday, and it was rotten luck that his uncle-father had finally found the courage to leave his estate. The only explanation for showing such fortitude was that the baron was a vainglorious buffoon whose craving to attend the prestigious coronation had finally outweighed his fear of travel.

Lucky me.

With an increasing sense of dread, he began his descent, the worn carpet beneath his boots speaking to how long it had been since the townhouse had been renovated while the wide wooden boards creaked in protest at his weight.

Why would the old man bother to keep the townhouse properly maintained?

It was a source of irritation to Brendan. One of many. That he was beholden to the baron, a mean-spirited old goat, was galling. Had events transpired as they should have, Brendan's own father would be Lord Filminster and Brendan himself would be a valued heir. Instead, he was an orphan and obligated to obey his uncle so he could access his allowance.

As he reached the front hall, Brendan's thoughts flittered to the last time he and the baron had corresponded. Three years earlier, Brendan had fancied himself in love with a lovely young woman until Lord Filminster had written to her father and informed him that Brendan would be cut off if a match was made. The baron had deemed the young woman unsuitable, being from a wealthy but untitled family.

Brendan would have proceeded despite the baron's interference, for he would eventually inherit the title and it would restore his finances. But her father had abruptly ended their courtship, so Brendan had buried his sorrows in the arms of a friendly widow, who had been flirting with him for some time, and vowed to never make a match that his uncle approved of. Unfortunately, he was afraid that their conversation today was to address this subject because he knew of no other reason for the baron to require his presence.

Shaking the thoughts from his head, Brendan noticed he had arrived at the study. He raised a heavy hand to rap his knuckles on the door.

"Come," intoned a disinterested voice.

Brendan entered and closed the door behind him, before finding his uncle standing by the fireplace. He choked back a laugh when he saw how the old man was dressed, raising a hand to cover his mouth as if he were coughing.

The baron was in heeled court shoes, which did little to raise his diminutive height in stature, his spindly legs revealed in white stockings while his white and gold striped trunk hose, an antiquated style of short voluminous breeches, ballooned around his hips. His doublet was form-fitting, which revealed a potbelly spilling over his codpiece while a velvet and ermine cape was fitted over his shoulders. A ruff around his neck made him appear to be all shoulders and head, while the gilt circlet on his head did nothing to disguise his thinning hair, which Brendan noted was brushed forward in the style of Napoleon. The baron was at once gaudy and clownish in the unbecoming attire.

Lord Filminster's beady eyes narrowed in suspicion, and he tugged at his doublet with a smugness that belied any awareness of what a humorous figure he cut. But the baron had always had a poor sense of fashion, and no one could accuse him of being a Beau Brummell, so perhaps he thought his attire to be handsome. Not for the first time, Brendan was grateful that he did not view the world through his uncle-father's eyes. He did not think he would enjoy the perspective.

"There you are, Ridley." Brendan grimaced. Was he going to be addressed as a vague acquaintance, then? "Is it customary for you to leave your rooms so late in the day?"

Brendan once again bit back a laugh. The man probably did not know how to pull on his own stockings, but he was to lecture on tardiness? Forcing a pleasant smile, Brendan walked forward to sprawl into an armchair facing his uncle. From past experience, he knew the old man was like a dog with a bone. If Brendan revealed any reaction to any of his vicious nips, the baron would gnaw at the offending subject relentlessly to wheedle further reactions.

The trick was to keep a friendly face and steadfast composure. He had not missed these biting conversations in the least, even when he had pined for his half-sister who was the sole family connection he cared about. Fortunately, Annabel and he had reunited after her marriage, Lord Filminster no longer able to keep them apart once she gained her autonomy.

"While I am in Town, I am arranging for you to meet suitable women."

Brendan kept the smile on his face, but mentally cursed. How long was the baron remaining? "My social calendar is currently filled—engagements with unsuitable women and whatnot."

Lord Filminster clenched his jaw at the supercilious tone, and Brendan squashed a kindling of delight to have raised a reaction from the man who loathed him so. "Those types of engagements will have to wait until you marry."

"You mean I should pursue the type of marriage you were attempting to force on Annabel? Her prospective husband knocking boots on the side while she waits for him in the country?"

The baron clenched his small fists, looking ready to stomp his foot in the manner of the old German fairy tale about Rumpelstiltskin. Brendan could only wish for his disappearance in such an event as the imp had done in the story.

"It is the way of high society," his uncle responded defensively.

"Not according to the man she actually married—*the duke*."

"The duke is obsessed with the hoyden for no reason I can fathom. She is a useless girl with no feminine accomplishments."

"I am not sure about that. My friends seem quite impressed with the duchess."

Lord Filminster broke eye contact, looking irate. He was not accustomed to his heir defending himself. Brendan had been a cowering boy the last time they had met in person, but he had found a measure of self-confidence in the intervening years, despite his uncle's attempts to belittle him at every turn in his youth.

"We will meet Miss Hartnett with her family tomorrow night for supper. And you are to meet with me first thing tomorrow morning so I can provide you a list of engagements we will be attending together."

"Miss Agnes Hartnett? She is seventeen years old!" Brendan knew he should not react, but his exclamation had escaped from his lips before he could stop it.

"And the daughter of a viscount."

"You mean the child of a viscount?"

The baron smirked, evidently enjoying Brendan's discomfort. "All the better for your pursuits with merry widows."

Brendan wanted to roll his eyes. He had no intention of pursuing the type of marriage where he and his wife would be strangers passing in the hall. When he married, an intelligent and beguiling woman would be his partner, and he would not stray, but this was not the time to reveal such ideals.

He needed to meet with the duke so he could formulate a plan to get rid of the baron as expediently as possible now that his motives had been revealed. Annabel and Halmesbury were among the few people who understood the baron, but unfortunately for Brendan, they would be occupied with obligations surrounding the coronation, so he would need to tolerate the old man's meddling for a couple more days.

"When would you like to meet?"

"I expect you to be here at first light."

Brendan forced an affable grin and stood up. "I will see you first thing, then."

The baron waved a hand in a gesture of dismissal, which Brendan took as his opportunity to escape. And think.

As he left the study, he almost ran into Michaels, their London butler, who was standing right outside the door. The older man straightened to his full height, which was several inches shy of Brendan's, bending his neck back awkwardly to stare down his nose like the little French emperor. With a haughty sniff, Michaels stalked away, leaving Brendan to wonder if the scornful servant might have been eavesdropping on the conversation.

* * *

WHEN LILY CAME DOWN for supper, she found her brother in the front hall. He was dressed to go out, with a beaver on his head, a coat slung over his shoulders, and gloves in hand.

Her spirits plummeted in disappointment. "You are not staying in with me?"

Aidan grabbed her hand in a cajoling manner as he smiled down at her. Lily cursed her height. Her brother was towering over her, and all she could do was stand about with the appearance of a child because she barely cleared five feet. If she displayed any anger that he was abandoning her for the evening, she would simply appear to be throwing a tantrum.

"You do not mind do you, Lily Billy? It is just that my friends have invited me to enjoy a game of whist at our club, and all the titled nobs are occupied with the coronation, so we will have the run of the place."

"I was looking forward to catching up, Aidan! You have barely spent a moment with me since you returned to London. I am going to be dragged to the country soon for a house party, and Mama will be throwing titled gentlemen at me every step I take."

"I swear I will stay in tomorrow, but tonight is too unprecedented to pass up. You would not want me to miss out, would you? Not after I distracted Mother from her ideas about Lord Ashby?"

"I did not know that would be an excuse to abandon me!"

"It is not abandonment. It is merely a postponement."

Lily relented. Aidan was clearly committed to his plans, and she did not wish to stand in the way of his fun. She wished she could go with him, but she was a young single lady and not permitted to do anything interesting. If only she could find a gentleman whom she wished to marry. As a married woman, her whole world would open up, but she was unwilling to compromise her standards by settling for an old or inferior gentleman. "Oh, very well! But I expect you to regale me with stories of your travels tomorrow night."

Aidan lifted a hand to chuck her on the chin. "We will spend the entire evening together in the library, Lily Billy. Thank you for this. You are a brick!"

Lily sighed, smiling as she watched him drawing on his gloves. "I am holding you to that, Aidan. No begging off tomorrow night."

Once he departed, Lily requested her supper tray be brought to the front drawing room, which overlooked the houses across the street and encompassed an oblique view of the square. She would feel silly eating alone at the dining table, and the window seat in the drawing room was her favorite reading spot. She could not help reflecting that she had been doing far too much reading this past year.

It was better than fending off elderly lords at a ball, but still. After three years, it was time she met a genuinely eligible man so she could enter a courtship, but that seemed as likely as sprouting a tail, after her third Season of no success. Where were the truly intriguing gentlemen? Not on the marriage mart, it would seem.

CHAPTER 2

"Carefully study the welfare of your men and do not overload them. Focus your energy and build up your strength. Keep your army constantly on the move and make unfathomable plans."
Sun Tzu, L'Art de la Guerre (The Art of War)

* * *

$\mathcal{L}$ily had called for Nancy, her father's former nursemaid, to sit with her while she worked on her embroidery. The dear woman was advanced in years. She was also as deaf as a post, which suited Lily because she could chatter her private thoughts to the servant without any concern for them being heard or remembered. This was infinitely preferable to being alone or, heaven forfend, chattering to herself like a madwoman. With Sophia gone, Lily had fallen into the habit of jabbering to Nancy far too frequently.

Dash it! She desperately needed to find a suitable gentleman. No debutante was meant to wander the social events for this long.

"It is all rather trying, Nancy. I have discovered that chattering to the gentlemen who are unsuitable has chased them away as I had planned. The problem is now I babble more than I ever have, so when I meet a gentleman who might be interesting, I become nervous and overtalk more than I would under normal circumstances."

"I thought you already attend formal dances, Miss Lily?" Nancy had looked up from her sewing, confusion on her wizened old face and her mobcap askew in her white hair, which gave her the appearance of having just risen from bed.

Lily hesitated, running her words back through her head before suppressing a giggle. "NORMAL CIRCUMSTANCES ... not formal dances."

The old woman nodded without comprehension before lowering her head to continue darning with arthritic fingers. Papa had many times attempted to pension off his beloved childhood servant, but Nancy was adamant that she wanted to remain working in their household and he had not the heart to reject her wishes. Her duties were minimal, mostly darning and companionship to Lily when she was wont.

"Lord Ashby was scared off, but then later that night, I met his son, Mr. Ashby. The gentleman was quite fine, and I was excited to share a dance with him. But instead of getting to know each other, I babbled like a fool about the flavor of the orgeat, which I thought was exceptional, until Mr. Ashby's eyes glazed over. He hurried me back to Mama and ran off as if his father's hounds were chasing him. How am I to make a meaningful connection when my nerves trip me up so? It was all very disappointing!"

"Mr. Ashby was pointing? Innit rude?" Nancy's raspy voice interjected.

Lily blinked, staring down at her needlework for a second while she tried to think what Nancy thought she had heard. "DISAPPOINTING. MY BABBLING ... is disappointing."

Nancy shrugged. "Yes, miss."

Lily gazed sightlessly at her floss, admitting the truth of it. She had quite been looking forward to meeting Mr. Ashby, a handsome gentleman of a similar age to herself. One of the very few braving the marriage mart in search of a bride, and she had frightened him off within seconds of meeting him.

Biting her lip, she sighed heavily. She needed to find a match so her life could begin, but she did not want to settle for someone for whom she shared no affinity. Her unfortunate habit of overtalking was a gift when it came to warding off unwanted attentions, a crafty stratagem she had developed after reading the book on military strategy her cousin had given her. But craftiness did not help her be any more measured or composed when she met a man she could genuinely consider marrying and a certain amount of shyness settled in.

Most men thought she was a silly flibbertigibbet. After three Seasons, she suspected they might be right. She was barely five feet short, had the general appearance of a young girl dressed in the ridiculous white and pastels Mama insisted she wear despite her over twenty years on this earth, and being a chatterbox reinforced the impression that she was merely an exuberant child.

"But I shall eventually meet the right gentleman. I could meet my future husband anytime, and be betrothed within two weeks. I simply must persevere. Sophia met the earl only twice, and they wed within a week of their second dance so my luck could change at any moment."

Lily was relieved that her usual optimism had caught up with her. Her thoughts had been taking a cheerless turn, and she did not want to dwell on the passage of time, nor her shortcomings. She was bright and friendly. When she wed, she could finally wear the rich colors that would accentuate her brown hair and chocolate eyes. Until then, she would need to persist in her quest to find the gentleman who would find her irrepressibly charming and make an offer to Papa.

"Is someone betrothed?" Nancy's question brought her back to the present.

"NO, NANCY! BUT I WISH TO BE. To the right man, of course."

Nancy nodded politely, clearly not understanding.

"Perhaps now that Aidan is home, he could introduce me to some younger gentlemen. I wish to make a match with someone I will spend a lifetime with, not an old man who can barely hold himself up without my assistance, or is as old or older than Papa."

"You wish to eat your supper?"

Lily frowned at the fabric in her hand, trying to work out what Nancy was going on about. "NOT SUPPER—PAPA!"

"Master Hugh is home?" Nancy swung her head round to the door to look for her young—old—charge, causing Lily to burst into a fit of giggles. Aidan could not leave her alone tomorrow night, because if she did not soon have a forthright conversation with someone who could actually hear her, she was sure to be committed to Bedlam before she could meet her match.

Noting the old maid stifling a yawn, Lily took pity and sent Nancy off with an affectionate shooing. She could not formally send her to bed so early in the evening, but she knew Nancy would find a comfortable spot to doze off until bedtime. Anyone who stumbled upon the old maid sleeping would simply turn a blind eye and wander off to a different part of the townhouse.

* * *

BRENDAN WAS ENJOYING a snifter of fine French brandy at his club when a horde of young men came in. With the lords occupied by the coronation, evidently the clubs were being overrun by green fools taking advantage of the usuals not being present to take the prime seating nor frown at their youthful antics.

A particularly spirited group of dandies dressed in elegant black coats and trousers were standing at the betting book, placing demented wagers about the King's coronation attire. Apparently, one of the gents was privy to the details.

Brendan had come for peace, to think what to do to get the baron off his back, and to enjoy a drink. Which had been a good plan until the lads had shown up to spoil his plan. He rubbed his temples, exasperated, as the group debated how much had been incurred for the crown hatband of George IV's plumed headpiece.

"Eight thousand pounds! I win!" A mild roar went up before an argument broke out between two of the bucks.

Brendan recalled making a few stupid wagers in his younger days, but carousing with his peers had been wearing thin this past year or so. Reuniting with his sister three years earlier, and observing the intimate connection between her and the duke, had sparked thoughts about the importance of family, especially with the arrival of his charming little nephew into the world.

The ennui with his current circumstances had really set in when one of his closest friends, the Earl of Saunton, had unexpectedly wed Miss Sophia Hayward the year before. Almost immediately, the earl's younger brother, Peregrine Balfour, had willingly raced into the parson's noose with a young woman from the country and left London to rusticate in Somerset.

Genuine friends were thin on the ground these days, with only him and Lord Trafford left from their group to represent the bachelors about Town. Reflecting on this, Brendan recalled he had gained a certain ace of spades from the events that had unfolded, which was an unexpected perk. Lady Slight had been so outraged at Perry's rejection in favor of a country mouse that Brendan had finally won a place in her bed after a prolonged pursuit of the intoxicating widow.

As each of his friends had done, he would one day like to find a woman who challenged and inspired him, but today was not that day and the baron would not be the one who shepherded him into a wedding. He would follow that path when he was good and ready—and found the right woman.

And not a moment earlier.

No one would make such a monumental decision on his behalf.

Brendan finished his brandy and stood, looking about for anyone he knew, but most of the set were a couple years younger than him. He might be only twenty-seven, but he felt decidedly mature compared to this bunch.

Pulling on his fob, he checked his timepiece, exhaling in relief when he noted the time. There was a certain scarlet minx on Grosvenor Square who had intimated that his spending the night would be well received. Pulling on his gloves and gathering his things, Brendan headed for the entrance, sidestepping when one boy stepped back with a loud exclamation, oblivious to who might be passing, in the usual manner of someone who had imbibed too much.

Brendan bit back his irritation, reminding himself that Harriet would welcome him to her bed this evening. He might as well take the opportunity to enjoy himself before he had to deal with the old man in the morning.

Behind him, the boy fell to the ground with a loud thump, and Brendan came to a halt. Looking about, he noticed none of the boy's cronies were paying the least attention to their friend passed out on the floor. Stepping back, Brendan dropped to his knee to assess the youth's condition.

Oblivious.

Peering at him closely, Brendan thought he might recognize the youthful face. Frowning, he tapped his cheek, which made the lad open his bleary blue eyes and attempt to focus on Brendan.

"Ashby, is that you?"

"Sizzme." Ashby's speech was garbled.

"Lad, you are not old enough to be here! How did you get in?"

The boy raised a limp arm to point at the group writing wagers in the betting book. "Mabruther."

Brendan whipped his head around to find that the older Mr. Ashby was indeed howling with laughter a few feet away. Shaking his head, he rose to his feet to approach the brother. "Ashby, your brother needs to be taken home."

"Bugger off. We are busy."

Brendan clenched his jaw and his fists, but taking in the brother's glassy eyes, he realized that the older Ashby was too inebriated to know to whom he was speaking. Or to do anything about his family lying on the floor. Or to be of any use at all.

Easing his stance, and growling in the back of his throat, Brendan returned to check on the younger brother who was passed out and snoring on the floor. The lad was no older than fourteen, if memory served, despite an obvious recent growth spurt that had added many inches to his heavyset frame. He had no place carousing with his older brother, but Lord Ashby was clearly too occupied with the coronation to be aware that his youngest son had been taken out on the Town by his heir. The club staff must have missed the much younger boy tailing the university-aged men.

Shaking his head in disgust, Brendan reached down and pulled young Ashby into a sitting position. He could hardly leave a child passed out in public. Certainly, if it were his family, he would appreciate someone stepping in and not leaving it to some strangers in a club. And the older Ashby was far too drunk to take care of his little brother.

Brendan heaved the heavy boy over his shoulder, then rose with effort to his feet, praying young Ashby did not hurl his guts without warning after imbibing so excessively.

Ye Gods, the lad must weigh twelve stone at least!

If the Ashby brothers had not arrived in their own carriage, Brendan was going to be a little late to Lady Slight because he would have to make a stop at the Ashby town-house on the way. Hopefully, there was a brawny servant on duty to assist him to get his unconscious load into bed, before Brendan left a note for the boy's father to apprise him of what had happened.

* * *

LILY LICKED her fingertip to turn the page of her book. The encounter with Mama earlier that day had been a moment of poor preparation on her part, and she had been fortunate that Aidan had intervened. The situation had compelled her to pick up her book for another read.

Each time she read *L'Art de la Guerre* by the general, Sun Tzu, she gained a deeper understanding of the military concepts which improved her skills managing her mother and undesirable suitors. It was why she had developed a habit of regularly revisiting the book.

Perhaps I should apply the philosophy of winning battles to the task of courtship, rather than the avoidance of such?

It was an interesting thought.

She was ensconced in the window seat of the drawing room. Her parents would be out until the morning, and after a Season of late nights, returning home at dawn, Lily knew she would not fall asleep until much later. The window allowed her to read without the oil lamps until sunset, at which time the servants had entered the room to light them up throughout the room. She had barely noticed, so engrossed in mentally translating the ideas from French, that the shift from sunset to night had passed her by.

Straightening up, Lily kneaded her neck, which had grown stiff from the position she was settled in. Peering out into the evening, she noted that the streetlamps were now lit, but the roadway was empty.

The carved ormolu clock over the mantelpiece chimed, methodically announcing the hour to be eleven o'clock. As the final chime died away, Lily heard carriage wheels striking the packed dirt of the road. She turned to watch with curiosity as a carriage bearing a coat of arms that was vaguely familiar entered the square, frowning when she observed it come to a stop in front of the Abbott townhouse.

Who could be visiting them, or rather her, at this hour without a prior invitation?

A footman scrambled down from the front and came around to open the door and lower the steps, before a polished Hessian boot emerged from the shadows inside the carriage. Soon buckskins were revealed, draped over the muscled thighs of a man, while Lily shook her head in amazement. Had she wished a gentleman into existence?

As she peered down, the lamp light revealed an unlikely person.

"It is Mr. Ridley," she whispered to the empty drawing room. He would have no reason to visit her, despite how much she might desire such an outcome.

Mr. Ridley was tall. Not quite as tall as Aidan or her papa, but perhaps as much as a foot taller than herself. He had a healthy bronze tone to his skin, in her memory, at least, because the night did not reveal such a feature, and the chiseled face of a handsome aristocrat. But it was the glorious chestnut curls that framed his face that had captured her fancy the few times she had encountered him.

He had always been friendly and tolerant of her chatter, but she could not be certain if it was only because they shared a distant connection—his sister being married to the duke, who was cousin to the Earl of Saunton, who was married to Lily's cousin, Sophia. Nevertheless, it did not signify because Mr. Ridley was obviously not on the marriage market, so he was not an option for her, no matter how intrigued she might be by the gentleman. This did not stop her from wondering if his mind was as fascinating as his person.

Lily had never found out because, despite the young man's polite discourse in the few moments they had interacted, his attentions were reserved for more sophisticated women.

Widows.

Which might explain why he is here!

At this thought, Lily peered back down to find Mr. Ridley standing on the side of the road, his carriage drawing away. As she suspected, once the carriage departed, he turned and loped across the street toward Lady Slight's home. Knocking on the door, while Lily wistfully watched and wished she could enjoy the courtship of such a man, he waited until the butler answered and stood back to let him in.

Sighing, she turned back to her book, pondering what it might be like to learn more about him. Was he as pleasant as his manner suggested? Did he think her a silly child, or would he recognize her as an eligible young lady, if he were marriage-minded?

She would probably never know. It was such a waste that someone so affable spent time with the viper, Lady Slight, who had angered her cousin with her attempts to interfere between Sophia's brother-in-law, Perry, and the woman whom he had eventually married.

* * *

WHEN BRENDAN finally reached Harriet's home, he was disappointed to learn she had not yet returned as promised. The butler did not bat an eyelid about letting a man in after he stated the widow was expecting him, showing Brendan upstairs to the first-floor rooms without comment.

In her personal drawing room, Brendan threw his gloves aside, then poured some wine and settled down in an armchair with his legs stretched out, to sip and stare into the empty fireplace. He placed the wine down on the end table next to the settee, thinking about how he had been up since very early morning and how carrying Ashby's dead weight in order to ensure the lad's safety had sapped his flagging energy. His lids slowly drifted shut and his thoughts faded to nothing as he fell sound asleep.

When Brendan came to, it was to the noisy arrival of Lady Harriet Slight returning home. Blinking rapidly, he swiped at his eyes with his fingertips, straightening up to the protest of his shoulder muscles. Groggy, he wondered how long he had been asleep. As Harriet ascended the steps, spouting instructions to her servants, a casement clock in the hall below announced the hour.

He tried to count the chimes, still bleary from being roused so suddenly from his slumber.

Was it four or five? Either of those would mean he needed to head home. *Blast!*

He rose to his feet as Harriet entered the drawing room, which led to her bedroom beyond. Coming to a stop, she stared at him, speechless for a moment while he drank her in.

Lady Slight, the widow of a decrepit viscount who had died within a mere couple of years of the union, was stunning. She had fiery red hair carefully set in ringlets around her face, but it was the low cut of her bodice that drew his appreciative gaze to the breasts threatening to spill out.

"Brendan! I quite forgot we made plans. I wound up at a soirée after the coronation." Harriet giggled, making Brendan wonder if she was half-sprung from the evening's entertainments. "Several soirées, if I am honest. I spent the evening conversing with the very best of society. I hope you found something to occupy yourself?"

Brendan suppressed his irritation. The widow was an entertaining partner for bed sport, but her inconstant behavior was not one of her charms. He appreciated why Perry had walked away from their dalliance without a backward glance.

Perhaps our time is drawing to a close?

The growing sense of ennui returned, a weighted cloak across his shoulders which made him wish he could sit back down on the settee and fall back to sleep. Then he remembered he had to see the baron this morning.

Not only was it time to leave, but finding a new paramour would be an inconvenience at the moment, so he should maintain this little understanding a while longer if he wished to have an escape from the Ridley townhouse. It was that or sleep at his clubs, but there would be no lush feminine body to warm his sheets if he chose the clubs.

"Of course!" He stepped forward to lean in and kiss her cheek, breathing in the scent of roses from her warm skin. No man could deny that the delightful Harriet was an alluring companion, with soft curves and provocative shadows that made a man think of the sensual activities to be enjoyed in the next room. Stepping back, he smiled down at her. "Did you enjoy your evening?"

"What unique events have unfolded this day! We shall never see another coronation as grand as this one. They are saying it eclipsed that of the little French tyrant himself. Did you hear a tailor went to Paris to study the emperor's robe?"

"I heard that a veritable fortune was spent on the day's activities," Brendan responded dryly, but Harriet failed to note the sarcasm.

"It was a day that shall never be rivaled," she continued, the red flags at the top of her cheeks displaying her excitement. Or, perhaps, she was tippled as he had thought moments earlier?

Brendan chuckled. "I am glad you enjoyed your day. And evening." He thought spending such a fortune on a single day was shallow and irresponsible, but it was nice to see her so ebullient.

"Evening, darling? I reached home at six o'clock in the morning! A sure sign of an excellent night."

Brendan gasped. "Six o'clock? I must go!" Grabbing his gloves from the side table, he cursed under his breath. He was not afraid of the baron cutting him off, or anything like that. The old man was too obsessed with maintaining appearances to allow his heir to emerge penniless. Nevertheless, he did not wish to exacerbate their tense relationship with no stratagem to run the baron off back to Somerset.

Making for the door, he ignored Harriet's offended expression at being put aside to stride out. He needed to get home immediately.

* * *

LILY OPENED HER EYES, finding her book had fallen to the floor when she had dozed off in the early hours. Sitting up, she peered out the window, blinking the blur of sleep away to find the first threads of dawn were stealing over the rooftops of Mayfair as Lady Slight's carriage drew up outside her home. The widow came into view after several moments when she walked to her front door in a cape and evening gown.

Lily's forehead furrowed in surprise. Had the widow left Mr. Ridley waiting all evening for her return? That seemed inconsiderate, even if their relationship was of the disreputable sort.

Stretching out in a manner that would have earned a rebuke from Mama if she had witnessed it, Lily stood up. If she had slept in the drawing room, her parents and Aidan must still be out and about at their various gatherings, or Mama would have woken her to send her to bed.

Suddenly, her attention was caught when the front door of Lady Slight's townhouse flew open and Mr. Ridley came striding out, heading down the street with a frantic demeanor. Had he fallen asleep as she had and failed to notice the passing of time? Apparently, he needed to reach somewhere in a hurry.

Leaning down to grab her book, Lily headed to the door. It was high time she went to bed. She hoped Mr. Ridley was close to home, because she doubted he would easily find a hackney at this time of the morning.

CHAPTER 3

"Be extremely subtle, even to the point of formlessness. Be extremely mysterious, even to the point of soundlessness. Thereby you can be the director of the opponent's fate."
Sun Tzu, L'Art de la Guerre (The Art of War)

* * *

JULY 20, 1821, THE DAY AFTER

*L*ily was eager for an outing with her cousin. After a restless night falling asleep in the front drawing room, she had gone to sleep in her bed and awakened fresh and ready for a visit to Hatchards with Sophia to peruse the latest novels. After yet another unsuccessful Season, Lily admitted she needed a respite from social events and meeting with people she barely knew. Sophia and she could relax and enjoy each other's company without Mama watching her closely like a falcon protecting its nest of hatchlings.

She was wearing a muslin walking dress in the customary white that her mama insisted on. Lily pulled a face at the figure in the full-length mirror in her room. White was not a flattering color for a pale young miss with brown hair and brown eyes. Ever since Sophia married, she had enjoyed the privileges of a countess, which included a flattering wardrobe of the blues and spring colors that suited her red-blonde hair and blue eyes. But even before marrying, Sophia had enjoyed more latitude as Mama's niece than Lily could ever hope for.

How was she to attract the attentions of a handsome—and young— gentleman when she looked washed-out and childish?

Shaking her head in disgust, she drew on a pastel blue spencer, which also did not suit. Mama wore rich colors, such as claret, saffron, and Egyptian brown. From their similarity of complexion and coloring, Lily knew these hues would elevate her appearance, but Mama would not relent about the whites and pastels, which she persistently insisted was the appropriate attire for a young debutante.

Not so young of a debutante any longer.

Lily grimaced at her reflection. Indeed. After three Seasons, she could no longer claim to be young.

Drawing on her kid gloves, Lily departed her room to head downstairs. Sophia would collect her on the hour, and Lily could not prevent a slight skip in her step at the opportunity to leave the Abbott townhouse without her family in attendance.

Reaching the hall, she checked the time on the casement clock before moving to the window overlooking the street, where she gazed out in anticipation.

And gazed.

And gazed.

Checking the time once more, Lily paced the hall. It was

not like Sophia to be late, and she had sent over a footman two days earlier to confirm their appointment despite all the coronation events her cousin was to attend as the Countess of Saunton.

When she checked the time again, Lily blew out sharply as her shoulders slumped in disappointment. First, Aidan had abandoned her the day before, and now Sophia was to leave her waiting.

Something must have happened.

Lily breathed in and decided that must be the case. Sophia would never deliberately leave her waiting without an explanation, so there must be a good reason for the delay. As she concluded this, she heard the rumble of a carriage on the roadway before it came to a stop, casting a shadow on the window of the entrance hall. Running over to the window, Lily peered out to find the Saunton carriage had finally arrived.

Without waiting for a footman to open the door, Lily pulled it open and almost skipped in her excitement to reach the carriage and depart.

The Saunton footman opened the carriage door, lowering the steps and assisting Sophia to step down. Lily bounded over, calling out, "There is no need to come in! I am here! We can leave immediately."

Sophia failed to respond in kind, causing Lily to pause. Her cousin had a grim expression, her face pale in the sunlight. "I am afraid I cannot go to the bookshop today. There has ... something has happened. I only have a moment to inform you of the change in plans."

Lily's spirits plummeted, her stomach clenching in trepidation about what would cause her cousin to appear so somber. Sophia was a warrior, a daring young woman who forged her own path. Whatever had happened must be a serious matter. "What is it? Is it the earl?" Then Lily had a worse thought. "Miles?" Surely nothing had happened to Sophia's babe!

Sophia looked about the square before taking Lily by the arm and escorting her back into the townhouse. They headed into the dining room, and Sophia drew the door closed behind them. "Richard and Miles are well. It is Richard's friend. Mr. Ridley."

"Mr. Ridley?" Lily's thoughts scrambled, veering off in different directions. She had just seen him a few hours earlier when he had fled Lady Slight's home at dawn. Surely harm had not befallen him?

"He returned home this morning to find his father had ..." Sophia bit her lip, evidently reluctant to impart the news. "The baron has been killed."

Lily's eyes widened, and she stepped back in shock. "What?"

"I hate to tell you such terrible news, but I am on my way to the Ridley townhouse to provide support to the duchess. Richard and the duke are there with her and Mr. Ridley to assist him with the authorities. She must be devastated." Sophia had grown close with the duchess, Mr. Ridley's sister. The earl and the duke were cousins and close friends, so she spent considerable time in the duchess's company. Sophia's eyes were stormy with her concern, her mind obviously on her friend's plight.

"I must come with you!"

Sophia returned to the present, tilting her head in question.

"I can provide assistance. Mama expects me to be with you, and your coachman can return me home later."

"Oh, Lily. What purpose would that serve?"

Lily straightened herself up to her full, though meager, height, with her arms akimbo. "Do not treat me like a child. I am twenty years old, Sophia Balfour! I am your friend, and I have a good head on my shoulders. The duchess is increasing, and she might have her son to attend to. Or I can provide comfort or ... or ... I can help." It was not the most persuasive argument, but Lily was frustrated with her situation. Until now, Sophia had been the only one who treated her as a person in her own right rather than a vexing child. If she was not permitted to accompany her cousin in a time of family crisis, Lily would feel utterly useless. And wretched, worrying about Sophia and the duchess when she could be with them to help.

Sophia's lips quirked into a smile, and Lily was relieved to see her cousin's customary irreverence returning. "My, my, Lily Billy. Such fire!"

"So I can accompany you?"

The countess sighed. "Not a word to your mama about where we went, you hear?"

Lily bobbed on to her toes as some fraction of her good humor came rushing back. "We should leave, then. Before she comes downstairs to break her fast."

* * *

BRENDAN SAT SLUMPED in a mild state of shock. They were in the library because the study was ... well ... it had a corpse lying on the floor awaiting the coroner's arrival. The metallic smell of blood in that room had quite given him a headache.

His brother-in-law, the Duke of Halmesbury, along with the duke's cousin and one of Brendan's closest friends, Richard, the Earl of Saunton, were talking with the runner who had arrived in response to Brendan sending a footman to summon the authorities.

They were standing a few feet away in the dim light, the blond duke towering over both men despite the earl being at least six feet. Even with his great height, the duke was small in stature compared to the large shelving and heavy furnishings of the room. The drapes and armchairs might have once been a rich green, but they had long since turned a greenish-gray, and Brendan reflected on how much he hated most of Ridley House, which had been decorated in a bygone era.

For some reason, the earl seemed to know the runner, Briggs. Brendan recalled vaguely that Richard had shot a man in his townhouse the year before, so perhaps that was how they had met.

"So Mr. Ridley—his lordship—found his lordship—the late baron—when he returned home this morning?"

Brendan grimaced at the awkward sentence. The runner was a stern, lean man in a crumpled great overcoat and a battered hat. He had the appearance of a man who had seen and done things that Brendan's set could not possibly comprehend, but his gruff voice stumbled hesitantly over the words as he grasped for the correct descriptors.

Yes, the baron was now dead.

Yes, that implied that he, Brendan, was now the new baron, but that had still to be confirmed by the Committee for Priviliges.

So the street-tough Briggs, a humble runner, was fumbling for the correct forms of address given these fresh circumstances.

"That is correct," Halmesbury responded, his deep voice firm and comforting. Brendan had still to gather his wits fully from finding the old man dead, so it was a relief to have the duke taking charge.

"And where was Mr. Rid—his lordship—the night before?"

The duke raised an enormous fist to cough uncomfortably into it. Richard noted the pause and interjected, "His lordship was with a friend overnight. A lady friend."

"Will she be able to confirm his whereabouts?"

Both Halmesbury and Richard glanced back at Brendan, still slumped in his chair. He shook his head in response.

"That will not be possible."

"Did any of the servants witness him arriving back this morning?"

All three men looked back at Brendan. He nodded. Soughing deeply, he spoke in a heavy tone. "I did not pay attention to who let me in the front door in my haste. I simply ran in without noting it, but it must be the butler or one of the footmen who let me in."

Briggs nodded, revealing a small scar over his right brow when his lank locks fell back. He had a thin face with a thick mustache that reminded Brendan of the stable master back in Somerset. "I shall question the servants and find someone to confirm your arrival, milord."

"Will that be sufficient to clear his lordship?" The duke's question made Brendan stiffen. It had been foremost on his mind since finding the baron on the floor.

Briggs stroked his mustache thoughtfully. "It might be, but I recommend speaking to the woman to persuade her to confirm his lordship's presence. It's not I, but the coroner who must be convinced."

Brendan grimaced. His affair with Lady Slight was not formed on the basis of her philanthropic nature. Rather, it was her talents in bed that lured her paramours. The notion that Harriet would confirm his evening at her home was inconceivable.

As it stood, both Halmesbury and Richard had displayed fleeting distaste when he recounted the events of the evening but refused to reveal the lady's identity. Brendan could not blame them for it, but their respective states of condescending marital bliss in the face of his goings-on had never been so annoying as it had been while waiting for the runner to arrive.

"Is he likely to suspect his lordship?" queried Richard, causing Brendan to straighten in his chair so he could lean forward to hear the runner's response.

The runner tugged at his mustache with an uncomfortable expression, staring down at his notebook for several moments before reluctantly replying. "Arnold Grimes is new to his post, but he strikes me as an ambitious man. It would be in his lordship's interests to address any suspicions quickly, and an alibi would be greatly in his favor."

Silence descended. The only sound was the ticking of the clock on the library table, which was darkened with the patina of decades of service. It was positively medieval in appearance. Finally, Richard sighed. "Thank you for your candor, Briggs."

"The baron has been dead for hours, and it is obvious to me that Mr. Ridley has been out, given his state of dress. If it were up to me, I would want to know who might have visited the baron last evening."

"But it is not up to you?" Brendan had never dealt with the authorities before, so he did not have a clear understanding of what the procedure would be.

Briggs looked over at him, an expression of sympathy on his weathered face. He shook his head. "I'm 'fraid not. The coroner is the final authority."

Brendan rubbed his temples, slumping back into the embrace of the library chair.

* * *

THE COUNTESS'S footman released Lily's gloved hand after helping her from the carriage, stepping back politely as she followed her cousin to the painted front door. A small brass plaque declared it to be Ridley House.

It was her first time visiting the townhouse, having had

no reason to meet the unmarried man in his home before. As a debutante, Lily did not get out very much. She went to social functions with her mama in attendance, and occasionally she went to Hatchards with Sophia or to her home.

A bachelor's residence, even if a grand family townhouse, was strictly forbidden. A thrill at this unexpected departure from the norm ran through her like a hot shiver. Despite the somber circumstances, this was the most excitement she had experienced since her cousin had married the year before, after a nefarious kidnapping attempt in the Abbotts' home.

Lily craned her neck back to peer up at the great house when she came to a stop behind Sophia. It was large, but she could not see anything more than that because the drapes were drawn shut, the only evidence that something untoward had happened inside. Soon the door was opened and Lily swept in behind Sophia, staring about the dark hall with open curiosity.

Sophia was looking the footman up and down. Since her troubles the year before, Sophia always noted the servants. It was a heightened awareness of security that Lily could not fault her for, considering how close she had come to being killed. Lily admonished herself for her inquisitiveness over the Ridley home and forced her attention to the conversation that the countess was having with the footman.

Lily noted that the young man was tall, with a friendly face and a smattering of freckles across his cheeks that spoke to his auburn thatch of hair.

"Have we met before?" The countess was questioning the footman, but Lily knew Sophia must have already noted that the servant was unknown to her.

"No, my lady."

"What is your name, pray tell?"

"Wesley, my lady. I have worked at Ridley House for

several years." He answered in a good-natured manner, apparently not offended by her cousin's interrogation.

"Where is the butler, Michaels?"

"He is making arrangements regarding our household's change in circumstances, my lady."

"Very well. We are here for the duchess."

"Of course, my lady. She is expecting you in the red parlor." Wesley bowed politely before leading them down a hall. Lily pattered behind, almost running to keep up with the taller countess and even taller footman. She barely had time to note the worn carpets and faded wallpaper when they came to a stop.

The footman knocked and then opened the door to announce their arrival before departing. As he left, Lily caught his eye and mouthed an apology for Sophia's earlier inquisition. The news of the baron's untimely demise must have set her cousin on edge after her prior experiences.

Wesley smiled in response as he drew the door shut, leaving Lily relieved that he appeared unaffected by the encounter.

* * *

MICHAELS SHOWED the coroner into the gloomy library, an expression of mild distaste stamped across his face. Brendan growled beneath his breath, his irritation with the servant particularly sharp today.

He had never gotten along with the man, who until today had been the baron's man. The butler's disdain for the baron's heir was subtle, but obvious. Something Brendan had refrained from confronting him with, but had been a source of aggravation these many years that he had resided at Ridley House since the baron had sent him away to London.

Once the butler departed, Brendan turned his attention

to the coroner, Mr. Arnold Grimes, and his heart sank. The man was medium height, with severely cut, receding iron hair and a graying close-cropped beard that put Brendan in mind of a Puritan. He wore a black coat and trousers with a white linen shirt. The overall effect was that of no color, while the sour expression on his face did nothing to belie that impression.

His cold presence sucked the very life out of the room, while the runner, Briggs, shifted away with a barely disguised revulsion.

Sniffing in an affected manner, the coroner addressed the duke and the earl. "Your Grace. My lord. I am honored to make your acquaintance."

Brendan rubbed his temple. The words were correct, but the tone did not match. The coroner's sneering dislike was obvious to all present, and he had failed to bow in respect to the high-ranking noblemen.

"Mr. Grimes, your reputation precedes you." The duke gave a slight nod, his gray eyes sweeping over the coroner without missing a beat. Halmesbury was a skilled negotiator, and his composure was practiced and aloof. Any candor he had displayed with the runner earlier had vanished, clarifying to Brendan that his brother-in-law recognized the coroner as a threat.

Brendan drew in a breath to steady his nerves and straightened from his chair to come forward to meet the man. It would not do to display any weakness in his presence.

The coroner frowned slightly at Brendan before dismissing him without bothering to greet him. "Briggs, let me hear the facts."

Briggs cleared his throat, then read from his notebook carefully. "The baron appears to have been killed sometime around midnight. The butler reports he returned home for dinner, and he was still dressed in his clothes from the coronation when he apparently encountered someone in his study. He was clubbed over the head with a horse statue, which was found bloodied and lying by the body. Mr. Ridley returned home just after dawn to meet with his father, finding the body about twenty minutes past the hour of six o'clock."

The coroner turned a stony stare to Brendan, who had to refrain from shivering at the blast of icy contempt. "And where were you?"

Brendan frowned, drawing himself up and responding in as haughty a manner as he could summon. This man clearly loathed the peerage. Or perhaps he just loathed everyone. "I was out."

"Out?"

"Out." Brendan refused to expound. It would not do to allow the coroner to get the upper hand.

Briggs cleared his throat. "One of the servants should be able to confirm his arrival once I question them."

"I certainly hope so."

Brendan kept a straight face at Grimes's response, but his stomach tightened in agitation and he wondered what it would take to persuade Harriet to have mercy on him and provide him with the alibi he needed.

LILY POURED a cup of tea for the duchess, adding a squeeze of lemon before handing Her Grace the cup and saucer. The duchess accepted it with a small smile of gratitude, her face wan in the dim room. She was an elegant young woman, with a riot of chestnut curls framing her face and brandy eyes that reflected the low light, but her eyelids were puffy and red.

Observing the signs of Her Grace's grief made Lily feel guilty for treating the situation as an opportunity to escape the monotony of her day. Lady Halmesbury had just lost her father in a brutal murder. Despite her renowned babbling, Lily could not find any words to comfort Her Grace.

She glanced at Sophia, who was staring out a window as if her thoughts were a million miles away.

The room had been silent since they arrived. No one spoke while they pondered the terrible events that had brought them together this morning. Lily winced, realizing she had talked her way into this gathering on a promise of providing assistance. It was time to enliven the ladies.

"I ... quite enjoy a cup of exotic tea. I particularly enjoy milk in my tea with one of those dainty biscuits that Cook makes. Do you know the ones I mean, Sophia? They have a hint of lemon and you can eat them in just two bites and they are light as clouds? One day it would be a wonderful thing to journey to the Far East and see fields and fields of green tea as far as the eye can see."

The duchess tilted her head, staring in wonderment at Lily, whose chattering had interrupted her reverie, before her shoulders heaved ever so slightly as if she were pushing a burden off. "I have often wondered about the lands where the tea is produced. What would acres of fresh, growing tea smell like? We only ever see the fragrant dried leaves that have been sealed in a tea chest and have journeyed for months over the sea. This tea"—Her Grace lifted her cup slightly—"traveled thousands of miles. It was grown in India, visited Africa en route, and arrived half a world away in London so that we might drink it as we discuss the events of the day."

Sophia turned back, appearing curious as she peered at the duchess and then accepted a cup of tea from Lily. "This tea is a tale of a different world. It allows us to travel farther than we can ever journey ourselves."

Lily picked up her cup and sipped, savoring the variety of notes while she thought about its journey, happy she could provide some solace. The three of them drank tea before Lily offered a saucer of biscuits. The duchess accepted one, and Lily was pleased to note Her Grace and Sophia appeared more present, breathing in the fragrant steam as they nibbled on the confections.

"I wanted to thank you … for sharing this time with me. My father and I were not close, but it is still a shock."

Sophia placed a hand over that of the duchess. "Of course, Annabel. We shall always be at your side when you need us."

"If I am honest, I grieve not so much for what we shared as father and daughter. I think … I mourn … for what we will never share. The baron was a hard man to please, and it was an effort to spend time with him. He never appreciated his family."

Lily bit a lip, surprised to hear such a private admission from someone such as the duchess. She felt positively mature to be included in such a discussion. "I am so sorry. Papa is everything a daughter could ask for. He protects us and dotes on us."

Sophia nodded. "Lord Moreland has been a better father to me than my own ever was. I regret if the baron never acknowledged how fortunate he was to have such an accomplished daughter."

The duchess quirked the corner of her lips into a semblance of a smile. "Fortunately, I have a wonderful brother."

Lily coughed gently. "I suppose Mr. Ridley is a baron now."

The duchess straightened in surprise. "I had not thought

of that. That is much responsibility to shoulder with such little preparation."

"The duke will guide him through the transition. And Richard will help him, too." Sophia's proffered declaration was more in character than her earlier solemnity, Lily noted with contentment. She was happy she had instigated the conversation, and the mood had subsequently lightened to her satisfaction.

Behind her, the door suddenly opened. Swinging her head around, she observed the men entering and noted their grim expressions with dismay as they made their way over to the women. The large duke lowered himself onto the settee next to his wife.

"Lily Billy," Richard whispered in greeting before settling down next to Sophia. Lily winked at him in acknowledgment, raising a slight smile from the somber earl.

Mr. Ridley, appearing pained, took a chair close to Lily. Despite the darkness of their gathering, Lily could not help a tiny thrill at being seated near to such a virile young gentleman.

In his upper twenties, he had chestnut curls to match the duchess. They also shared those riveting brandy eyes, but Mr. Ridley was a man through and through, with his lean body, broad shoulders, and chiseled jaw. He scraped six feet, which meant he towered over her dainty form, and she could not help but wonder what it would be like to waltz with such a fine specimen of manhood, rather than the doddery old men she was usually required to dance with.

"That Mr. Grimes is pugnacious and unlikeable," Richard grumbled after several moments. Sophia frowned at her husband in question. "I believe he will pursue Ridley for this murder."

"I agree. I talked with Briggs in private before he left, and he said it is imperative that we find an alibi. Apparently,

Grimes has political ambitions and does not admire the aristocracy. To make it worse, the little upstart has powerful friends in the House of Commons, so this could be a proper fight, despite Brendan's connection to me." The duke's tone displayed his concern as he took a cup of tea from his wife and sipped.

"Who is Grimes?" The duchess sounded alarmed.

"The coroner," the duke responded.

Mr. Ridley groaned. "Why me?"

Richard puffed in disgust. "Why not you? Grimes sees an opportunity to make a reputation for himself by bringing the first peer in sixty years to the scaffold. The baron has been absent from Town for two decades, so it is simple to accuse you of being the only man with a motive. The narrative writes itself. Estranged heir murders peer in a fit of rage to obtain the title and income. We must obtain an alibi so he is forced to look elsewhere, or we will have a serious fight on our hands."

Lily realized that her presence had been forgotten, and the situation was being openly discussed in front of her. Or had she been accepted as a confidant into this tight circle of friends? Either way, she would not ruin it by reminding them she was present!

Mr. Ridley sighed heavily. "The lady in question will never agree to come forward, and I cannot name her without her permission."

"Can you speak with her?"

"Not without revealing her identity under the current circumstances. There is a possibility that Grimes will have me under observation."

Lily peeked over at him, noticing the pallor of his face. She bit her lip, wondering if she should confess that she had witnessed him arriving at and leaving Lady Slight's home. But the word of a young debutante, especially one who had been up till all hours reading in the drawing room, might not hold much weight.

"What if someone else saw you arrive ... or leave?" Lily almost clapped a hand over her mouth at her display of audacity, asking such a question in a room full of important peers, but she held her hands together to quell the urge.

Mr. Ridley tilted his head in question at the duke, who shook his head. "It would not settle the matter because they could not confirm Brendan was there the entire time. It would have to be the lady."

"Or, perhaps, her servants?" responded the gentleman, a flush rising out of Mr. Ridley's collar and spreading to his ears, which turned a fiery red. Lily wondered what it was about until she recalled that he had been at Lady Slight's, but the widow had not been there. Presumably, he did not want to reveal that his paramour had abandoned him all evening, which was why he was musing about the servants in her stead.

"I suppose that the woman in question would need to be agreeable or her servants will not come forward." The duke was pessimistic in his reply.

Lily stared down at her hands, trying to think of a solution. She knew Mr. Ridley had been at Lady Slight's the entire evening, but young ladies like her were practically invisible until they wed. And she could not attest for certain that Mr. Ridley had not left Lady Slight's in the middle of the night. Only Lady Slight's servants could attest to that, which they would only do with the widow's permission. If Lily admitted her knowledge, it was certain her cousin would dissuade her from getting involved to protect her from a scandal that might affect her eligibility for a good marriage. But if Mr. Ridley could not request help, perhaps Lily could visit Lady Slight to convince the widow to step forward?

Not, she suspected, if she forewarned the others of her

idea. And Mr. Ridley clearly did not wish to reveal the widow's identity. Conferring with him in private would be impossible and, regardless, he would probably decline her offer to assist him.

"So Mr. Grimes is likely to issue a warrant of arrest for Brendan?" The duchess's voice was even but thick, and Lily suspected she was on the verge of tears.

"I think it is possible. Briggs is questioning the servants, but so far none of them have confirmed they let Brendan in this morning. Even so, I believe an alibi is the only certain method to have Grimes move on to find the true murderer."

"What would happen if he arrests me?" Mr. Ridley sounded haggard with worry.

"You will probably be imprisoned and ..." The duke stopped, looking away with a pained expression.

"And?" Her Grace queried.

Sophia responded reluctantly, stating what each of them was thinking. "In the last century, the Earl of Ferrers was imprisoned at the Tower and then he was condemned to death by Lords for killing his agent. If Mr. Ridley is tried and found guilty of murdering a peer of the realm ..." The countess bowed her head, the room descending into silence with only a low sniffle from the duchess to acknowledge the dire nature of her brother's predicament.

To Lily's right, Mr. Ridley collapsed his head into his hands with a groan. "So I am to be arrested, tried, and hanged based on the assumption that I am guilty?"

His anguish was palpable, but unlike earlier, Lily did not think her babbling would lighten the mood. She had never been involved in such an adult conversation, and she was afraid she had nothing useful to offer. Perhaps she was a silly child, after all.

Her frustration rose to engulf her body, a physical sensation that made her skin itch. She finally had a chance to participate in a mature matter, and she found herself speech-less. Even so, if it would help Mr. Ridley out of his predicament, she would stand as a witness. But the witness that they needed was not her, it was the widow.

I must find a way to help the duchess and her brother!

CHAPTER 4

"Quickness is the essence of the war."
Sun Tzu, L'Art de la Guerre (The Art of War)

* * *

JULY 21, 1821

"*M*iss Lily, I ain't sure about this. Your mama is going to have words with me." Nancy was plaintive, her eyes furtively searching the street to ensure no one saw them approaching the widow's door. "The talk belowstairs is that Lady Slight is a bit of a fusty luggs!"

"A WHAT?"

Nancy scowled, her wrinkles settling into deep lines as she mumbled under her breath.

"FUSTY LUGGS?"

The old nursemaid huffed before replying with obvious reluctance, "A mean-tempered trollop."

Lily's eyes widened in feigned surprise. "Never say there is gossip amongst the servants!"

Nancy leaned forward to hear better. "Hey?"

Lily tossed her an impish smile and turned back to raise the knocker on the door, bringing it down with a determined rap. She needed to be quick about this before her family noted her absence.

Lady Slight's rake-thin butler opened the door, sweeping his gaze over her before rotating his head to take in old Nancy, with her disheveled hair and drooping mobcap. His lips curled in disdain. "May I help you, miss?"

Straightening herself to her full height, Lily adopted the haughty tone she had heard Mama use on those she deemed unworthy. She offered him one of her calling cards. "Miss Abbott to see Lady Slight."

The butler's nostrils flared as he read the card. "Lord Moreland's daughter?"

"Indeed. Show me in." The butler's cold eyes flickered, and Lily realized she had him.

"Follow me."

Lily grabbed Nancy by the arm, dragging her in behind her. The old woman waddled behind her as the butler's long legs ate the distance faster than Lily could keep up with.

He stopped, opening a door. "Lord Moreland's daughter, Miss Abbott."

Lily skipped in behind him, slightly breathless from attempting to keep up while navigating Nancy with her. Coming to a stop, she found herself in a small, gilded parlor.

Every surface had been covered with intricately painted floral patterns and Greek deities frolicking. On the smooth vertical space of the mantelpiece was a frieze of Romans going about their business while a musician strummed some sort of string instrument. She caught herself gaping at the lavish room, barely registering Lady Slight's presence as she peered up and around her at the elaborate room.

By the time Lily noticed the redheaded viscountess sitting in a regal blue-green armchair with a gilded frame, the lady's irritation was on display, along with her ... assets. Lily forced her eyes up from the low bodice, wondering how the widow could breathe in such tight stays. The lady's bosom was thrust so high, it was practically hitting her in the chin!

Dropping a curtsy, Lily opened her mouth and forged ahead. "I have come to speak to you about Mr. Ridley—Lord Filminster!"

The widow frowned. "Lord Filminster?"

"The baron is dead. Mr. Ridley is likely to be accused of his murder. You and your servants are the only ones who can clear Mr. Ridley—Lord Filminster. You must inform the authorities that he was here in your home last night, before he is arrested and taken to the Tower. The runner says that he must have an alibi as swiftly as possible. You must send for the coroner, who is Mr. Grimes, and he is the one you must inform straightaway of Mr. Ridley's presence here!"

Lady Slight's jaw dropped open in evident amazement. Lily realized she might have said too much, too quickly. Her cursed babbling could hit with velocity when talking to someone who was not familiar with her verbosity. Leaning back on her heels, Lily commanded herself to breathe.

Several moments passed, during which Lady Slight slowly closed her mouth and appeared to be gathering her wits. "Mr. Ridley is to be accused of murder?"

Lily nodded, keeping her lips firmly together.

"And you wish me to speak to the authorities to clear his name?"

Another nod.

"Why on earth would I do that?"

"Because he was here. All night."

The viscountess narrowed her eyes. "How would you know that?"

"I witnessed his arrival and his departure from my window."

Lady Slight rose, walking over to a window, her scarlet silk skirts rustling while a waft of expensive perfume tickled Lily's nose. "Lord Moreland's daughter? He lives across the street, I suppose." The viscountess leaned to peer outside.

Abruptly turning, she moved to where Lily was standing. Using her superior height, she gazed down her nose at Lily with an expression of distaste.

"Why would I be concerned about some silly little chit dressed in her silly white lace?" Lady Slight reached out an elegant hand to fiddle with the ruffle at Lily's neck. "Mama still dresses you, does she not?"

Lily's heart fell from her chest into the pit of her stomach. It was humiliating to have such icy disdain thrust upon her. The older woman was an alluring Aphrodite, while Lily was … not. Nevertheless, despite the threatening emotions, she was going to hold her ground and convince this viper to do the right thing. At the same time, Lily was afraid she had made the situation much worse with her lack of strategy in visiting. She should have prepared a more compelling argument.

"You know he is innocent! You have a responsibility to speak!"

Lady Slight lifted a hand to her mouth and tittered, but her eyes remained hard and icy. Lily welcomed the fury that rose through her like a hot tide of righteousness to provide her fortitude.

"I shall stand as a witness. I shall inform the coroner where Mr. Ridley—Lord Filminster—was that night!"

The viscountess shrugged gracefully, highlighting the dainty lines of her creamy naked shoulders. "I shall deny it."

Lily gritted her teeth. "The coachman who dropped him off will confirm my testimony."

Lady Slight's painted lips twisted into a wintry smile as her eyebrow arched. "The coachman knows nothing about the matter. Ridley promised his carriage would draw up in front of what turns out to be your townhouse, not mine, and he would have awaited its departure before crossing the road."

"You do not deny he was here, then!"

"Why would I? Your word is inconsequential, so …"

"You will not help Mr. Ridley, despite his innocence?"

"I think … not." The reply was callous. Heartless. The viscountess seemed to enjoy toying with her, entertained in the manner of a horrid little boy pulling the wings off an insect.

Lily clenched her hands lest they fly into the air to slap the shameless hussy across the face. The widow was several inches taller than her and merciless, so an attack seemed ill-advised. "But why? You must care for him? You were to spend the night with him!"

Lady Slight sneered. "Your naïveté is too obvious, dear. If I provide him an alibi, I shall be forced to wed him to save my public reputation. I would never marry a mere baron. I am the widow of an important viscount, with the freedom to conduct any affairs I wish, you ridiculous girl."

Lily stuck out her chin, squaring her shoulders. "You have no honor, my lady!"

The viscountess froze, her jaw firming. An ormolu clock on one of the side tables ticked in the silence as Lily stared Lady Slight in the eye. Eventually, the other woman blinked and turned away. "The opinion of an unwed chit does not signify."

With that, she moved back to her seat, floating through the air like a leaf dancing in the wind. Lily watched her carefully drape her skirts as she sat down and realized she was being dismissed. Turning, she grabbed Nancy by the arm, who was standing close to the door with wide eyes and craning to hear the exchange.

"We are leaving, Nancy."

"We are grieving?"

"LEAVING!"

Lily stalked through the door as thoughts collided in her head. Had she made matters worse? How was she to fix this? Mr. Ridley was innocent, and the dreadful viscountess would not lift a finger to help him!

* * *

"You must inform the coroner where you were. It is the only way." The earl's frustration with Brendan was rising.

"Who is the lady you were with, Brendan? Perhaps I can visit and persuade her to assist." The duke's tone was even, but his concern was drawn in the lines between his bronzed brows and in the slight narrowing of his eyes.

Brendan shook his head. He could not reveal that without the lady's consent.

Be honest with yourself.

He winced. Wishing to speak to Lady Slight before revealing her identity was part of it. However, the truth was his affair with Lady Slight embarrassed him. Richard despised the woman for her involvement with his brother, Perry. Brendan could not blame him. He knew that it had been a dishonorable move to knock boots with the ace of spades because of the vacancy left by Perry's marriage.

You were thinking with your Thomas.

This was hard to refute. Lady Slight, while an elegant presence, certainly did not provide scintillating conversation or challenge him as an educated man. There was a reason

Perry had fallen in love with a woman who bore no resemblance to the widow.

Richard stood with a grunt of disgust, stalking over to the library windows to gaze sightlessly. Shaking his head, he turned back to bark the question Brendan had been dreading. "Who is she? It must be someone we know or you would not be so reticent! We are your friends! Your family! We cannot help you unless you tell us all that happened."

Brendan shook his head again. "The lady does not signify."

Lady Slight might be interesting to bed, but he knew without a doubt that the woman was selfish and would never agree to be involved in his troubles at the cost of her reputation. It was one thing for her to engage in affairs privately, and most of polite society was well aware of her behavior. Admitting such formally would be ruinous. The lady would be shunned by the same nobility who had visited her in her boudoir, or had tittered behind their fans with her as they gossiped about their respective liaisons. The hypocrisy of their set was not lost on him.

If he had been more honorable himself, he might now have a legitimate alibi to call on. He could not blame Lady Slight for being in this predicament. There were only his own damned choices at fault.

"We must focus on finding the suspect instead."

The earl shook his head in disgust at Brendan's proclamation. "How are we to investigate while the taint of suspicion lies on you?"

The duke sighed, sitting back in his chair and resting his hands on his long, muscled legs. "I agree. I looked into this Grimes, and he has important supporters, as Briggs asserted. There could be serious repercussions to this if we do not clear your name quickly. Even now there is talk of your guilt running through the halls of Westminster, which could severely detain your confirmation as baron. Meanwhile, the household and tenants of Baydon Hall, along with the rest of your people, are without representation. There is no lord to sign any documents, or to approve any matters. No method to pay any wages. We must prevail on this woman to come forward, even if we must provide enticement."

Brendan sat back, rubbing his temples as he tried to think. Two days ago, he had been an heir to a barony, spending his allowance and chasing skirts such as the widow Slight. Now he was on the cusp of being accused of murder, and facing possible confinement in the Tower.

How many leave the Tower as free men once they are imprisoned?

Brendan shivered at this question.

"It will not come to that. We simply need to find the actual perpetrator. I am sure having a servant attest to my arrival earlier this morning should stave off any imminent accusation, so we might proceed with hunting for the perpetrator ourselves. Perhaps we can hire Briggs to look into it further, even if the coroner will not do his duty."

Halmesbury ran a hand through his hair, his disquiet evident.

"What is it?"

Richard returned to his seat, dropping into it heavily before fiddling with his cravat. Brendan's tension tightened, making his head throb with the force of it.

"What is it?"

Halmesbury cleared his throat, sitting forward to lean his wrists on his knees. "None of the servants have admitted to opening the door for you this morning."

"What? I came in just past six o'clock, and I certainly was not carrying a key! Someone opened the door when I knocked on it."

Both the earl and the duke were silent.

"You believe me, do you not?"

Halmesbury's head snapped back. "Of course we believe you. The old man was horrible. I wanted to throttle him myself on many occasions for how he diminished Annabel, but you are a civilized man and we are practically brothers. There have been no thoughts in my head that you did this terrible thing."

Brendan's chest heaved in relief. "Thank you."

Across from him, Richard chuckled. "Personally, I am not so magnanimous. I did briefly wonder if you may have done it."

A glance of rebuke at the earl only caused him to chuckle harder.

"I appreciated your old man for allowing me to escape my circumstances at home during my troubled youth. Visiting with you over the holidays saved my sanity, but he did send you to Cambridge, after all."

Brendan gave a half-laugh, amused despite his panic and the burdens he had been carrying since finding the baron in the study. "Cambridge is a fine university, you dolt."

Richard shrugged. "Ah, the defensive lament of all those who did not attend Oxford."

Brendan kneaded his temple with a thumb, chortling at the ridiculous distraction. His entire life might be in crisis, but at least he did not face it alone.

"Is it possible that the truth of my relationship with the baron might come out?"

Halmesbury flinched. "By Jove, I hope not! That would certainly provide further motive for Grimes to pursue the matter."

"Is there anyone other than us who knows the truth?"

Richard fidgeted in his chair, drawing their attention. "The rumors are true, then? The baron is not Brendan's father?"

Brendan slumped, groaning as he collapsed back into his chair and furiously rubbed at his temples.

"You know of the matter?" Halmesbury's question was almost inaudible, denoting his worry.

Richard nodded. "I heard whispers of it while we were at Eton, and again at Lords, when the baron would come up in conversation. It was not my place to question Brendan about it."

Halmesbury shook his head. "I am afraid we might be buggered."

Tension was boring through Brendan's head. He almost expected to find a hole in his temple, but there was no physical evidence of his torment as he kneaded the area.

"What is it that Grimes can do? As coroner?" Brendan addressed the question to the duke. He was helplessly out of his element, never having dealt with any criminal matters before.

"If he thought you were a legitimate suspect, he could arrest you, while we await a coroner's jury to confirm that the baron was murdered and that you are the primary suspect. It is promising he did not do so today. It suggests that the jury will be called to review the facts of the case, which means there will be more parties involved to advise prudence."

Brendan felt a flood of relief. Perhaps Grimes would continue to investigate until more suspects were found. The man's disapproval of him had been palpable, and Brendan had been fighting off panic since their meeting.

"Unless ..."

Brendan and Halmesbury both turned to Richard, his unease stamped across his features.

"Unless he wanted to confer with his supporters. He could still arrest Brendan once he has secured their approval to proceed."

* * *

LILY PACED UP AND DOWN. She had been doing so since dawn. After leaving Lady Slight the afternoon before, she had been scrambling for a solution to Mr. Ridley's plight. Somehow, knowing where he had been the night of the murder made her feel personally responsible for his well-being, along with that of his sister, Lady Halmesbury.

Lady Slight would not do the right thing, and perhaps visiting the widow to beseech her to intervene should have assuaged Lily's conscience.

Yet ... she still felt accountable. Lily should step forward and state what she had witnessed to the authorities, but Lady Slight had thwarted this path. The widow would simply deny it and then it would be Lily's word against hers. The statement of a widow would hold far more weight than that of an unwed young woman, especially when that widow was a viscountess.

Lily stopped to stomp her feet in frustration before stalking over to her dressing table to stare at the news sheet. Reports of the baron's death were now in circulation, along with mentions of the estrangement between him and his son. They had not spoken in seven years, according to the article, which Lily had not been aware of.

The temerity of the widow still grated on her nerves. The woman had admitted to having Brendan stop in front of Lily's home as a decoy to the true destination. Clearly, the viper had no concern over the possibility of tainting her or Mama's reputation if passersby had spotted him in front of the Abbott townhouse. How despicable the woman was!

What if ...

Lily raised her head to stare at herself in the mirror. Brown eyes, which she hoped were the color of chocolate— mostly because Mama and Aidan had attractive chocolate eyes—stared back at her. The inkling of an idea took shape in her mind, but her stomach tightened in dismay. Surely Mr. Ridley would find a way to address this matter? He had the help of both a duke and an earl at his side.

Except ...

The duchess sniffling quietly during their tête-à-tête echoed in her mind. She had appeared genuinely concerned.

Surely they will come up with a plan to deal with it ...

Lily tried to squash the recollection of Sophia recounting the tale of the Earl of Ferrers—a nobleman who had been imprisoned at the Tower, tried at Westminster, and then hanged.

There must be another way ...

What if there was not? What if an innocent man was tried and hanged because Lily would not act?

It will ruin me ...

Was maintaining her reputation worth the cost of her self-respect? A man could be arrested. A good man from an excellent family, all because Lily stood by and allowed it to happen. He was the obvious suspect, had no defense to offer, and Lily believed her when Lady Slight stated she would not help.

What of falling in love? What of being wed, and having children, and the freedom of a married woman?

What would it matter if she achieved these goals, but lost her sense of self in the process? The truth was, she could not seek counsel in this matter. She simply had to decide what was the right path and take it. It was the very essence of being an adult who stood on her own two feet.

Lily fell to her knees, the weight of responsibility too much to bear. And she wept, her shoulders shuddering with her despair as she faced the burden of growing up.

For the longest time, she had wished to be an adult, to be treated with respect and behave with maturity. Lily had imagined marrying a man who loved her, as Sophia had done. Bringing her first child into the world, as Sophia had just done.

Now Lily wished she could return to her childhood, where heavy decisions did not weigh upon her.

If she discussed the matter with anyone, even Sophia, she knew she would be dissuaded from doing the right thing. She would hear arguments about how her reputation was paramount. How she must make a successful match. How it was someone else's problem to deal with.

But if she did not do the right thing and protect Mr. Ridley, despite the knowledge she had of his innocence, it would rack her with guilt.

If she buried the guilt somewhere in the deep recesses of her soul, she would become a heartless hussy such as the one who lived across the street, who enjoyed a parade of men through her home but possessed no integrity, no humanity, and no true joy. A beautiful but empty shell in an exquisite room with no sign of vitality.

Her optimism would die a slow and painful death, and she would no longer be … Lily—a spirited young woman who may not quite fit in, but who had cheer in her heart and in her words.

I must do what I know in my heart is right.

She wept for the end of her hopes and dreams, and for the beginning of a frightening path into the unknown. Her reputation would be destroyed, and she could only hope that Mr. Ridley might save her in turn.

Finally, once the tempest of emotion had passed, Lily slowly rose to her feet to dry her face and ring the bell to summon Nancy. It was time to leave before Mama and Papa arose for the day.

CHAPTER 5

*"Secret operations are essential in war; upon them the army relies
to make its every move."*
Sun Tzu, L'Art de la Guerre (The Art of War)

* * *

JULY 22, 1821

"The runner is here to see you." Disdain dripped from the butler's words, as if to point out that Bow Street runners were not the class of visitors that the late Barons of Filminster would have tolerated.

Brendan's temples throbbed at Michaels's dour announcement.

"Where is he?"

Michaels's forehead wrinkled as he peered down his nose at Brendan. "In the entrance hall." The unstated *of course* was practically audible. Evidently, the butler thought it was beneath his station to show a visitor such as Briggs into the baronial library.

Brendan nodded in dismissal. Once the butler left the room, he rubbed furiously at his temples. He could not think of anything but being transported to the Tower since Richard had pointed out that the coroner might still press for an arrest once Grimes had acquired the approval of his cronies. It had been another sleepless night, staring at the ceiling with racing thoughts.

As he stood up to find out why Briggs was here, a thought struck him. Brendan collapsed back into his chair.

They had assumed he would be treated with the privileges of a peer because he was the baron's heir. However, no one had seemed to realize that he might be dealt with as a commoner because the Committee for Priviliges had not yet confirmed him!

What if they take me to Newgate?

Brendan groaned as his headache doubled in intensity. Newgate had a reputation for being filthy, overcrowded, and ridden with parasites. Fingering his hair, he contemplated having to shave it off to rid it of lice. Dropping his face against the table, he groaned again as he knocked his head against the mahogany surface in frustration.

Why could he not have been carousing with friends instead of napping in Harriet's boudoir? A simple life choice which might get him a turn at the gallows unless he could find a defense.

Halmesbury was wrong about waiting. We must immediately hire a runner to investigate the matter!

Brendan realized he should have been acting more swiftly to defend himself. Inking his quill, he jotted out a note to the duke. He sprinkled pounce to dry it, then blew before folding it up. Ringing for a footman, he sent it off. He hoped the duke was available to visit him. Yesterday, they had been too complacent. It was time to take matters into his own hands instead of waiting for this Grimes to do his job.

Finally, he stood at the library door and steeled his nerve. Finding his composure, he strode out to find the runner.

Briggs was standing by the shadowed staircase, his hat in hand. The runner looked tired in the flickering candlelight of the hall, and Brendan wondered what hours the man kept. Was he investigating other cases? That seemed likely. Crime had not stopped because of the Ridleys' crisis.

"Briggs, how are you this morning?" Brendan's attempt to be hearty sounded too loud in the empty hall.

"My lor—Mr. Ridley." The runner was hard to read with the thick mustache that obscured his lower face, but the discomfort in his tone was unmistakable.

"What can I do for you?"

"I'm 'fraid the coroner asked me to be present. He's running late."

"Late for what?" Alarm chased through him as he accepted the runner was here to deliver bad news.

"To arrest you. I am to wait for the coroner."

Brendan heard this as if from a great distance. The runner's reluctance was palpable, making it clear that the man did not believe they were taking the right action. But Brendan had somehow expected this very thing would happen the moment he had discovered the baron lying dead on the floor.

At just twenty-seven years of age, his entire life might be over. Reaching out a hand to lean on the banister as his knees weakened beneath him, Brendan's hopes and dreams for the future rushed before his eyes like a play at Covent Garden.

He did not want it to be over. He wanted to find a good woman and wed. He wanted to have children and spend time with them like his mother had once done with him. He wanted his real life to begin, rather than to be an idle heir frolicking around Town. He wanted … to live.

As Brendan's internal crisis peaked, Michaels rudely disrupted him. The butler tread with heavy steps and a mild look of distaste to open the front door. Brendan realized in a daze that there had been a knock.

Fuck! Is the coroner here to take me away?

He nearly swooned with relief when he caught sight of Halmesbury and Richard entering. He came rushing back from wherever he had been transported to, sound and color a painful cacophony as he returned to the present.

The duke stood near the door, sunlight framing him from behind, and Brendan realized he was talking. He frowned quizzically, struggling to make out the words in his shock.

The duke spoke again. "Are you well?"

Brendan shook his head. "Briggs … is waiting for the coroner to make an arrest."

Halmesbury stepped forward. "Saunton, see to Briggs. Ridley needs a drink."

The duke grabbed him by the arm and steered him to the library, where Brendan dropped into the large, worn armchair he had been using since they had sealed the study. "I just sent a footman to find you. We need to find an alternate suspect, Halmesbury!"

"I agree. That is why Richard and I are here. We realized we spent too much time lamenting the situation yesterday and we need to take more action. This Grimes is bad news, from what my men tell me, and we cannot rely on him to investigate this matter properly."

Brendan nodded, taking the drink that Halmesbury had poured and gulping it down. The shock slowly dissipated, and his wits slowly returned. "We need to put as many men as we can on this. I did not do this, I swear it."

The duke had dropped into a seat next to his. "I know you

did not do this, and we will do whatever it takes to clear your name. Annabel and I will not allow this travesty of justice to occur because this weasel coroner is too focused on his political ambitions to do his job. Besides investigating this matter, I have tasked my men with finding out about this Grimes. He does not strike me as a man who is aboveboard, and we might uncover evidence of his true motives."

Brendan cleared his throat. "Am I to be taken to the Tower or to … Newgate?"

The duke frowned. "I have not heard they intend to do that, but I will definitely insist that they take you to the Tower. Lords will not wish a matter of this import to be tried at lower courts. You might not be confirmed as the baron, but it is well known that you are the legitimate heir."

"Even with the news of my parentage being discussed?"

"It does not signify. The law recognizes you as Josiah Ridley's son, no matter the circumstances. He was married to your mother at the time of your birth. The prosecution may introduce that as motive, but it does not alter your legal status."

Brendan nodded, leaning back in the armchair to rest his aching head. He had never been more thankful that the duke was his brother-in-law. Halmesbury would leave no stone unturned to defend him, and Richard was a tenacious friend. Somehow, they were going to navigate this disaster and he would be cleared of this terrible crime.

* * *

LILY WAS the smallest member of the Abbott family. A fact that she could use to her advantage under normal circumstances. It allowed her to remain hidden when she wished, as long as she kept her mouth shut.

These were not normal circumstances.

"Lily Beatrice Anne Abbott!"

Her heart sank. Mama had found her out.

"Where have you been, young lady?"

Lily slowly turned on the stairs, pinning a bright smile on her face. It was usually easy for her to smile, it being second nature to embrace the world with good humor.

Today she had to force it.

Today was not a normal day.

"Mama! I am so happy to see you. I feel as if we have barely spoken, what with the coronation and everything happening this week! So many late events without me. Did you enjoy ..." Lily, for the life of her, could not think where her parents had been last night. "Last night?" she finished, barely stopping herself from cringing at her weak delivery.

Usually, she would attempt to chatter for a greater length of time, but words were currently failing her. She had discarded one burden of guilt to hoist a new one on her slim shoulders. She would eventually have to work up the courage to break the terrible news to her marriage-minded mama.

But not now.

Now she wanted to make it to her room, throw herself on the bed—after she scaled the step to reach its lofty heights— and mull over her new future now that she had ruined herself so thoroughly.

All because of that awful man, Grimes! If he had done his job and investigated properly instead of targeting Mr. Ridley ...

Lily shook her head to focus on her glowering mother. It was too late for regrets.

"Where were you?" Her mother's uncharacteristic heat made Lily step back, almost stumbling on the stair. She grabbed the banister to right herself, and spread her lips back out. Her smile had been slipping, and it would not do to give her mood away. Not yet.

"I took a constitutional with Nancy."

"On your own!" It was less a question and more a cry of distress.

"Nothing happened. I am here, all safe and sound." It was a bald-faced lie which would soon be revealed, but Lily needed to compose herself before the next battle of discourse.

Speaking with Grimes had been an exhausting experience, especially after a sleepless night of tossing and turning. She had had to dig deep to find every ounce of insouciant chatter she could muster while his cold, beady eyes had surveyed her with patent disgust.

"What if someone had seen you? Of course, someone saw you! How will we explain this? What if it ruins you entirely, young lady?"

Lily withheld a grimace. If Mama thought that walking in the street with Nancy as chaperone was enough to destroy her reputation, she was going to have an apoplexy when she discovered the truth. She hated that she was going to cause Mama distress, but she could not have it on her conscience that they tried an innocent man for patricide. Mama would eventually get over it and turn her attentions to marrying Aidan off.

In the grand scheme of things, Lily was a rather inconsequential piece of the Abbott family heritage. Her making a good marriage would have meant one more connection, but Viscount Moreland, as all his predecessors before him, was very well-connected already. Mama would recover from the disappointment, and Mr. Ridley would be a free man.

"Mama, I had a chaperone, and I was in a good neighborhood in broad daylight." Another bald-faced lie, but Lily really needed to end this conversation so she could go to her room and think about how to break the news to her family. One day, she hoped, they would accept that she had made the right decision. The adult decision.

"Oh, Lily! Why would you do this?"

Lily bit her lip, watching her distraught mother lament her inappropriate behavior, and she felt sad for the coming changes. Mama had always been a good parent. A little too suffocating, a little too worried about what high society thought and about keeping up appearances, but at heart Lady Moreland was a loving parent who wanted what was best for her daughter. They might disagree on what that was, but Lily had never doubted that her mother's concerns were founded on genuine love.

She swallowed the knot that had formed in her throat. Lily sincerely hoped her mother might come to understand the decision she had made, and accept that she had taken the only path she could under the circumstances.

"I needed some air because I have been cooped up all week with all the coronation happenings."

"Is this my fault? Have I neglected you?"

Tears sprang to her eyes. She had not thought about that as a possible consequence—Mama would blame herself once the news broke. Hurting her slightly overbearing parent had never been part of the plan. Not that much planning had been done.

Lily descended the stairs to stand in front of Lady Moreland. Reaching out to take hold of her by the arms, Lily stretched up on her tiptoes to plant a kiss on her mother's smooth cheek. "You are the very best of mamas, and you have never neglected me."

Dropping to step back, and trying to ignore the look of utter astonishment on her mother's face, Lily turned away and ran up the stairs, holding her skirt up with both hands.

"Do not run! It is not ladylike!"

Lily huffed a laugh as she continued her course to her room. Running was the least of her problems now that she had taken such a defining action as she had done this morning.

* * *

"GRIMES IS HERE," Richard intoned from the window.

The earl was a handsome man with an amiable smile. Before his marriage the year before, he had been a renowned skirt-chaser, with women practically lining up to enter his bed. Now that the former rake was tamed, he was no less charming than he had been. Rather, his affability seemed more genuine than it had before he had seen the error of his ways and taken steps to correct his past mistakes.

Currently, there was no sign of Richard's amiable smile.

Reluctantly, the duke rose along with Brendan, whose body felt so heavy it was a struggle to lift it. He briefly kneaded his temple and then carefully reconstituted his composure as a mantle over his face and limbs as he squared his shoulders.

Stiff upper lip, Brendan Ridley. It is time to face your accusers.

The three of them filed out of the library while Brendan wondered if he would be allowed to pack a bag. Perhaps his valet would be permitted to attend him. Then he pulled a face as he thought about convincing the man to enter a prison.

Nay, you will have to do for yourself.

When they reached the entrance hall, Briggs was alone with Michaels, who had the sour appearance of a man who had been sucking on lemons. Brendan deflated slightly, his shoulders sagging just a fraction of an inch. He had just gathered his best masculine solemnity, and the coroner was not even there to witness his bravado in the face of adversity.

Richard peered up and down the hall and stairs as if

expecting the coroner to jump out of the shadows. "Where is Grimes?"

"He has left," Briggs replied. Brendan noted the man's change in demeanor. His earlier reluctance had disappeared. "There will not be an arrest today."

Brendan swayed slightly. The duke caught hold of him, bracing him with his considerable strength and turning to Michaels. "Take Mr. Ridley back to the library!"

Michaels scowled, pursing his lips before stepping forward. Brendan shook his head. "I am all right. I ... shall be in the library."

As soon as he entered the room, he headed for the spirits, pouring a short brandy. He had already had one, and being inebriated at this time seemed like a bad idea, but he at least needed to fortify himself after so many shocking turns of events. He quickly threw it back, swallowing with difficulty while his thoughts swam about.

Why has Grimes changed his mind?

Brendan trudged across the room to drop into the battered armchair which had become his residence over the last few days. Leaning forward, he hung his head while he tried to reconstruct his thoughts. Through the open door, he could hear footsteps approaching.

Brendan rose as the duke entered, his questions only half-formed.

"The woman you were with stepped forward as an alibi. All charges have been dropped," the duke announced.

Brendan clapped a hand over his mouth in relief as Halmesbury approached him. Near the door, he saw Richard talking in a low voice with Briggs.

Brendan sucked air into his constricted lungs. "And here I was hoping to get a tour of the Tower." His quip was weak, mostly just his wound-up nerves speaking on his behalf.

Halmesbury shook his head, a slight grin twisting his lips.

His brother-in-law seemed to be as relieved as he over the change in circumstances.

Presently, the earl finished speaking with the runner. As soon as the door closed behind Briggs, Richard turned to glare at Brendan with livid hatred before storming across the room in a rage. Before Brendan knew what he was about, the Earl of Saunton's fist flew into his face.

The room faded as he saw the large duke springing forward, his tails flapping in his haste to intercede.

"Brendan?"

Darkness. Oblivion.

"Brendan?"

Slowly, he opened his eyes. The duke was looking down at him, his gray eyes reflecting his concern.

Groggy, Brendan recalled the events of several moments ago. Or was it minutes? He had lost consciousness, so he could not know for certain.

"Why is Richard angry with me?"

"It came to light why you would not name the woman you were with. We are both rather ... appalled." Halmesbury's expression was pained.

Brendan squinted in confusion. *Perhaps my wits are addled?* He had known they might judge him if they knew whom he was with, but appalled was rather strong. "About Lady Slight?"

"Nay, you blackguard! About Lily! She is my wife's cousin! An innocent!" Brendan had never seen the earl enraged before, but his face was set into hard lines and both pale and reddened with the force of his emotions.

"What about Lily?"

"You debauched her, you treacherous lech!"

"Who is Lily?"

Richard surged forward with murderous intent in his eyes.

The duke gestured him away, still looking down at Brendan. "Hold off, Saunton! I think there is more to this."

Brendan lifted a hand to rub at his throbbing jaw. "I was with Lady Slight that night. I knew if I named her without her approval, she would simply deny it. And I did not want to tell you who it was because I found myself embarrassed."

Halmesbury considered this announcement, confusion marring his face. "You are saying ... Moreland's daughter lied about being with you. Why would the young lady destroy her reputation for you?"

"I do not know."

"What is this? Never say you believe this scoundrel?" The earl was clearly still in a tither. Likely he anticipated his wife's family descending on him, not to mention his countess's distress that her cousin was ruined.

"Which one is Lily, exactly?"

Richard growled menacingly before stomping over to look down at Brendan, who was relieved that the very large duke rose from his crouch to stand between them. The earl looked fit to do him an injury. "My wife's cousin, you bastard!"

Brendan frowned, attempting to recall who the girl was.

"My god, man! She was with us in this room just two days ago!" Richard threw an arm out to indicate the chair in which she had presumably sat.

Brendan realized he needed to think harder before his friend punched him again. "The little one who looks like a fairy?"

The earl growled, pressing forward, but the duke held up a hand to hold him back. "She is lovely!"

"The one who never stops talking?"

"She is a lively optimist! And she barely spoke when she was with us the day of the murder."

"I barely know her. I hardly recollect she was here after all that happened that day!"

"You will have plenty of time to correct that when you wed!"

Brendan's jaw sagged. "I cannot marry her!"

"You bloody will! The young woman has destroyed her reputation to save your neck!"

Brendan sat up, lifting a hand to cradle his throat in reflex. He could have hung. The coroner had been about to arrest him and transport him to the Tower. Without an alibi, no one would believe he had not committed the murder, not even he, if he were an outsider hearing the facts of the case.

What her unknown reasons were for providing a false alibi did not change the facts. That he had barely noted her presence was irrelevant. The little slip of a girl had saved his bacon in the nick of time.

Collapsing back on the floor, Brendan nodded with resignation.

* * *

"WHAT HAVE YOU DONE?" Her mother's wail interrupted Papa's explanation of Lily's situation.

Aidan careened from the intricate fireplace, his face as white as a ghost, to fall into a plump armchair. "This is all my fault ... If I had been here as agreed ..."

Lily stared into the empty hearth, blood thudding in her ears as her family assimilated the news of her impending scandal.

"There is no time for regrets. Lily felt compelled to act, and it is our place to support her." Viscount Moreland's voice was low but firm as he admonished her mother and brother.

"But, Hugh, she is ruined! Lily will never make a good

match when the peerage believes she was bedded by ... by ... by a murderer!"

Lily winced, clasping her fingers so tight that they ached. She felt terrible for the ordeal she had created, but she could not regret following her conscience to rescue an innocent man.

You did the right thing! There was no other choice.

"Christiana, Mr. Ridley is not a murderer. Lily has provided him with an alibi to clear his name because she has knowledge of his innocence."

"But, Hugh—"

"Our child will be secure because we will stand with her!"

Lily flinched. She had never heard Papa raise his voice before. He was usually accommodating to her mother's wishes, but there was one subject on which he always stood firm. Family loyalty always came first.

Lily supposed she was fortunate that this was the case. When she had knocked on the door of his study, she had not been certain how he would react to what she had to tell him, but she should have known. Papa had immediately called for the rest of the family to join them so he could break the news. Even now, he stood by her side.

She looked up at her father, towering above her. His face showed the signs of aging, but his square jaw was firm and his expression resolute.

Blowing a deep sigh, Papa relaxed his features before continuing. "I know you wanted Lily to make a good match —the best match—but her conscience dictated that she take action. Now our family must work together to help her forge a new path."

Her mother lifted a hand to cover her mouth, a sob escaping as her chocolate brown eyes glistened. Lily's heart wrenched in her chest. Her own eyes prickled with the threat of tears as she dropped her head to stare at her twisting fingers. "I am ... so sorry. I ... did not know what else to do."

"Nay, this is my fault!" Aidan jumped to his feet, pacing back and forth and flinging his hands into the air. "If I had been here that night, I would have seen him myself and been able to step forward as his alibi. It is my fault that Lily was alone. If not for me, she would never have been in this situation in the first place."

"Aidan."

Her brother continued to pace in front of the large fireplace, mumbling about his culpability.

"Aidan!"

He stopped to look at their father, who said, "Lily made her decision, and there is no unringing that bell. News of her spending the night with Ridley will spread through the *ton* shortly, and we must prepare ourselves."

Aidan nodded dully, still pale from the shock of recent revelations.

"Will ... will Mr. Ridley offer for her?" Mama's voice was fretful, and guilt stabbed Lily.

"I shall contact him forthwith to learn his intentions."

"And if he does not?"

Papa firmed his jaw at the question.

Please, Lord. Mr. Ridley must help me!

"We must find a gentleman willing to marry her."

Lily nearly choked at Mama's declaration. What kind of man would be willing to marry her now? Surely not an upstanding one?

Papa shook his head, much to her relief.

"Aidan will take her to the Continent until the scandal dies down?" Her father glanced her way, and Lily nodded in agreement. She had contemplated many alternatives over the course of the night, and that was the only one which appealed.

But Mr. Ridley will do the right thing. He must!

Aidan came to sit by her side, his boyish face gaunt in the morning light. "Whatever you need, Lily Billy. I will pound Ridley until he comes up to scratch, if you wish. Failing that, we will visit the wonders of Europe together."

Lily pulled her lips into a halfhearted smile as she dropped her head against his shoulder. She was grateful that her family would support her over the coming days.

CHAPTER 6

*"The principle on which to lead an army is to establish a standard
of courage that all must achieve."*
Sun Tzu, L'Art de la Guerre (The Art of War)

* * *

JULY 23, 1821

*R*ichard's voice was still ringing in his ears as
Brendan's carriage came to a halt in front of the
Abbotts' home. Through the window, he noticed Lady
Slight's townhouse across the street.

Miss Abbott's strange decision made a little more sense
now that he could see that it was her home where he had
disembarked several nights earlier. Practically a stone's
throw apart.

A footman opened the door, lowering the steps for him.
Brendan descended the steps and then peered up at the
modest home of Viscount Moreland. Three bays wide and

three stories high, there was no ostentatious display despite the family's wealth. Brendan knew Lady Saunton, the viscount's niece, had boasted a large dowry that had led to all her troubles the year before. The earl had saved her from a dire situation unbeknownst to the Abbotts and had nearly been killed for interceding.

Which reminded him of Richard's agitated admonishments early this morning. Butterflies set flight in his stomach as Brendan once again thought about his looming proposal. His lack of sleep, and the shock of the baron's death followed by his almost arrest, had his head aching. There were moments where he felt entirely disoriented, something he had been battling since the runner had informed him of his imminent arrest the day before.

Now he was to offer for a young girl he did not know.

Brendan had always promised himself that he would never allow the baron to trap him in an unwanted marriage. When he learned the truth about his parentage—and realized that his mother had married Josiah Ridley out of necessity, to save Brendan from bastardy—he had vowed to never find himself in similar circumstances. His mother had been beauty and grace, and she had deserved better than the marriage with his uncle-father.

Brendan had resolved himself to one day marry a woman of his own choice, one he would cherish. Somehow, he would know her when he met her. Know that she was the perfect woman for him. She would make him forget the widows of his past and remind him what it was to be loved unconditionally in the manner that his mother had loved him before her untimely death more than ten years earlier.

Yet, here he stood, ready to enter the Abbott household and make an offer for a young chit whom he barely knew. A child.

Brendan did not want to be a man who said his vows and

then philandered around London, as many members of the *ton* did. But how was he to make a marriage with a veritable stranger who was barely out of the schoolroom?

It was his worst nightmare. He had evaded the baron to ensure he would not be forced down this path. The old man would have been ecstatic to learn that Brendan was to marry the daughter of a wealthy and powerful viscount, a step above the two of them in rank. It was galling to contemplate Josiah Ridley's glee if he had been here to witness Brendan's descent into propriety and ascent in social status.

It had been several days since he had found the baron on the floor of his study, with sleepless nights to make his temples throb. His eyes were gritty from the lack of rest, and his chest tight from being forced down this path.

Steeling himself, he donned his beaver and approached the door, resolutely raising the brass ring to bring it down in a loud knock.

A tall footman answered the door and accepted his card. Peering down at it, the polite expression receded. "Mr. Ridley."

It was a statement, not a question, and there was no mistaking the hard look the servant threw at him. Brendan had always made a point of getting along with servants, something his mother had instilled in him. This one was not receptive to the friendly smile he attempted. The servants here must be loyal to the household, and it was clear that knowledge of Miss Abbott's circumstances had made its way belowstairs.

"I will see if Lord Moreland will receive you."

Brendan winced at the tone. Clearly, the man was not concerned that Brendan would complain to Lord Moreland about his behavior, casting a scathing glance back over his shoulder as he walked down the hall.

When Brendan was finally shown into the viscount's

study, he noticed the elegant quality of the room. Overt signs of wealth were not on display, but the exquisite furnishings could only be Chippendales and the wood panels cladding the walls were of fine quality indeed.

Lord Moreland rose from behind his mahogany desk to greet him, gesturing for Brendan to take a seat. "I confess I am relieved you are here, Ridley. My daughter has taken an extraordinary risk to see to your freedom, and I hope you appreciate her sacrifice."

Brendan nodded. "I am here to discuss terms of marriage."

The older man's forehead puckered. "Marriage? Lily must accept your offer before we can discuss terms."

The throbbing in Brendan's temples was at a fever pitch, and it took him a few seconds to comprehend what the viscount had said. "Surely she has no choice, given the circumstances?"

Moreland was a large man, tall with wide shoulders, dressed in conservative but expensive clothing. He had a handsome, square face and a calm manner, but his face firmed at Brendan's question. "I appreciate you are here, and taking steps to correct this situation. However, I want to be clear about this—my daughter has bravely acted on your behalf, and she enjoys the full support of our family. It is her choice whether she wishes to proceed with a wedding."

Brendan lifted a hand, no longer able to ignore the pounding at his right temple. Besides being a child barely out of the schoolroom, apparently the chit was spoilt by a doting father.

Perfect! Not only a bride I did not wish for, but an interfering family to contend with.

At this point, he could safely claim that this was the worst week of his life. Worse than the week his mother had died, leaving him and Annabel to the baron's discompassionate mercies. This was the week he had been accused of patricide, and now was forced to wed a girl he did not know with an idolizing family in the wings.

"Do I have your permission to speak with her, then?"

"I am looking into you, Ridley, but I am not pleased with what I know thus far. Your history with your father does not demonstrate honor in regards to one's blood."

Brendan's breath hitched, and he had to calm himself. "That was the baron's choice, my lord. He sent me to London and bade me never to return to Somerset."

Lord Moreland's face softened. "Your father is the cause of the estrangement?"

Father! Huh!

"Yes, my lord."

"That is something, I suppose. However, any man who visits the widow Slight would be a cause of concern for me. It is hardly the action of an honorable man."

Brendan gritted his teeth as the throbbing in his temples ratcheted up. The irony that he was defending his right to marry a girl whom he did not know was not lost on him as he sought a response. Many fathers of the *ton* would not care, as the late baron had made clear when Brendan's sister had once found her former betrothed *in flagrante delicto*. But Lord Moreland apparently had strong thoughts on the subject of fidelity.

"The actions of an unwed gentleman, I assure you. I have no plans to continue with Lady Slight if—*when*—I am wed." Brendan had caught himself, but Moreland cast him a baleful eye at the slip. Truthfully, he wished he could visit Harriet, but he would not do so if he were to marry. Had the widow heard of his predicament? Perhaps not. Perhaps she would have stepped forward to save his neck if it had come to that.

Moreland stood up. "It does not signify. Lily is aware of your affair, so it is for her to reach a decision if she wishes to proceed with a wedding. I trust my daughter, and since she thinks you are worthy of her intervention, then I will allow you to speak with her to come to terms. Thomas will show you to the drawing room."

The viscount rang a bell, and behind him the door opened. Brendan took to his feet, wondering why an established man like Moreland would think that a young girl barely out of pigtails could make such an important decision regarding her future. Brendan could hardly comprehend how Miss Abbott had made her way to visit the coroner in the first place.

* * *

IT WAS with a heady sense of relief that Lily had observed Mr. Ridley arriving. She had quickly fixed her silly lace and muslin gown and checked her hair in the mirror. She had not slept in several nights. Her head was heavy and her eyes burning, but if Mr. Ridley had come up to scratch and was here to offer for her hand in marriage, this terrible week would end on a positive note.

It was not how she had hoped to approach a marriage, but the gentleman was young and handsome. More importantly, he was affable and from a good family. Given their mutual connections, she could do much worse than tying herself to him.

Lily bobbed up and down the drawing room that overlooked the street, trying to contain her excitement that Mr. Ridley would salvage her reputation. Mama would stop weeping, which would make Lily feel better about what she had done. And, hopefully, Aidan would stop lamenting it was all his fault that his sister was ruined.

Some semblance of normalcy would return, and Lily would embark on a new journey as a married woman of the *ton.* She could finally make her own choices, order her own clothes, and attend events with Sophia, rather than her mother domineering her every decision. And she and Mr. Ridley would find some common ground and perhaps even, one day, fall in love.

Checking the clock, she wondered what Papa might be saying to Mr. Ridley.

Finally, there was a knock on the door. Lily quickly rubbed her scratchy eyes and called out for the servant to enter. Thomas stepped in to announce Mr. Ridley, before bowing and departing the room. Unexpectedly, the footman closed the door behind him and Lily realized that this was it. She was alone with a man for the first time because he was to propose marriage.

Her eyes sought the gentleman out. He had come to a stop in front of the fireplace, gazing down while Lily studied his reflection in the mirror above the mantel. Mr. Ridley's tanned face was pale and drawn. She appreciated how handsome he appeared in the afternoon light, in his impeccable buckskins and green coat, but it was obvious that he was weary. Likely, he had not slept in many days, and her heart ached on his behalf. What a terrible week the young man had experienced.

Is he devastated over his father's death? He has not had an opportunity to mourn!

Mr. Ridley cleared his throat. "I wanted to thank you, Miss Abbott. Your intervention was quite timely. I was about to be arrested when you met with the coroner."

"You are welcome, Mr. Ridley! I was quite beside myself over your situation. Lady Slight's choice to not step forward was most unacceptable, and I found myself consumed with guilt. I believe it was the only method I had to assist you!"

In the mirror, Lily could see that Mr. Ridley had frowned at the mention of Lady Slight, causing her stomach to tighten. Was the gentleman still intrigued by the widow? How did he feel about making an offer of marriage?

I am afraid I do not care. If he offers me marriage, I will accept!

"Lady Slight likely does not know of my predicament."

Lily bit her lip. The widow most assuredly did know about Mr. Ridley's plight, but Lily was uncertain if she should inform him of the ill-advised visit to beseech Lady Slight to step forward. Lily was still rather embarrassed by how she had dealt with the matter, so perhaps it was poor timing to confess her knowledge of the widow's thoughts.

"Nevertheless, I am so happy you are here! You are here to offer for me, correct? I lay awake all night to reach this decision, and I must say I am quite worn out. But here you are, to do the honorable thing! I knew you would! You are a gentleman through and through!" Lily clapped her hand over her mouth to quell the babbling before any more words could spill from her overenthusiastic lips. Mr. Ridley would not be accustomed to her chatter, and she did not wish to put him off during such a crucial conversation.

Looking back at the mirror, she noticed the gentleman was frowning again. Slowly, he turned to stare at her, an incredulous expression on his face, and her heart skipped a beat in her chest. Had she already put him off with her babbling?

"Did you provide me with an alibi"—Lily dropped her hand from her mouth, leaning her head forward in her eagerness—"to trap me into marriage?"

All the nights of lost sleep, and the strain of consoling her distraught mother, along with the abandoned hopes and dreams of a love match that she had been so eager to find, came crashing down on Lily.

The force of it had such weight that she raised a hand as if to protect her head from the falling debris, before dropping it down at the realization that there was no tangible evidence of the destruction in her mind. She took a step back, nearly falling over an end table in her haste to put distance between them.

"Is ... is that what you think of me?"

Mr. Ridley narrowed his eyes, his suspicion evident, while Lily fought off a wave of nausea. "You must admit you had unusual knowledge of my circumstances if you wished to trap me into marriage, Miss Abbott?"

Lily had been so excited to see his carriage draw up, and to believe that her prayers had been answered. But this relentless nightmare was not yet over.

Tears sprang into her eyes while she frantically sought a resolution. Agreeing to a marriage with a man who mistrusted her to this extent, who believed her capable of providing an alibi with the purpose of forcing a marriage, was untenable. A simple solution was not to be found.

"Surely you know me better than that, Mr. Ridley? We have several mutual acquaintances and—"

"Miss Abbott, we do not know each other at all. I have no knowledge of what you might be capable of, given the right incentive. I could not make sense of why a young woman would risk her reputation to defend me, but now ..."

Lily pushed back the emotions raging through her, straightening up while an eerie calm stole over her. Defending Mr. Ridley had been her decision, and she would deal with the consequences. "Are you here to make an offer, Mr. Ridley?"

She was proud of how even her voice sounded, and she refused to let any additional words spill from her lips. He would have no option but to answer her.

"What choice do I have?"

Lily gave a curt nod. "Then I shall respond. I am pleased for your sister's sake, and for our mutual connections, that your name has been cleared. I stand by my decision to do the honorable thing on your behalf. In regards to your offer, the answer is no. No, I will not wed you. No, I do not wish to receive you in my home. No!"

With that, Lily turned and strode away. At least she hoped she was striding, and not merely running off like a silly girl, because inside, her heart was cracking into a thousand pieces and her pride was all she had to defend herself from the onslaught of pain. She wondered if visiting the Continent would soothe the tempest in her soul, or would she forever mourn the marriage she would never attain now that her reputation was ruined and Mr. Ridley had disappointed her hopes.

Exiting, she shut the door on Mr. Ridley, and the past, before heading for her bedroom.

She and Nancy would need to pack her things, because she had a long journey to prepare for. She must leave as soon as possible so she would not have to witness Mama suffering, and healing for all could begin.

CHAPTER 7

*"Confront them with annihilation, and they will then survive;
plunge them into a deadly situation, and they will then live. When
people fall into danger, they are then able to strive for victory."*
Sun Tzu, L'Art de la Guerre (The Art of War)

* * *

Brendan stood in the street, his head reeling. He suspected that he might have handled the situation with Miss Abbott in a less than exemplary manner. Raising his hand, he rubbed his temple once again, attempting to alleviate the tension that had built and built over the past few days.

He had barely had time to be relieved that he was not being arrested before the next crisis had presented itself. The earl was livid about Miss Abbott, presumably because his countess would be distraught at the news regarding her cousin.

The young lady's act had been so generous, so unprecedented, he simply could not believe it had been altruistic.

Unfortunately, revealing his sentiments had brought her to tears, and Brendan was fighting off gut-wrenching shame for mishandling the discussion. Even if she had plotted to trap him, she was just a child. She barely looked old enough to be out of the schoolroom, and perhaps she had had grand ideas of marrying a baron.

His head throbbed, a stray thought bouncing around his skull. Miss Abbott must be older than she looked, because he seemed to recollect that he had been introduced to her the prior year. In her lacy dress, and her girlish ringlets, he could have sworn she was not old enough to be having a Season. But if he recollected their first meeting accurately, the young lady would be on at least her second Season, which simply was not possible. That would make her almost of an age with Lady Saunton, but she barely came up to his chest. He could not even ascertain if she had curves in the flouncy gowns she seemed to favor wearing.

Perhaps Lady Moreland had brought Miss Abbott out early?

Squinting against the bright sunlight, Brendan's vision was blurry from the pain in his head. He had sent the carriage away, requesting it return after an hour, because he thought he would be negotiating a marriage contract with Lord Moreland. His options were to walk home, or ...

Or to visit Lady Slight until my carriage returns.

Brendan did not think it was a good idea, especially in sight of the Abbotts' townhouse, but he felt quite unsettled about the past few days and he could not suppress the urge to call on the widow.

Before he knew it, his feet were moving across the street and his hand was raising the brass ring to knock. Matters felt incomplete with Harriet somehow, and he wanted to resolve their relationship.

When the butler opened the door, his eyes flared ever so

slightly in surprise. Brendan knew it was unseemly to visit the widow in broad daylight, but he could not find the will to care about being proper.

"Lady Slight," he asserted.

The butler hesitated, but acquiesced and opened the door wider to allow him entry. Probably the servant thought it better to allow him in quickly rather than have a gentleman loitering on the front step. Once in, the older man led him toward the painted room. The drawing room was Harriet's favorite, most likely because she knew it exhibited her in the best light—a beautiful woman seated in a beautiful room.

Somehow this thought caused a slight irritation, reminding him that he had been contemplating ending their arrangement. The viscountess was far too enamored with her own appearance, posing frequently in a manner that suggested she had practiced her nonchalant gestures in front of a mirror. A gilded mirror.

The butler knocked on the door, then entered the drawing room to announce Brendan's arrival. Following him into the room, Brendan stopped and took in the perfection of his redheaded paramour, attired in silk with her bosom revealed in eye-popping proportions, surrounded by her room of intricate painting. On her left, a naked Venus frolicked with several cherubs in a large oil painting, mirroring the impressive bosom of the painting's owner.

"Brendan! It is so lovely to see you. I was not sure if I would see you again."

He arched an eyebrow in question.

"I heard you might be arrested," she offered as an explanation.

Brendan frowned. "That little *on-dit* spread rather quickly?"

Harriet waved her hand. "I heard about it from the oddest little chit who came to call on me. Can you believe she demanded I reveal your whereabouts—she even threatened me!"

His pounding headache vanished in an instant, and Brendan took an involuntary step forward.

"Whom do you mean?"

Harriet giggled, fluttering a hand toward the window. "Lord Moreland's daughter … or niece … or something or other. From across the street. The little hoyden tried to intimidate me, but she was barely larger than a squirrel and I set her in her place. As if anyone would believe a child over the word of an established widow of an important viscount."

Miss Abbott had tried to convince Harriet to assist him?

What did that mean?

If the girl had been trying to trap him into a marriage, why would she attempt to have Harriet step forward as a witness to his innocence?

The headache came rushing back, and Brendan raised a hand to rub his temple. It never paid off for him to be ill-tempered, but this blasted week had him on edge. Now he had accused a selfless young lady of nefarious intentions, and the embarrassment slammed hard like a blow to his solar plexus. Dragging in a ragged breath, Brendan sought a seat. He dropped into a spindly gilded chair with a loud creak.

"Miss Abbott attempted to have you step forward as an alibi?"

"Miss Abbott! That was her name! Hardly a miss, more of a child muslined up to her chin. I would not leave the house if I were dressed in that peagoose concoction. Quite puritanical, I must say!"

The widow's laughing chatter grated on his nerves, and he raised his fingers to his temple once more.

"How did you reply to her request?"

Harriet giggled again. "I put her in her place, I will have you know. I told her that if she accused me, I would deny it.

She even had the gall to threaten me with your coachman as corroboration, but I pointed out that the only fact that he could attest to was that he had delivered you to her home across the street. I did not state it, but it was clear she would compromise her own reputation if she attempted such a tactic with me."

Brendan bit back a groan. Apparently, the mystery of Miss Abbott's decision was revealed. She had reached the conclusion that the only method of assisting him was to pretend he had spent the night with her, rather than with Harriet. Instead of appreciating her integrity in preserving his freedom, perhaps even his very life, he had accused her of deplorable subterfuge.

He had not thought this week could get any worse, but discovering his own perfidy when he had always prided himself on treating people fairly—

"Were you not concerned for me, Harriet? Would you have allowed me to hang?"

The widow had been so self-absorbed, she had barely noticed his reaction, but the question had her leaping to her feet. Rushing over, she grabbed him by both hands. "Of course not, Brendan! I knew you would find a solution. You are an intelligent man with powerful connections."

So, yes. The widow would have carried on with her meaningless pursuits while I was tried and hung.

Brendan recalled how he had questioned his life choices when he had found the baron's body. Since then, he had convinced himself that Harriet cared for him more than he had postulated in the distress of that moment. That she had simply been unaware of his predicament.

The truth was now revealed, and he had to admit that the one person who had risked everything to save him was a young girl who barely knew him. Miss Abbott was a warrior. A woman of integrity. Willing to act on behalf of a veritable stranger. Lord Moreland's decision to allow his daughter to exert her will regarding her future now made perfect sense.

And I am an idiot. A spoilt, narcissistic idiot. The sort of man who finds the soulless Harriet alluring.

He must repair the damage he had done to Miss Abbott's pride. But how?

* * *

LILY HAD BEEN LYING on her bed, staring at the ceiling for several minutes. Her prideful storming from the drawing room had lasted until she had entered her bedroom, at which point she had hoisted herself onto the bed and collapsed in a state of numbness to consider her future.

A knock at the door barely registered. "Go away!"

She could not bear any more of Mama's remonstrations. She knew it came from a place of love, that Mama was distraught by Lily's change of circumstances, but she could not bear it at this moment. Her certainty that Mr. Ridley would come up to scratch and rescue her from scandal had come to naught, and she had no energy left to deal with her mother's stricken regrets.

The handle clicked open and a red-blonde head peeked around the door. "I really would rather come in."

"Sophia!" Lily sat up in a rush, bursting into tears to see her best friend.

Her cousin rushed over, joining her on the bed and pulling her into an embrace. "Shh, Lily. Everything will work out."

"You heard?"

"Of course! I would have come sooner, but Miles had colic and I was up with him and the nurse all night."

"I am so happy to see you! Mr. Ridley was here, but he said such awful things and I sent him away!"

Sophia pulled her closer. "Your mother informed me. Apparently, I missed the performance by a few minutes."

"How would Mama know what happened? Mr. Ridley only just left."

"I am sure she was listening at the door. She seemed quite affronted with the gentleman, complaining about his ingratitude."

Lily pulled back to stare at her cousin in amazement. "She did?"

Sophia nodded. "She was quite livid, ranting about how no man can treat an Abbott in that manner."

"Huh! I thought she would blame me for not accepting the offer."

"Nay, Lily. Your mother wants what is best for you. She just needs time to adjust to all these happenings. Her hopes were high for an excellent match, and now she must contend with broken straws. Just give her some time to figure things out."

"I am ever so glad you are here."

"What happens now? Are you certain you do not wish to marry Mr. Ridley?"

Lily wailed, burying her face back in Sophia's shoulder, which was damp with tears. "I am not certain of anything! I do not wish to be snubbed by good society. Now I must leave London in shame and travel to places unknown just so I can show my face in public, far from everything I am familiar with. How did it all come to this?"

Sophia patted her on the shoulder, while several moments passed.

"I feel I should warn you that the gossip rags mentioned you this morning."

Lily groaned. "My presence in high society has finally been noted."

"I am afraid so."

Lily heaved her chest in distress. "What am I to do?"

Sophia turned her head to Lily, her blue eyes sympathetic. "Would you ... permit me to speak to Mr. Ridley?"

"Oh, I think that is impossible. It is clear he does not trust me."

"I feel confident we can make this arrangement work, but the gentleman has been under great pressure these past few days. He always struck me as a kind man, spending time with his nephew and playing with Miles when he visits our home."

"You believe I should provide him with another opportunity to make his offer?"

"I believe we need a little patience. Mr. Ridley's belligerence is understandable. He found his father dead, was accused of patricide, and then was forced to come here to offer you marriage in the course of four days. The poor man is reeling. It does not excuse his behavior, but I believe we should try this again."

Lily sucked on her lower lip, staring out the bedroom window while she thought. "I am not sure."

"Mr. Ridley only had Richard to advise him this morning before his visit here. As much as I love my husband, you and I both know that Richard is still learning how to handle the intricacies of emotional ties, and Mr. Ridley is inexperienced in courtship. I am certain that he is the best solution to your debacle but might require some guidance in such a trying time."

Nodding, Lily fell back on the bed. "We shall try this one more time."

Sophia settled down beside her, and they both stared at the ceiling just as they had done as girls. "It was exceedingly brave of you."

"I had to do it. Seeing the duchess in such despair ... I had to follow my conscience."

"You gave up much."

Lily sighed. "I shall never have a suitor bring me hothouse flowers, or accompany me to Gunter's for ices. I will never have my first dance with a man and realize that he might be my future husband."

Sophia's lips twisted. "Neither of us has had an easy time of it, have we?"

"Richard did bring you flowers that day you compromised him!"

Her cousin huffed. "And he drove me to Gunter's the day we wed to flaunt our connection in front of the *ton*."

Lily smiled, remembering the strange course of Sophia's wedding to the earl. They had overcome much to find their way to love.

Slowly, her high spirits trickled back, and Lily felt optimistic for the first time in days. "Perhaps it could all work out!"

Sophia reached out to clasp Lily's hand. "I will do everything in my power to make it so."

* * *

BRENDAN STEPPED out into the bright sunlit street at the same time as another man departed Lord Moreland's home. Stopping to stare at each other, Brendan realized this must be Moreland's heir. The young man was the image of his father. Tall. Broad shoulders. Square, handsome face. However, the gentleman had the coloring of Miss Abbott. Chocolate brown hair and eyes which were currently glaring at him.

Before Brendan could move away from the widow's door, Abbott came striding across the street to confront him.

"What are you doing at this ... this ... this harlot's home? Why has Lily turned you down?" Reaching out, the outraged brother grabbed him by the lapels.

Blazes! I need to visit Gentleman Jackson's! This is the second time I have been manhandled.

He blamed his lack of sleep. His reaction time was too slow, and the pounding in his head a distraction he could not set aside. "I was here for ten minutes! Nothing happened."

Abbott stopped. Slowly, he released Brendan, who tugged at his waistcoat and jacket to set them to rights.

"My sister is ruined, and it is my fault for leaving her alone that night. You have to fix this, Ridley!"

The torment in the brother's face was apparent to Brendan, even in his compromised state, and he was once again stabbed with shame. If it were his sister …

"Miss Abbott refused my offer."

"Why? What did you do? She hoped you would take care of her after what she did for you!"

Brendan broke eye contact, staring over Abbott's shoulder. He was hardly going to admit his cruel accusation or fumbled proposal. "It is not what she wants. And what about you? Would you marry a child?"

Abbott's face hardened. "She is no child, you scoundrel! What Lily lacks in stature, she makes up for in heart! She is kindness and joy. And, fortunately for you, she is the epitome of honor, or even now you would be imprisoned. This woman"—Abbott gestured at Harriet's home—"is a vicious viper. Yet you visit her while my sister has retreated, facing certain ruin. I am to take her to the Continent to outrun this scandal. Lily is a young woman with her entire life ahead of her. What is she to do if you will not assist her?"

Brendan winced. The more he learned of the girl, the more ashamed he felt about how he had treated her earlier. He must aid the young woman who had discarded a promising future to help him, but how he was to do that was unclear. She had practically thrown him out.

"I will work something out."

Abbott narrowed his eyes, looking Brendan over carefully. He stepped back, giving Brendan room to breathe. "I spoke with some of the chaps this morning, and they tell me you are a good sort, Ridley. You must wed my sister to save her from this shame. Lily does not deserve this. Everyone she knows will give her the cut direct. It is inconceivable that this happen to her." Abbott hung his head, overcome by emotion. "She is the very best of sisters, and if I could restore her reputation, I would. You must help her."

Brendan raised a shaky hand to rake it through his hair. He had no inkling of how to repair this, and he was so damned tired he felt he might collapse like a dog in the street. "I will try to make it right, Abbott."

It was not much to offer as consolation, but it was all Brendan could think to say.

WHEN SOPHIA LEFT, Lily followed her downstairs. After bidding her cousin goodbye, she entered the fateful drawing room, where she had not only witnessed Mr. Ridley enter and then depart Lady Slight's home, but had also anticipated his proposal, then rejected him. Mama was sitting in Lily's favorite spot by the window and watching the street intently, flinching in surprise when Lily's footfalls disturbed her.

"Lily!" Mama jumped to her feet, crossing the room to pull her daughter into an embrace. Lily froze, her face squished into her mother's shoulder while her arms hung uselessly at her sides and she tried to make sense of what was happening. "We shall find a way through this. I cannot believe what Mr. Ridley said to you! I was so relieved when Sophia arrived … I would have come upstairs, but I was not sure what to say and I thought she might address it better than I."

Lily lifted her arms and embraced her mother back, hiding her face as tears once again threatened to flow. Mama's unexpected shift to one of support was welcome. Lily had been feeling terrible about how she had affected her mother with her news. "Sophia and I had a good talk. Thank you for … Thank you."

They broke apart awkwardly, neither making eye contact. "Mama, I would prefer not to attend the Townsend dinner this evening. Perhaps you can inform them I have a headache?"

Something flashed over her mother's face, too fleeting for Lily to comprehend it. "Our invitation was … rescinded."

Remorse twisted in Lily's belly. Word of her scandal must be spreading rapidly, as Sophia had warned her earlier. "I am sorry."

Mama shook her head. "I never liked Lady Townsend that much anyway."

Lily smiled wanly, not wanting to refute her mother's declaration. Mama and Lady Townsend had been friends for as long as Lily could recall, but pointing it out would not help anything. "Sophia informs me that I was mentioned in the gossip rags."

Mama blew out her cheeks, shaking her head again. "Sophia was minimizing the truth. There was a drawing of you in … an inappropriate state … with Mr. Ridley."

Lily swallowed hard, mortified and unsure how to respond. "I am so sorry, Mama."

"We will prevail. Perhaps Sophia will talk some sense into Mr. Ridley."

"I hope so. I truly do."

* * *

"Briggs is here."

Michaels's disapproving tone was all too obvious. Brendan gritted his teeth. The source of the butler's animosity was unknown to him. It had been present the very first night he had arrived in London, freshly booted from Baydon Hall by his uncle-father on his twenty-first birthday. He should be accustomed to it by now, but now that he was to be the new baron, perhaps he should retire the supercilious servant.

"Show him in."

The duke shifted in his seat while Richard turned from the towering stacks of musty books he had been glaring at since his arrival a few minutes earlier. The earl was still bristling with umbrage over the situation with Miss Abbott, but he had arrived as promised to meet with the runner. Now that Brendan's name had been cleared, the true identity of the baron's killer needed to be uncovered.

Kneading his temples, Brendan steeled himself. The lack of sleep, along with the altercations at the Abbotts' home, were draining the last of his energy, but this matter had to be dealt with urgently.

The runner finally appeared in the doorway, bowing slightly. "My lord."

Apparently, now that Brendan was not under arrest, Briggs had settled on how to address him. He supposed that was a good omen.

"Please, have a seat."

The runner walked up, looking uncomfortable but taking a seat next to the duke and removing his battered hat.

The duke cleared his throat. "We wish to hire you to pursue the matter of the baron's death."

Briggs nodded. "I was hoping you would, because I have concerns for Lord Filminster's safety."

Brendan had barely been listening, the pressure in his

skull distracting him, but the statement had him straightening in his chair. "What?"

"Before I raise my concerns, I must ask ... Would your father have answered the door himself?"

Frowning, Brendan shook his head. "Never. The baron would not lower himself to fulfill the duties of a servant. He was ... a vain man."

"I was afraid of that."

Halmesbury leaned forward in his armchair, his concern clear. "What are you thinking, Briggs?"

"Lord Filminster"—Briggs bobbed his head toward Brendan as clarification—"spoke of being let in early in the morning. None of the servants admitted to being the one who opened the door for him. That is suspicious in itself, but ..."

Brendan's impatience got the better of him. He had been living on a knife's edge, and his equilibrium was long since eroded to dust. "But?"

Briggs tugged at his mustache, his expression displaying his reluctance to continue. "The baron was murdered by one of the servants, or a servant knows who killed him because they provided the killer access to your home."

Brendan groaned, dropping his face into his hands. Of course! He had been so consumed by problems, he had not applied logic. Vaguely aware that the murder must be solved, Brendan had failed to realize the perpetrator was close to hand, or a traitor was in residence in his home.

"Bloody hell," the earl muttered beneath his breath. "We have been contending with family pressures, so we did not stop to think about the implications."

The duke sighed. "I, on the other hand, have had time to think on it, which is why I insisted we meet with Briggs. Annabel reached the same conclusion that the baron would never lower himself to answer the front door. Michaels informed me that the door had been locked, and verified as such, because there have been reports of break-ins."

Briggs nodded in agreement. "I do not wish to cause any panic, but I think it is imperative that the servants be questioned again. With Grimes overseeing the investigation, I was not free to act, but he is tart about how things have turned out, so he is focusing on the inquest. I wish to speak with them again without supervision, so I might compile a list of suspects."

"What of Grimes? Is he likely to pursue me?"

Halmesbury shook his head. "Fortunately, since Miss Abbott has provided you with an alibi, I was able to persuade the Home Secretary to intercede with Grimes about pursuing proper lines of inquiry."

The anxiety Brendan had been feeling dissipated at this news. "Briggs, you may have whatever you need. The safety of my household must be secured."

He made arrangements with the runner, offering him double his usual fee along with a bonus, so he would turn over his cases to other runners. It was imperative the man prioritize the baron's murder.

Calling Michaels back to see to Briggs's needs, Brendan found himself alone once more with the duke and the earl. Silence had fallen the moment the door closed, and Brendan realized that the subject of their discussion was to shift to Miss Abbott.

Resuming his seat, he rubbed his eyes, which were still gritty from exhaustion, waiting for the barrage of words to come.

"When is the wedding?" Richard's hard words cut through the room like a firm slap across the face.

"There is not to be one."

The earl's face fell into a scowl, a low growl emitting

from his throat. Brendan stood up and moved behind his chair in preparation for another enraged attack.

"What happened?"

Brendan had almost forgotten the duke was present, but it was a relief to hear his voice. Richard was so angry, angrier than he had ever seen his longtime friend, and Halmesbury was definitely needed to bank the fires.

"I … may have … accused the young woman of deliberately trapping me."

Brendan was staring at the wall, but there was no mistaking the snarl from the direction of the stacks.

The duke sighed heavily. "What do you plan to do?"

"I do not know. Miss Abbott refused my offer. I must confess I was relieved because I am not ready to marry a child."

"You are the child, Ridley! And it is time for you to grow up!" The earl's angry interjection was followed by a scratch at the door.

Michaels entered, prompting Richard to recede farther into the shadows of the room and away from Brendan. "Lady Saunton is here."

The earl froze, turning to stare at his wife, who had entered during the butler's announcement. "Sophia! What are you doing here?"

The countess tilted her head, smiling benignly at her husband, whose prior rage had dissipated like snow melting in the hot sun. "I am here to speak with Mr. Ridley about Lily, of course."

CHAPTER 8

"There has never been a protracted war from which a country has benefited."
Sun Tzu, L'Art de la Guerre (The Art of War)

* * *

JULY 24, 1821

*S*heer exhaustion from several days of insomnia had finally carried Lily off to the land of sleep. It had been a relief to have her thoughts fade into black for the first time since the night of the murder. By the time she opened her eyes, it was midmorning.

Sitting up, she stretched her arms out and breathed in deeply while wiggling her toes. She felt a million times better now that she had had rest. The strange aches and pains of fatigue had vanished, and her usual optimism had returned to fill her head with possibilities.

"Lily! You have a visitor."

Spinning toward the door, which now stood open, it startled Lily to find Mama with a broad smile on her face.

"My abigail is here to assist you to get ready." Lily noticed the lady's maid was standing in the hall behind her ecstatic parent.

What on earth?

When Mama had initially heard the news of Lily's ruin, she had wept and lamented Lily's future in plaintive tones. Then, after Mr. Ridley's accusatory proposal, Mama had become angry, ranting in an agitated manner about the state of young men and their deplorable manners. Dinner had been a torturous affair, with her brother staring numbly at his plate, evidently still blaming himself for what had happened while Papa had been called away on an urgent matter.

Now she is joyful?

What could cause such a drastic shift in mood? "Who is it?"

"It is not for me to say. Quickly, we must get you ready." Mama clapped her hands together and her lady's maid rushed in.

Lily was still feeling groggy from just having woken up, but she reluctantly left the embrace of her comfortable bed. She had hoped to take her time rising, and perhaps enjoy a cup of tea before descending the stairs, but it was not to be.

Mama headed for Lily's wardrobe, looking through the gowns inside and muttering until she pulled out a creamy confection of lace and cotton. Lily pulled a face. It was the one the least suitable for her complexion, but Mama insisted it was perfection.

With all the bows and flounces, the gown made Lily feel like a child preparing for a formal portrait—the kind where the wealthy family dressed in costumes from bygone eras. Perhaps, if Sophia failed to bring Mr. Ridley up to scratch and Lily was forced to leave for the Continent, Aidan would help her replace her wardrobe far from Mama's prying eyes.

Please, Lord! These clothes are hideous for me.

Her prayer was interrupted by the maid, who began to vigorously brush out Lily's hair, causing her eyes to water.

Twenty minutes later she was ready, her hair in the hated ringlets, and Mama dragging her by the hand down the hall. Once they reached the staircase, her mother started descending, almost pulling Lily off balance with her longer stride. "Mama, I am short!"

Her mother paused. "We must hurry. It has been an age."

Lily nodded, taking up her skirts with one hand in order to hasten her descent. As they approached the first floor, her nose tickled. Raising her hand, she quickly pinched it to fight off a sneeze, almost tripping on the last step. Mama hurled out an arm and steadied her.

"Achoo!"

Mama ignored her, racing toward the drawing-room door and flinging it open.

"Achoo!"

Lily sniffled before stepping into the brightly lit room and gasping in surprise.

On every surface were vases of lilies. On every table, the mantel, even the wide windowsills were beautiful, fragrant lilies of every kind. She had never seen so many flowers outside of a flower market!

"Achoo! Achoo! Achoo!"

And across the room stood Mr. Ridley, looking ever so handsome in the sunlight. His features were relaxed and his tanned face returned to normal. Mr. Ridley must have finally gotten some rest!

"Achoo! Achoo! Achoo! Achoo! Achoo! Achoo!"

Lily swiped her fingertips at her streaming eyes while her heart filled to the brim. Flowers! He had brought her flowers!

"Achoo! Achoo! Achoo!"

"Oh, Lily! I forgot!" Mama was stricken, throwing her hands up in her despair.

Mr. Ridley had stepped forward, concern marring his eyes. "Are you all right, Miss Abbott?"

"Achoo! Achoo! Achoo! Achoo!"

"She is not, Mr. Ridley. I forgot that Lily has some sort of sensitivity to lilies. I am afraid we must leave the room!"

"Of course, I shall take her for a drive in my carriage, as we discussed. I believe your maid is waiting for us there."

"Achoo! Achoo! Achoo!"

Mama took a firm hold of Lily's elbow, quickly pulling her from the room to escort her to the staircase and down to the lower hall where Lily took deep breaths. A handkerchief appeared in front of her face.

"I am so sorry. I quite forgot. The flowers will be gone when you return."

Lily wiped her streaming eyes and blew into the handkerchief. There was no denying the inelegance of the moment, but nevertheless, she could not wipe the huge grin from her face.

She had a suitor! And he had brought her blooms! So many, many, many blooms!

Everything will work out for the best!

Mr. Ridley appeared at her side. "My apologies, Miss Abbott. It was intended to be a thoughtful gesture, but I am afraid it has gone rather awry."

Lily shook her head, craning her neck to bestow a smile on the tall gentleman. "Not at all, Mr. Ridley. I would not have missed it for all the world!"

He stared back at her in wonder, light reflecting in his brandy eyes to highlight the gold glints buried in the amber-brown depths. Shaking his head, he chuckled. "I do believe you are telling the truth."

Lily creased her forehead in admonishment. "I always tell the truth, Mr. Ridley." She winced. "Except when I exaggerated to the coroner, that is. But that was justified, considering I knew your whereabouts."

Mama groaned from her other side, clearly quelling an urge to admonish her.

"Shall we?" Mr. Ridley offered an arm, and with a thrill of delight, Lily weaved her arm around his. In unison, they walked to the front door, which Thomas was holding open.

The past few days might have been a nightmare, but she had awakened to a lovely dream and the joy of it was so powerful it bubbled through her veins.

Mr. Ridley led her to his carriage and assisted her up the steps. Inside she found Nancy waiting, huddled in a corner and appearing nonplussed to be taken along for a courtship ritual. Lily settled in while Mr. Ridley sat on the bench across from her. Turning to the open door, she gaped at the sight of Mama standing in the hall. Her parent was allowing her to leave with only the old nurse as accompaniment?

Mr. Ridley's footman closed the carriage door, and Lily realized that her suffocating Mama was indeed sending her off with only Nancy in attendance. Her heart thudded in her chest, and looking back to Mr. Ridley, she found him smiling at her.

"Where are we off to?"

"It is to be a surprise. You shall have to wait and see."

Lily bit her lip before scooting toward the window to watch as the carriage pulled into motion.

"I want to apologize, Miss Abbott. Yesterday … was an aberration. The baron has interfered with my marital prospects in the past, so it has long been a sensitive topic. Added to everything that has happened … But I should not have displaced my umbrage on you. You have been extraordinarily generous to me, and I am afraid I behaved reprehensibly."

Lily turned her head to study him. "It was reprehensible, but I can understand that you have been under great strain. What with everything that has happened, and the shock of it all. Any person could behave poorly when confronted with so many challenges so swiftly."

"You are too kind."

Her lips curved into an impish grin, and she shrugged. "The alternative is to be cruel, and where is the fun in that?"

Mr. Ridley chuckled, revealing a slash of pearly teeth, which Lily noticed with fascination. He really was a perfect physical specimen of manhood. It was a wonder that he was yet unmarried.

"I must apologize that we are in my carriage, which requires we bring a chaperone." Mr. Ridley gestured to Nancy sitting in the corner. "My curricle is being repaired."

"Nancy? Do not worry about her. She cannot hear a thing, CAN YOU, NANCY?"

"I think the footman's name was Beasley, not Yancy."

Lily's lips twitched. "She will probably nod off soon. Nancy cannot stay awake in carriages."

"Ah. Your mother had a bit of a spat with Lord Moreland when she suggested Nancy as the chaperone. Apparently, he wished someone else to accompany you."

Lily's brows shot up in surprise. "Then I suppose Mama wished for us to have the opportunity to speak freely."

It would appear her parent was taking steps to stack the deck in Lily's favor despite the departure from propriety. She could only imagine her father's chagrin at sending his daughter out without a proper chaperone.

"What did you wish to speak on?" If Mr. Ridley wanted them to be alone, there must be something to declare.

Mr. Ridley shook his head, his chestnut curls swaying. To

avoid reaching out to touch the silky locks, Lily carefully sat on her hands. Sometimes they had a mind of their own. "Later. We have something to do before we ... discuss the future."

Lily's heart leapt in her chest. The gentleman was going to state his offer again, just as Sophia had predicted! She was light-headed with relief at the possibility. Traveling would be a grand adventure, but she would rather do so with a husband at her side and not under a dark cloud of scandal in which everyone she ever knew believed her to be an unchaste young woman.

Turning back to the window, she craned to peer at the homes and shops passing by and tried to calculate their destination from the direction of their travel. After many minutes of watching the traffic passing, she still did not know where they were headed until the carriage slowly turned into a crowded street.

"Berkeley Square!"

"Indeed."

"We are visiting Gunter's for ices?"

"Your cousin assured me you would appreciate it."

"Was it her idea? The lilies?"

Mr. Ridley grimaced ever so slightly. "Not precisely. She mentioned some hothouse flowers would not go amiss, but I am afraid I quite overdid it, considering your sensitivity."

Lily clapped her hands, falling back into her seat. "I have never been! The other debutantes speak on it incessantly. Mama visits with her friends, but we seldom go out in public, except for the theatre or fittings at the mantua-maker's."

"And I have never accompanied a young lady to Gunter's, so we are on equal footing, I suppose."

The carriage pulled to a stop in the shade of the trees. Lily could see gentlemen lounging against the iron railings, while young ladies fanned themselves perched high on curricles. Servers from Gunter's were in attendance, delivering ices in goblets.

Mr. Ridley's footman—Wesley, the one Sophia had interrogated on the day of the murder—opened the door and lowered the steps. Shortly, a server appeared in the doorway to request their order.

Lily's mind raced with possibilities. The moment of reckoning was here. She would need to pick a flavor!

Mr. Ridley opened the other carriage door while the server listed off the flavors, allowing for a breeze through the small space. The fragrances of grass and oak trees wafted through the door as Lily listened intently to the choices. "… chocolate, lavender, maple, Parmesan cheese, Gruyère, and bergamot."

Her mind reeled. This was something she had imagined many a night, and now the moment had finally arrived. What if she made the wrong choice and did not like it? She would never have another opportunity to try Gunter's ices for the very first time!

"Um … lavender?"

"It is an excellent choice, miss."

"Agreed. I will have the same," Mr. Ridley concurred across from her. Lily swung her head back to find that he was staring at her with a bemused expression on his face. "Would Nancy like one?"

He bobbed his head to the old woman, who was leaning at an alarming angle in the corner. Her mouth hung open and a bleating snore was Mr. Ridley's only response. Lily pressed her lips together not to giggle, throwing a glance at Mr. Ridley as if to say, *I told you so.*

Mr. Ridley chuckled before dismissing the server with their order.

* * *

BRENDAN WATCHED Miss Abbott relishing her lavender ice. He and his valet had locked themselves into his rooms the night before to prevent any nocturnal disturbances, which meant he had finally enjoyed a full night's sleep. Now that his general outlook had markedly improved, he had to admit that the countess Saunton was right. Miss Abbott was an exuberant young woman who embraced life wholeheartedly.

He supposed he was very fortunate, because she had committed to the role of his scandalous paramour so enthusiastically that Grimes was utterly convinced that Brendan was the licentious debaucher of gently bred virgins. Under normal circumstances, he would consider it a calamity that people would believe he was a scoundrel of the highest order, but given the alternative, an accusation of patricide, he supposed he could withstand it. Soon their wedding would divert society's whispers from his apparent perversions to whisperings about a grand passion.

He knew it was the only honorable path forward. The two of them would have to make the best of this.

But, hang it all, she is of such tender years!

Even now she scooped her ice with the focus of a child eating cake. He could not even detect the rounding of a bosom underneath all that frothy lace. If the young woman had curves, her attire did a distinguished job of disguising them. It was a mystery why debutantes dressed in a manner least likely to lure a man's interest when their entire existence revolved around dragging him into the parson's noose.

But it did not signify. This marriage must proceed for both their reputations. It was a matter of honor. Miss Abbott had taken a monumental risk in saving him from the ordeal of an arrest and trial. Even if he had been found innocent, rumors would have persisted that he had murdered his own father. Because of what she had done, the conversation had been well and truly shifted to the subject of seduction, and once their betrothal was announced, it would shift to talk of love matches.

Despite her obvious youth, Miss Abbott's zeal and integrity were growing on him, so forging a strong partnership should be possible.

If only I found her physically appealing.

This was the crux of the problem. Brendan knew that once he was wed, dallying was not an option. He had witnessed too many marriages of the *ton* turn cold and distant, where marital partners could barely stand to be in the same room while each conducted illicit affairs. It was not a future he was willing to accept, so somehow he would need to reconcile himself to bedding this immature girl within the bonds of marriage.

When they had finished their ices, and the maid was still sleeping in the corner of the other bench seat, the server came to collect their goblets. The carriage doors were closed, but they did not depart. This was it. It was time to do the honorable thing.

"Miss Abbott?"

She turned those large brown eyes on him, and he briefly wondered how she might appear in the richer colors that Lady Moreland wore that offset her coloring so well. Miss Abbott had the same rich, brown hair framing her elfin face. Her eyes were remarkable—lively and bright—but the pale, lacy confections she wore were abysmal. He could only hope that she would order a new wardrobe with more flattering colors once they wed.

"I am deeply ashamed of my reactions yesterday, and on speaking with Lady Slight, I very much understand the depths of my misunderstanding of your character. It must have taken great courage to visit the widow and demand allegiance on my behalf."

Miss Abbott's eyes rounded. "She confessed to our conversation?"

Brendan nodded. "I want you to know what a great honor it would be for me to wed a courageous young woman such as yourself. If you were to do me the honor of consenting to be my wife, I shall spend every day of our lives displaying my respect for your admirable integrity in assisting me as an innocent man."

The young lady cocked her head, contemplating him thoughtfully. "What if I wish to visit the Continent?"

"Then we shall plan a trip. I could take you to Florence, if you wish."

Surprise spread over her features. "You would do that?"

"If we wed, I consider it will be a partnership. Your wishes would be as important as my own."

She sighed. "That sounds lovely, and I suppose I have little choice. I had always hoped to make a love match, but it would seem a marriage of convenience is in order."

"Perhaps ... it would be better to think of it as a marriage of friendship? What you did for me ... My late mother would have lauded it as a selfless act. An act from the heart. I can never repay such kindness, but I can attempt to do so. Providing you the protection of my name is the least I can do. Beyond that, I hope we shall build a strong marriage."

"Is it to be ... a faithful marriage?"

Brendan puffed in surprise at Miss Abbott's frankness. She was an unusual girl, to be sure. "I assure you that Lord Saunton would rip me limb from limb if I even entertained the notion of infidelity. There is no risk of an affair if we wed."

Miss Abbott nodded. "A marriage of friendship, then." Sticking out her gloved hand, she waited. Brendan looked down at the appendage in confusion. "Friends shake hands, do they not?"

His lips quirked into a smile. Extending his hand, he took her delicate one and gave it a brief shake, surprised by the firmness of her grasp. She might be so slight that a strong puff of wind could carry her away, but there was no doubt the girl had a backbone made of steel. "It is a bargain."

At his knock on the ceiling, the carriage soon pulled into motion. Brendan settled back into the squabs of his bench while Miss Abbott watched out the window with avid interest. It was settled. He was to marry the young woman to protect her.

This thought pricked as he recollected his other troubles.

Confound it! What if I get her killed?

Brendan suppressed a groan at the reminder that there might be a murderer lurking in his home. Perhaps he should delay the wedding until the investigation was complete?

CHAPTER 9

"Victorious warriors win first and then go to war, while defeated
warriors go to war first and then seek to win."
Sun Tzu, L'Art de la Guerre (The Art of War)

* * *

JULY 25, 1821

*L*ily examined herself in the mirror. Soon she was to take her vows, but her critical eye informed her that she still had the appearance of a child. The flouncy gown she currently wore was hardly ideal to set the pulse of a man racing, though she had no wish to appear a harlot such as Lady Slight with her scarlet silk which the widow wore for daywear. However, the widow with her revealing gowns and bountiful diddeys threatening to escape from the bondage of her bodice ... Lily was well aware that her betrothed found the woman appealing.

Soughing, she stepped back to lean against the foot of her very tall bed.

It would not do. How was she to compete with such obvious charms while attired like a virginal debutante? She wanted to light the fire of passion in Mr. Ridley's eyes. To make him notice her as a woman and not as a ... friend.

Sophia and the duchess were utterly captivating, but not obvious. Each wore the colors and styles suitable to their complexions, which were as disparate as one could achieve— the duchess had the chestnut hair of Mr. Ridley with brandy eyes, while Sophia was a reddish-blonde with stormy blue eyes. Certainly, the hues Mama wore would suit Lily better than these pastels and whites.

Customarily, one simply wore an existing gown, but ...

"Bah! I need a new gown for my wedding."

"I agree." Sophia came to lean beside her. "And I know just where to get one."

"What do I say to Mama?"

"You say you are a grown woman who needs a new wardrobe fit for a married woman, and you will not take no for an answer."

"And then?"

"Then we hike our skirts and race for the front door where my carriage is waiting before she can argue and waste valuable time."

"We should tell her from across the hall, then, so we have a head start."

"I think we wait at the foot of the stairs and as soon as she appears at the top, we inform her where we are going. That will give us more of a head start."

Lily nodded. "We must go to a modiste. Mama's mantua-maker makes gowns for matrons. I need something ... alluring. Mr. Ridley is a handsome man, and I do not want to be viewed as ... less. Society must believe that our so-called tryst was inspired by great passion."

"I made an appointment with Signora Ricci for this morning."

"You knew?"

"Of course I knew. No self-respecting woman wants her mother to choose her wedding gown for her. Especially not ..." Sophia bobbed her head at Lily's bodice, which was adorned with tiny bows. Lily looked down and thought about how similar she looked to one of those elaborate Twelfth Night cakes confectioners displayed in their windows during Christmastide. She was veritably ... festive.

But not alluring.

She needed to make Mr. Ridley's pulse race. He should be ecstatic with his choice of bride, rather than reminiscing about his former paramour when he bedded her for the first time.

"There is not much time. Papa insisted we wed soon to abate the scandal. Mr. Ridley has already applied for a Common License."

"Signora Ricci will work it out. Now that the nuptials are proceeding, it is imperative we attract Mr. Ridley to you as a woman. You deserve more than a marriage of friendship."

Lily inhaled deeply, then blew out a shaky breath. "Mama will descend shortly. We should be waiting if we wish to catch her on the steps."

Sophia grinned broadly. "I do enjoy a good caper!"

Straightening up, Lily gathered the courage to ask the question that had been bothering her. "How bad is it?"

Sophia twisted her lips, looking away. "The gossip?"

Lily cleared her throat in affirmation.

"Let us say ... it is a good thing you are to wed soon."

* * *

"YOU NEED to apply to the Home Secretary for a writ of summons." The duke's announcement halted Brendan's pacing.

He had secured Miss Abbott's agreement to wed, thus assuaging his conscience. Now his thoughts had turned to protecting his bride when she entered his home. Briggs would brief him later today about his interviews with the servants. The only positive was if the runner had found anything, it was not dire enough to rush into the library to inform Brendan of his imminent death.

"For what?" His response was not a denial. He simply could not think what Halmesbury was talking about.

"To take a seat in the House of Lords." The duke responded in a pragmatic tone, his gray eyes on Brendan, who tried to absorb this declaration.

"I do not think this is the time for politics!"

Richard snorted from the window. "Dunderhead! It is not about politics. At this moment, there are hundreds of tenants and servants who have no landlord. Not to mention thousands of constituents with no representation. There is more than yourself to think of. You are a leader of men now ... or at least you will be once the Committee for Priviliges confirms you as the new baron. Funds must be authorized, documents must be signed, people must be managed. Even funds for your household are affected, or do you think your late ... benefactor ... will release funds from beyond the grave?"

The pressure at his temples increased once more. Brendan slumped into an ancient sofa to stare at the dingy crown moldings framing the ceiling. "Lawks! We only just buried the baron!"

The duke's lips pinched, and he drummed his long fingers against the arm of his chair. "Annabel wished to attend, but ..."

"But women do not attend funerals."

Halmesbury nodded, and Brendan realized he had been so absorbed by his own troubles, he had barely noticed the strain his brother-in-law was under. The duke's face was grim when he finally continued. "I told her I did not care about conventions. She should attend if she wished to, but she awoke feeling poorly this morning. The distress has not been good for her, and she is so far along ... she opted to rest rather than brave the reactions of the other men in attendance. I wanted her to have the opportunity to say goodbye, but she said her health and the health of our babe must come first."

Brendan felt guilt flickering to life once more. He had been so consumed that he had not thought about how his sister was holding up. "I should pay her a visit."

Richard moved from the window to take a seat. "Perhaps we can all have dinner together. We could talk, and perhaps reminisce about the baron to provide an opportunity for her to close that chapter."

Halmesbury cocked his head, thinking about what his cousin had proposed. "I would like that. The five of us, then? You and the countess, plus Brendan?"

Richard nodded. "Yes. I shall cancel our plans for this evening."

"I appreciate it. An intimate dinner with family, rather than the fops that the baron spent his time with. We can tell anecdotes perhaps and give her a chance to air her thoughts."

"Sophia will be gratified to assist the duchess."

Brendan closed his eyes. The light was worsening his headache, and he had much to think about.

A few days ago, he had been a carefree heir, running about Town and carousing with his friends. Now he was to be responsible for a wife. *Not just a wife. Tenants! Servants! The people of my district!*

He was ill-prepared for this. The baron and he had been estranged. It was no small matter to step in as the new baron and attempt to take hold of the reins. Brendan had never been apprenticed into these matters. He barely knew their steward and only knew their solicitors from meeting them once or twice. "Let us not forget we have a murder unsolved, as yet."

Halmesbury sighed heavily. "Thunder an' turf! This is a grim week."

Richard leaned back, fidgeting with his cravat and chuckling humorlessly. "Which part? The grotesque crime, the unexpected death in the family, the averted arrest, or the betrothal born from scandal?"

Brendan laughed his disbelief at how the week had unfolded. "All of it. Every last bit of it."

The duke broke the ensuing silence. "I would advise you to stay vigilant and continue to take precautions until the matter is resolved."

"I am, but it is daunting to think of introducing a bride into this muddle."

"There is no choice. The so-called tryst between the diabolical seducer and a highborn debutante is all that is being talked about. I have been announcing this wedding far and wide to help dispel the outrage."

Brendan made a choking sound, butting his head back on his chair in disgust. "I am trying to put out house fires with only a teaspoon to transport the water."

Richard chuckled. "It will eventually blow over. Just forge ahead with the wedding. Once that happens, some new travesty of good judgment will be undertaken to distract the *ton*."

CHAPTER 10

"All men can see these tactics whereby I conquer, but what none can see is the strategy out of which victory is evolved."
Sun Tzu, L'Art de la Guerre (The Art of War)

* * *

JULY 29, 1821

"*H*ugh! It is not suitable attire! You must tell Lily to change."

"I think Lily looks lovely."

"But ... but ... it is red!"

"More of a burgundy, I think."

"And gold!"

"What is your issue with gold? She wore gold ribbons with her ball gown last week?"

"It is not the same!"

Lily peered down at her dress. Despite Mama's distress, she could not contain the huge grin of joy that had her cheeks spread so widely, the muscles in her face were aching.

Signora Ricci had not disappointed. The talented modiste had created a gown that was utter perfection for Lily, and she could not be happier.

"It is clearly not meant for wearing during the day!"

"It is her wedding, Christiana. It is customary for a young woman to wear one of her best gowns for such an occasion."

"And her hair! It is far too inappropriate!"

"She has beautiful hair. Quite like yours, wife."

Lady Moreland stamped her foot in outrage. "I forbid this! Lily shall not leave our home wearing such a frock! She must change and do her hair in a manner appropriate to a debutante."

Lily paid no mind, still stunned by how mature she appeared. The gown was better than even she had envisioned when Signora Ricci had first described it a few days earlier.

"Aunt." Sophia's voice was calming amid the family chaos. Her cousin had always been calculating in her approach to life, clear in her goals and acting with decisiveness. Since her marriage, Sophia's confidence had grown to make her a formidable countess of the realm. "Lily has selected a gown that is appropriate for her complexion. She is no longer a debutante." Lily ran her hands over the tulle overskirt in reverence. "She is a bride."

The occupants of the entry hall froze, then turned to stare at Lily. She looked up in amazement, staring back at Sophia, who was smiling gently at her. "I am a bride."

"And a bride should choose what she wants to wear." Lord Moreland's deep voice cut through the silence that followed. "Now I believe it is time to leave. We have a wedding to attend."

Lady Moreland was still wailing her distress as they bundled into their carriage. Sophia joined them, taking a seat next to Lily. She had promised she would accompany her so she could dissuade Mama from interfering. Lily had every intention of forging a happy marriage, which included mutual attraction, and the gown was crucial to a successful start. She must light the spark of passion in Mr. Ridley before it was too late.

"Signora Ricci is a genius." Lily kept her voice low out of respect for Mama, who sat across from her with twin lines between her brows marring her handsome face.

"She understands color and form superior to other modistes. I was fortunate that Richard sent me to her." Sophia's reply was unapologetic, causing Mama to cry out once more.

"Hugh! Why would the earl know a modiste?"

This time Lord Moreland appeared rather uncomfortable, shooting a glance at Sophia, who smiled blithely in response. She shrugged slightly. "My husband was a rogue. Thankfully, he has excellent taste and I have the advantage of his past in my present. Signora Ricci is a veritable artiste who makes her customers look like the subjects of great art."

Lily giggled. "Lady Slight would agree with you."

"Lady Slight!" Mama's voice was shrill in the confined space.

Sophia colored, turning to look out the window at the passing traffic. "The viscountess frequents the dress rooms."

"Dash it, Hugh! We must turn this carriage around."

Papa shot another pained glance at Sophia, who was studiously watching the street. "Be that as it may, Lily's gown is modest compared to Lady Slight. She is embarking into marriage and she deserves to feel beautiful, Christiana. And she is. Beautiful. I have never seen her look lovelier than she does at this moment."

Lily peered at her reflection in the side window, scarcely able to credit her transformation. She had always suspected that the modest colors and virginal flounces she wore were a hindrance to attracting the attentions of handsome young gentlemen. Surely their first impression of her must be that she was dull and shapeless. There were so few young men on the marriage mart, and the fashionable colors for debutantes and Lily did not suit. It was a match made in the depths of hell, exaggerating Lily's youthful looks so that she had appeared inconsequential. Only the oldest codgers were attracted to her at the balls. Why that was, was a question she did not like to ponder. Lily was just gratified to discover now that she might actually be pretty. Sophia had brought her own abigail to style her hair, which was the perfect finishing feature for her new appearance.

An entire wardrobe was being created for her, but Signora Ricci had moved mountains to deliver several new gowns in record time.

The one she wore now might be more suitable for the theatre than for a ceremony, but it was Lily's favorite and Sophia had encouraged her to wear it. She wanted to walk into church with her head held high, and ignite Mr. Ridley's passion, so she needed every weapon she could muster to distract her groom from the paramour he had given up to wed her.

"Mama, I love you dearly. But this is my wedding day, and I barely know Mr. Ridley. It is imperative that I do everything in my power to set our marriage on the path to success. I wish to enjoy the companionship that you and Papa share, and to do that, my groom must view me as a grown woman and not as a charitable gesture. This will be a happy marriage if I make it so."

Her family, barring Aidan, who had left for the church earlier, turned to gaze at her. Mama's face crumpled into an expression of tearful adoration. "Oh, Lily! My little girl is all grown up."

Zooks! I hope Mr. Ridley agrees!

The gentleman was sartorial elegance in his perfectly tailored clothing. What would he think now that Lily finally had a competent modiste to dress her?

* * *

BRENDAN STOOD at the altar with the vicar, awaiting the arrival of his bride. Near him, Richard fiddled with his cravat and checked his timepiece. From the pews, Annabel watched on with her hands folded over her rounded belly while the duke stretched his broad shoulders. Brendan's friend, Lord Julius Trafford, sat behind them in the next pew. Trafford had been indignant at the news he was to marry, but had begrudgingly shown up for the ceremony dressed to the nines in the latest fashion. Frankly, Brendan thought the elaborately embroidered coat and waistcoat looked rather uncomfortable, not to mention the intricate knot of his cravat that tilted Trafford's chin to a haughty angle.

On the other side of the aisle was Miss Abbott's family, including her brother, and Mr. and Mrs. Thompson, who were related to Richard.

"My lord, I have services soon." The vicar shuffled on his feet, a pained expression on his dour face. "I need to prepare."

"They will be here any minute." Brendan's assurance was thin. He did not know his bride. It was his assumption that the wedding was imperative to mitigating their scandal, but how well did he truly know the Abbott family?

What if they do not arrive?

Brendan shifted, raising a hand to knead his temple and shield his eyes from the light pouring through the stained-glass window above the altar. For some reason, the thought that Miss Abbott might not appear was disappointing, which he needed to make sense of. He supposed that Miss Abbott had struck him as a genuine person. She certainly possessed integrity in spades. When he had imagined his future marriage, it had always been to someone sincere and enlivened. Someone with grace like his late mother, and someone with courage like his sister, not to mention someone who engaged in strategy such as Richard's wife or the wife of Richard's brother, Perry.

It seems Miss Abbott fits the bill.

The young lady was everything he admired in a person. The lack of physical attraction was his only objection, but surely that was a minor issue in something as important as a lifetime partnership. He was an experienced man in the matter of bedding. There would be some sort of solution to that problem.

Confound it!

That thought turned to the expectations of later that evening. He would need to consummate his marriage with a girl who reminded him of playing with his sister in their youth, with her frothy lace and childish form.

Brendan pressed his thumb down on the pressure in the indented temple area, but it did not ease the mounting tension in his skull.

The vicar shuffled again in agitation, reminding him that their ceremony was running late, just as a commotion at the front doors had Brendan whipping his head round. The countess entered along with Lady Moreland, quickly striding down the aisle to sit in the pews alongside Abbott. Swinging his head back, Brendan watched Lord Moreland enter with an unknown woman on his arm and, for a second, stood still.

My God! If only I were marrying her!

The young woman was breathtaking. Her glossy brown hair was piled high, with tendrils escaping to frame her face. She had creamy skin offset by a deep red gown, which was overlaid by tulle with gold shots that brought out the warm tones of her complexion. Her bodice modestly covered her breasts while framing her milky décolletage, pushing a man's thoughts to notions of slowly unwrapping her silky clothing to reveal the rounded mounds beneath, while her skirts flowed softly from a slim waist over curving hips.

Brendan shut his eyes, admonishing himself. It was his wedding day, and he was noticing a woman other than his bride? It was deplorable. Was he a ravening beast who could not control his ardor?

Opening his eyes once more, he found Lord Moreland had moved down the aisle with the young woman. Brendan frowned, tilting his head to look back at the doors, but Miss Abbott was nowhere to be seen.

Lord Moreland arrived at the front pews, and the woman let go of his arm, coming to stand near Brendan and smiling gently in greeting. Brendan smiled back in perplexity, glancing back to find his missing bride.

The woman raised a quizzical brow when he turned back. "Shall we begin? The vicar surely needs to prepare for service."

"Miss Abbott?"

"Were you expecting someone else?"

Brendan hesitated, his eyes surveying her quickly. She was undeniably petite. The approximate size of the woman he had visited at the Abbott home. She had a heart-shaped face with huge brown eyes, a pointed chin, and delicate ears. If he imagined her with ringlets and ruffles, he supposed these might be the same elfin features that he had been in conversation with a few days earlier.

Damn it! Do I not know what my bride looks like?

Brendan swallowed a wave of mortification. Perhaps he had never had sufficient interest to really look at her, not as a vague shape and conglomeration of debutante hair and gowns, but actually see her. His only defense was that negotiating the marriage contracts, and getting them signed, along with meeting with Briggs regarding the murder, had taken up all of his time and wits while hasty plans had been made for the license and ceremony.

Feeling foolish, he refrained from shaking his head to clear his thoughts and took his place by the vicar, who was peering at him with an impatient expression. The fragrance of honey teased his senses, and he glanced at his bride, wondering if the scent was hers.

Brendan's strange week had grown even stranger. Each time he thought he knew who Miss Abbott was, a surprising new facet was revealed for him to admire. He felt the worst scoundrel, cringing at his failure to recognize her, and to have momentarily been distracted by someone he believed to not be his bride. It was high time to change his ways, and the events of the past two weeks had certainly set him on a better course.

Fancy that! She is gorgeous under all that childish adornment.

* * *

THE WEDDING BREAKFAST had been a success, despite the aged state of the room, many members of their party already being familiar with each other. The room had been filled with hothouse flowers, providing bright spots of color alongside shining crystal and glinting silver. Lily's groom had expressed his doubts about hosting the breakfast, but Sophia had insisted that the Abbotts needed to feel welcome in Lily's new home to set their minds at ease. Personally, Lily preferred Ridley House for the event because it was set off on a side street close to the square, rather than the Abbotts' home which was directly across from Lady Slight's townhouse.

Lily thanked each person as they took their leave, struggling against a suffocating embrace from her weeping mother before Papa had taken her by the arm to depart.

Brendan's odd-fish friend, Lord Trafford, walked up. He had a bizarre thatch of blond hair, while the lower portions of his hair were more of a contrasting brown, and Lily wondered if it was an affectation that his valet had somehow bleached. If so, the heir to Lord Stirling might have too much time on his hands.

The gentleman bowed deeply, his frothy cuffs flittering around his wrists, with the air of a man who had stepped off a fashion plate. "Congratulations, Lady Filminster. Ridley is a good chap. Take care of him, you hear?"

Lily smiled tentatively, unsure how to respond to such a remark. Lord Trafford strolled away to join the duke and her husband, who were standing in the dim hall, leaving the duchess alone with Lily in the breakfast room. Like the other rooms Lily had been in, the breakfast room had ebony wood paneling cladding the walls, worn carpeting, and fading wallpaper. The furniture was large and brooding, and the townhouse needed to be renovated.

My townhouse!

The duchess rose from a heavy hardwood chair and made her way to where Lily was standing.

"Your Grace." Lily sank into a curtsy. "Thank you for attending."

The duchess shook her head, smiling down at Lily, whose head barely cleared her chin. "We are sisters now, Lily. You may address me as Annabel."

Lily's jaw dropped. She quickly shut it.

You will catch flies if you allow your mouth to hang open like that. Mama's admonishment from childhood echoed in her ears, while Lily's thoughts scrambled at the idea that a duchess viewed her as a sister. "Thank you, Your—Annabel."

"It is I who must thank you. I appreciate what you have done for my brother. It was a remarkable sacrifice, and I am pleased to welcome you to the family. Sophia regards you very highly, and it is a wonderful day for the Ridley family to welcome such an exceptional young woman into our midst."

"Um—I—thank ... you." Lily was rarely speechless, but she had always been somewhat in awe of the duchess, so it was going to take time to accustom herself to being on a first-name basis.

Annabel smiled, leaning over to buss her on the cheek. "Welcome to the family, Lily Ridley."

Lily Ridley!

Lily Beatrice Anne Ridley!

Lady Filminster!

She was a married woman. And she had found herself a young, handsome gentleman who had many fine qualities, according to Sophia and Richard. Now all that remained was to orchestrate some love in their union, and she would have achieved the future she had planned for herself, despite the recent debacle.

Lily watched the duchess walk away to join her husband, the butler opening the front door for their departure with a haughty demeanor. Soon they took their leave, and Mr. Ridley—*bosh!*—Brendan returned down the hall to the breakfast room to find her waiting in the doorway.

"Miss Ab"—Brendan winced—"Lily, you are ... radiant today."

Lily blushed, staring down at her slippers in embarrassment. She had not failed to notice her groom's interest had been piqued. First at the church, where he had evidently been taken aback by her transformation, and then over breakfast when he had frequently glanced in her direction. She had not missed that some of his surreptitious glances had fallen to her bosom, which Signora Ricci had modestly revealed with the simple beauty of her gown.

But is it enough to make him forget the voluptuous Lady Slight?

* * *

BRENDAN ESCORTED MISS AB—HIS bride to a drawing room down the hall. It was a small sitting area overlooking the garden and mews to the back of the property, which he had preferred to the large one on the next floor. The light was better in this room, his primary reason for favoring the study, which was currently restricted, and this room.

Lily was radiant in the early afternoon light. The change in attire and coiffure had revealed a lovely young woman beneath all those layers—a person who had not been far from his mind since seeing her in church that morning. She might be a petite woman, but she certainly was inducing monumental musings, which was an unanticipated turn of events.

Burn my buttons! Is there something to the whole matchmaking business where one is introduced to appropriate potential matches?

Brendan's only foray into the marriage market had resulted in the baron's interference through the Royal Mail, leaving a bad taste in his mouth and an unwillingness to proceed. He had fallen in with widows, living a careless existence, which recent events had proved to be a poor choice. When he had needed support, he had received it from an unexpected quarter, and his desire to eventually find a wife in the vein of his friends had come to fruition despite his roguish behavior.

However, the weight of responsibilities was a new burden to bear, and before he could build a new life with his bride, he needed to secure their safety. Lily was a virtuous and kind woman who may have saved his neck from the hangman's noose. He must do everything in his power to secure a long and happy future for her.

"I have some news to impart, I am afraid. It is our wedding day, and I wish to focus on the celebration of such, but there is a ... situation ... that I must inform you of. For your safety."

Lily was swallowed by the red, faded settee she had taken a seat on. She leaned forward, her attention on him fully while he stood hesitantly, gazing at his polished boots.

How to broach the subject? His bride had undertaken so much risk on his behalf, and now he was to inform her that there were further risks to overcome?

Brendan was momentarily distracted when he noticed that her leaning forward had revealed the hollow between the swell of her breasts, and his thoughts drifted to peeling her gown from her lithe body.

Good grief, she was an entirely unfamiliar creature in the new gown. His bride's skin was glowing with health, and the rich hues she deserved had replaced the unflattering colors of their prior encounters.

"What is it? Is there something wrong? Are the duke and Richard aware?"

Brendan snapped back to the moment, realizing he had been staring at Lily's bosom like a green youth discovering women for the first time. How could a girl with such strength and integrity be so ravishing? He had grown accustomed to beautiful women who were selfish and self-absorbed and had accepted it as a matter of course.

Lily was not, strictly speaking, a fashionable beauty by societal standards, but she was very attractive in her own right. All soft curves and indentations that made him think of—

"It is regarding the matter of the baron's murder. Halmesbury and Richard are well-informed. We have discussed the matter, along with the countess, and I do not wish to alarm you, but I feel it is imperative you know what has happened so you might be alert and take measures to protect yourself."

Lily's eyes rounded, but she maintained her composure despite the serious nature of their discussion. Before he could stop himself, he blurted out the thought running through his mind. "Exactly how old are you, Miss Ab—Lily?"

When he had first met with her, he had been certain she was no more than seventeen. Then he had recollected that he might have met her the year before, which would make this her second Season. Now that she was dressed in adult clothing to reveal the matured form beneath those ridiculous gowns that high society mothers made their marriageable daughters wear, he could not help but wonder if his assessment was entirely incorrect.

His bride sat back in surprise. It was not customary for ladies to discuss their ages, and he supposed he could have looked her up in Debrett's *Peerage*, or simply questioned Lady Saunton on the matter, but here he was. Married and questioning his bride about details he should probably know.

Finally, she grinned, and the small, pearly white teeth and the perfect symmetry of her soft pink lips fascinated Brendan. Her enormous eyes shone with unrepressed humor, and Brendan found himself captivated by the lively woman before him.

Ye Gods! Are you a carnal beast? It is a mere three weeks since

...

"I am older than I appear—twenty years of age, and this was my third Season. Another Season or two and I would have been on the shelf, so I suppose this was a strange but fortuitous turn of events." Her face fell in sudden alarm, her hand flying up as she turned a deep shade of red to match her dress. "Oh, no! I swear I was not attempting to take advantage of your situation to trap you!"

Brendan shook his head, raising a hand to rub the back of his neck in abashment, but deep down, he admitted it set his mind at ease to know she was a mere seven years younger than himself. Their difference in ages was far less than he had erroneously calculated the previous week. "I am still deeply embarrassed about that accusation. Lady Saunton made the quality of your character clear to me, and Richard certainly seconded her opinion."

Lily's face revealed her profound relief as her color returned to normal. "What is the concern regarding my safety?"

The shift back to his earlier allusions stirred anxiety in his gut. He had been contending with feelings of inadequacy. Brendan was ill-prepared to manage the people who were counting on him. Considering that Lily's honor was greater than his own, he barely deserved her vows of commitment. It was time for him to prove his worth and become a man he could respect. His days of idle carousing were in the past.

Moving over to the sideboard, he picked up a decanter. Spirits would not go amiss to steady his nerves if he were to impart this news. "Claret?"

"No, thank you."

Brendan froze, staring down at the decanter in his hand. Young ladies had few opportunities to drink and, in his experience, they did not miss a chance to do so. Turning, he raised a quizzical brow.

Her gaze skittered away from his, and her expression was apologetic. "My family does not imbibe. After Sophia lost both her parents and came to live with us, Papa got rid of the drink in our home out of respect for her and her brother. And after what her brother did to her last year, and because Richard was nearly killed by that drunk lord breaking into their home, I made a pledge to Sophia never to drink spirits.

She has seen too many loved ones destroyed, and it was the least I could do."

Brendan grimaced at the decanter. He had forgotten the sordid affairs of the previous year. *I am an absolute ass.*

"But you are welcome to enjoy one, if you wish."

He huffed at this, turning to deposit the decanter back on the surface behind him. "I should probably reduce my drinking. There will not be a lot of time for that now that I am to manage the baronial estates."

"What was the problem you wished to share?"

Brendan walked around the room, eventually sitting beside her on the settee with several feet between them. "It is possible that the baron allowed entry to his killer. However ..."

After a few moments, his bride started when she clearly perceived what he had left unsaid. "One of the servants might be involved?"

Brendan was impressed. She had reached the conclusion faster than he had. "It is a possibility. The runner we hired, Briggs, has questioned the servants. There are only five in ... our ... home who attend to the front door."

Lily leaned toward him, evidently intrigued. "Who?"

"There is Michaels, the butler. And the two footmen— Wesley, whom you have met, and Stephen. In addition, the baron brought two footmen with him, Stanley and David. And there is a coachman who brought them to London, but he did not have access to the house. The baron's valet was away that night and did not return until the next day. My valet assisted the baron but had been sent to retrieve an item that the baron had misplaced earlier in the day and was absent for several hours."

"And whom does the runner suspect?"

"He ruled out Wesley because he was not on duty that night. Stephen was sent out on an errand by the baron, which kept him away overnight with the baron's coachman. The other footmen deny attending to anyone that evening, but it is Michaels whom he is most concerned about."

"Michaels? The butler? What motive would he have?"

Brendan sat up slightly. He had not known what to expect when he announced the potential danger, but Lily possessed a backbone. She was asking intelligent questions and paying acute attention. "I did not know, but Michaels has been with us since his youth. His father was the gamekeeper at our country seat, Baydon Hall. The father was killed in the woods, perhaps by poachers, and apparently his mother blamed my grandfather for his death. It is a long time ago—"

"But Briggs thinks it might be a motive for Michaels to either have lost his temper with your father, or assisted someone else to cover up the murder?"

"There is no evidence, and Briggs is still investigating Stanley and David, but I need you to be vigilant until this matter is cleared up."

Lily nodded, apparently musing over what he had divulged before turning back to look at him with those big brown eyes. How had he never noticed how lush her lashes were? They swept down in a fan as she blinked, which led him to notice the sweet roundness of her cheek. She was rather soft and delicate. It made him want to reach out a hand to caress the creamy curve of her jaw.

"I am sorry for your loss." She whispered it in a low voice, the throaty quality drawing him closer, and before he knew it, he had closed the gap between them on the sofa. Sitting this close to her, he once again noted the fragrance of honey, and he wondered if it was some sort of skin cream that she used. The urge to lean down and lick her jolted through him, and he had to hold himself back from startling his virginal bride with such amorous advances.

"I suppose I must confess a secret. The others are already

aware, and you might hear about it with all the gossip that is making the rounds." He sighed deeply, leaning back as she gazed up at him with a concerned expression. "The baron was not my father."

Lily hissed, drawing back, and Brendan quelled his alarm. Was she horrified by this revelation?

CHAPTER 11

"Supreme excellence consists in breaking the enemy's resistance without fighting."
Sun Tzu, L'Art de la Guerre (The Art of War)

* * *

*L*ily had thought that her new husband might have been thinking about kissing her. His gaze had centered on her mouth, and his brandy eyes had grown languid when he had suddenly made the shocking statement. She had wanted the kiss, to feel his firm, sculpted lips against her own and discover what it was to have a man desire her. Not just any man, but her husband.

His announcement wiped these thoughts away. Lily gaped at him, aghast. "What?"

"My mother was betrothed to his older brother, Lord John Ridley, who died just weeks before their wedding. My uncle stepped in and married her to deflect the scandal."

Lily's forehead creased in distress, despite Mama's perpetual warnings that she would develop lines. "That is awful. Your father died before you were born? How did you cope with that situation?"

Brendan was studying his hands, his profile not revealing his thoughts, but he appeared to be peering into the past. "I did not know. I only learned the truth a few years ago, so I believed the baron was my father for my entire youth."

Lily had recently mulled over the pressure of adulthood, of no longer being shielded from the pains of the world. Their discussion was a lot to comprehend, but she felt somehow encouraged that she was sitting with her husband and having a serious conversation about their lives. It felt more ... genuine ... than sipping tea and discussing pointless *on-dits* with Mama's friends and their daughters. This was real. This meant something. How she responded would help to set the tone for their marriage.

Shifting closer, she laid her hand over his on the sofa, enjoying the largeness of it as heat seeped in to warm her. "Thank you for discussing these matters with me. You made mention of us being friends, and this has certainly demonstrated your commitment to forging a strong partnership."

Brendan turned to look down at her, and he appeared relieved by her reaction. "I am committed. We must make the best of this situation."

"As am I," Lily responded, watching with fascination as his gaze once more moved to her mouth.

She scarcely dared to breathe as he lowered his head and his lips brushed against hers, her eyes closing in anticipation. It was fleeting, and she thought her first encounter was over, but then she felt his lips brush hers once more, before settling against her. His powerful arms banded around her, one wrapping around her waist while he raised his hand to cup her head and he deepened their kiss.

It began with a fluttering tingle in her lower belly, but as his warm lips pressed against hers, the tingle ignited into flames and Lily moaned, pressing back as if they could attain even closer proximity. As her lips parted, she felt his silky tongue lick, causing her to jump slightly before parting her mouth to allow him entry. Sophia had explained the intricacies of making love to a man, so Lily was aware this type of kissing existed, but knowing it in theory and experiencing it firsthand were decidedly different.

As his tongue explored her mouth, she moaned once more. Curving her arms up to clutch him by the shoulders, she tugged him even closer. He resisted for just a moment, before pulling her even closer, her breasts now pressed against his chest as he twisted his body to accommodate. He emitted a low growl, mumbling something about honey as their kiss continued, before he trailed his mouth against her jaw. Lily thought she might have felt the swipe of his tongue once more as he reached her earlobe and suckled, provoking her into bucking against him and keening at the sweet sensation spreading out in every direct—

They let go at the same time and shot back to stare at each other, both flushed and breathless.

"Did you hear that?"

Brendan nodded, springing to his feet to race across the creaking floor and throw open the door, their moment of heated passion forgotten as they tried to make sense of what they had heard out in the hall.

Lily craned her neck, but beyond the door there was only darkness. Ridley House was a home caught in the mists of history, a brooding château lifted from the pages of an Ann Radcliffe novel, and a sense of foreboding crept up Lily's spine. That a murder had occurred a week earlier did nothing to dispel the dread icing her veins.

Michaels stepped out of the shadows, peered down his nose at her new husband, and made a decorous announcement in his dour tone. "Lady Filminster's room is ready."

* * *

MICHAELS HAD SUMMONED WESLEY, who was leading her up the steep staircase. Apparently, the house had been operating with a reduced staff, just enough to maintain it and take care of her husband, who likely had not entertained. Which meant there was currently no housekeeper at Ridley House, Michaels directing the maids himself.

Reaching a landing on the second floor, the footman veered down a poorly lit hall. Dour portraits of Ridley ancestors stared down at Lily in stony disapproval, while their cold eyes seemed to follow her as she hurried to keep up with the much taller servant.

Wesley must have noticed her haste, adjusting his stride for her much shorter legs, and Lily smiled up at him in gratitude. "Ridley House is much bigger than it appears from the outside."

"I believe the darkness exaggerates the size, milady."

"It is very dark in here. The house has not been used much, by its appearance."

"Until now, Mr. Rid—Lord Filminster is the only one who has used the house in years. Many of the rooms have been shrouded, but Mr. Michaels directed us to open them up when we received news that Baron Filminster was coming to London for the coronation."

Lily listened to this with great interest. The question she wished to ask was about Brendan. Had his paramours visited him at Ridley House? Had Lady Slight ever spent the night?

If Lily were at home in the Abbott household, she would know which servants to press for the belowstairs gossip, but as a newcomer to this household, she could hardly accost poor Wesley with such an interrogation.

Lud! Her need to know was overwhelming, but she must ignore it.

"And my room?"

"Lord Filminster has been moved into the baronial bedroom, and your room connects. Your room has not been occupied in many years, but Mr. Michaels has replaced the bedding and we have thoroughly cleaned the rooms in anticipation of your arrival."

Wesley came to a stop at the end of the hall, which was dimly lit by a window. From what she could see in the poor light, everything was clean, but the windows were clouded with age and thousands of cleanings, so not much light made it through. Not to mention the drapes framing the window that were faded from decades of service. Lily could not make out the carpeting, which may or may not have included a pattern in its weave.

Ridley House was long overdue for a renovation.

The footman opened the door and stepped out of the way for her. Lily tentatively entered, swinging her head from side to side. There was a large stone fireplace and a couple of cloudy windows framed by ancient drapes of a heavy fabric that made them appear to be carved out of stone. A worn rug adorned the floor, and an enormous four-poster bed boasted a cheerful coverlet in bright colors—the new bedding that Michaels had obtained, she surmised. And on the chest next to the bed lay her books, a French dictionary and her book on military strategy.

But it was the door across the room that held her attention—the one that must connect to Brendan's room.

"The maids have unpacked your trunks." Wesley walked over to indicate the towering ebony wardrobe. "And there is a dressing table and washstand over here. The bell is here if you need anything."

She nodded in acknowledgment, eyeing the tall bed with concern. "Wesley, is there a bed step?"

The top of the mattress was so high it almost cleared her

waist. She had severe trepidations about being able to reach it on a nightly basis without doing herself an injury.

The footman frowned, walking over to the bed to hunt around, his face slowly drifting into a pained expression. He raised a hand to rub his jaw, before finally admitting, "I do not believe I have ever seen one in the house, now that you mention it."

Lily sighed, trying to think what to do. "Is there a spare chair I can use while steps are ordered?"

"Of course. I will bring one from another room and inform Mr. Michaels of the issue."

"That would be excellent!" She beamed at the servant, who headed out the door. Within a few minutes, he returned to place a chair at the foot of the bed before shutting the door as he left.

Exhaling heavily, she walked around the room to explore her new home. She opened the wardrobe to find all her new gowns, along with some of her old ones. Those would definitely be donated because she had no intention of wearing them again.

Raising her fingers, she brushed her lower lip, where she could still feel the impression of Brendan's mouth against hers. Considering her new gown had lit the flames of interest in her husband's eyes, and she now stood a chance of making him forget the voluptuous Lady Slight, she would not risk wearing the gowns that gave her the appearance of a child. Her husband's blunt question about her age proved the point categorically, if there had been any doubt over the matter of her attire.

Sophia's abigail had shown her how to simply dress her hair, while her cousin was interviewing prospective lady's maids on Lily's behalf. If all went well, Lily would have someone to attend to her within the week, which would not be a moment too soon. She wondered if there was a maid assigned to take care of her until then.

Lily used the chair to climb onto the bed, dropping back to stare at the ceiling and think what she should do next. She would need to speak with Brendan about Ridley House's necessary renovations, not to mention hiring a housekeeper to take care of their home. Unless he intended to use the housekeeper from Baydon Hall?

She sighed heavily. There was a lot she did not know about her new life as yet.

* * *

BRENDAN PACED THE LIBRARY, not sure what to do. He had a bride upstairs, something he would need to grow accustomed to. Michaels had informed Lily that they had no housekeeper earlier, and it had rather mortified Brendan to realize that he had not taken the time to address the issue of Ridley House being shorthanded. Not to mention, was there a maid to attend to Lily?

The house had stood empty for the better part of two decades, with only Michaels and a handful of servants to take care of it until the day that Brendan had shown up and taken residence. Michaels had then added additional servants, and they had an acceptable cook, but the staff were not accustomed to having a young lady in residence. Or a lady of any age, for that matter. The staff had been merely maintaining the home and taking care of its solitary resident these past six or seven years.

What did he know of such matters? He had managed no one, simply being an heir who came and went as he pleased. He was going to need to ask questions of Halmesbury and Richard. For all intents and purposes, he might as well have been an orphan for his entire adulthood, for the amount of interaction he had had with the late baron.

Perhaps he should set a meeting with his man of business. Perhaps he should discover if he had a man of business and who that might be.

Once a quarter, he had visited the baron's solicitors to receive his allowance, so truly he did not know. If someone specifically handled the finances, he would need to find out who that was. What did a man of business do, as opposed to the solicitors? And should he write to the incumbent steward at Baydon Hall?

Brendan groaned, running his hands through his hair and kneading his temples.

Then he walked over to the library table and sat down. He needed to make a list, and later seek the duke or Richard to gain clarity on how to proceed. It was time to pick up the pieces of his inheritance to make sense of his role. He had people depending on him, but what that meant in actual definable terms, he would need to find out.

* * *

LILY CAME DOWN for dinner wearing the same gown from that morning, deciding it was acceptable and not wanting to relinquish it after such a successful unveiling earlier that day.

She had perused the several floors of Ridley House and could now confirm that every room was filled with imposing furniture, tired and ugly drapes, worn carpeting, and faded wallpaper which was peeling from the wall in some of the lesser-used spaces. Not to mention a litany of ominous creaks, creeping shadows, and a parade of stern-faced portraits in heavy gilded frames that made her nerves twitch and sent her imagination down brooding paths. She had not found any recent paintings of her husband or the duchess in any of the rooms, and she was fairly certain that the youngest painting was several decades old.

It was appropriate to assert that their home needed some attention, and she was going to take charge.

Opening and closing doors, she eventually found the dining room, but it was empty.

Fumbling around the hall, she found her way to the library, which was the only door displaying any light. Entering, she quickly located Brendan at the library table, surrounded by piles of books. Walking over, she noticed they appeared to be accounts.

"What are you doing?"

Brendan flinched in surprise, straightening up. "I am not precisely sure. These are the household account books, and I thought I might get familiar with ... well ... anything. I know nothing about how the Filminster barony is managed, so I have made a list of questions to pursue. This was the first afternoon I have not been consumed with other matters."

Lily pulled a face, then took up a seat at the table. "We are both rather new at this, are we not? I just explored the house to get some notion of the state of it. The entire residence has been unused, except for the small drawing room, breakfast room, and your bedroom ..." Lily blushed, realizing what she had just alluded to. Her habit of speaking without thinking really needed to be tempered.

Brendan cocked his head, grinning quizzically. "Did you enter my room, Lily Ridley?"

Hearing him say her new name in his husky voice sent a frisson of pleasure chasing through her body, even as she lowered her gaze down at her fingers. "I may have."

"Hmm ... You did, or you did not. Which is it?"

"I did! I wanted to see what it looked like. I went in every room, except the study, of course. And I think I found your old room, too!"

Brendan reached over, using his finger to tilt her chin up so she looked him in the eyes. He gently brushed his thumb over her lower lip. "I want to explore your room, too."

Lily gazed into his brandy-colored eyes, fascinated by the specks of brown and gold, and her breathing slowed as she thought about inviting her new husband into her room. Lily licked her lips nervously, drawing Brendan's gaze to her mouth. He exhaled slowly before releasing her to sit back.

"We should eat some dinner, I suppose."

She nodded, but Lily's mind was on their fiery kiss from earlier and how soon she might expect another.

CHAPTER 12

*"Do not repeat the tactics which have gained you one victory, but
let your methods be regulated by the infinite variety of
circumstances."*
Sun Tzu, L'Art de la Guerre (The Art of War)

* * *

They ate their dinner in the breakfast room, which
he favored over the austere dining room down the
hall. It surprised Brendan to find he was enjoying Lily's
company. He had never spent any great length of time with a
woman—other than his mother and sister, in his youth—
wherein he was not pursuing them for the purposes of
seduction.

The widows he had spent his time with had been sensual
creatures, and eventually he had grown weary of them when
the lust had worn off and left nothing but ennui in its wake.
He had reached that stage with Lady Slight, he recollected.
The widow's charms had been fading after he realized she
was a rather thoughtless harpy who spoke only of other

151

members of the peerage, fashion, and social gatherings. There had been no substance to their conversations, which had made him eager to leave once they had spent their passions.

Lily was different. He discovered that she was fun to talk to, had an intelligent mind for conversation, and was kind and optimistic. Her tendency to babble, which had seemed so intimidating at first, turned out to have depth. She was genuinely interested in many things and chattered as her thoughts flittered about.

Watching her over the dinner table, her face lively with good humor in the candlelight, while she spoke about what she had found exploring their home, was more captivating than any interaction he had had in recent times. She seemed to relax in his company, and her conversation turned out to have more weight than one initially might think when assailed by a wall of words.

Brendan recalled their passionate kiss from earlier that day, while she told him of the improvements that were needed, and thought about how delightful it would be to school such an enthusiastic woman in the art of lovemaking. Would she be as bright and interested in bed as she was in conversation? She certainly had responded with eagerness to their kiss.

Suddenly, it did not seem too terrible to enjoy a wedding night with his virginal bride.

He noticed she had stopped talking and was staring at him.

"I ... am sorry. What did you say?"

Lily frowned slightly, clearly believing he was woolgathering while she talked. Which he had been, he supposed. About her.

"I asked if you would like dessert?"

Brendan felt his lips spread into a reluctant grin.

Reaching over the table, he covered her ungloved hand with his.

"I would, indeed," he purred suggestively, stroking his fingers over hers. Not entirely appropriate for an innocent young miss, but he suspected Lily would understand his point while not being offended.

She tilted her head, obviously perplexed by his tone. "What—oh! You mean ..." She waved her free hand in the air before turning a deep red. He watched with fascination as the color climbed her neck to settle across her face.

Brendan could not help it—he was charmed. He was beginning to understand why Richard had left his life of roguery behind to marry Lady Saunton, a strong-willed woman who would not tolerate a husband who strayed from his vows. There was something to this committed partnership with an intelligent and attractive woman. He had to admit he had never thought to look so close to home as Lady Saunton's own cousin. Perhaps if he had not been dragging his feet about marriage, he would have uncovered this delightful companion sooner. She certainly was far more entertaining than his paramours of the past few years.

* * *

A BUXOM KITCHEN maid with apple cheeks had come to Lily's room and assisted her out of her clothing.

After refreshing herself at the washstand, Lily pulled on the night rail that Sophia had helped her order. It was a deep golden color, in the fashion of the French. Standing in front of the full-length mirror marred by age, Lily released the plait that the maid had assisted her with before departing. As her hair fell in a curtain around her face, she nodded in approval. Letting her hair swing loose was an improvement.

Racing over to her bed, she awkwardly scaled the chair

onto the towering mattress, where the coverlet had been pulled back. Kneeling on the exposed sheets, she waited with bated breath for Brendan.

A knock on the connecting door announced his arrival, and she called for him to enter. She was transfixed when the door opened to reveal her husband in loose-fitting trousers and an embroidered banyan which accentuated the breadth of his shoulders. There was not an ounce of superfluous flesh on his frame to be seen when he closed the door and approached the bed.

To her great satisfaction, she noted how his glinting eyes surveyed her face before dropping to take in the sight of her golden night rail, taking his time with the bodice, which revealed an unseemly amount of décolletage and the top of her sloping breasts. Lily withheld the urge to glance down, resolutely holding up her chin to stare back at him.

Brendan reached the bed and slid a hand around her waist to gaze down into her eyes. "You are ravishing," he informed her in a low, husky voice.

Lily licked her lips, inadvertently drawing his eyes as she had done earlier in the evening. "Thank you."

"Do you know what to expect?"

"I know everything!"

Brendan's lips quirked into a crooked grin. "Everything?"

"I asked Sophia many questions because I ... do not want to disappoint!" Lily admitted breathlessly.

Her husband's face grew serious. "If there are any issues this evening, it will be I who disappointed."

Lowering his head, he captured her mouth with his own. Lily's head fell back as she parted her lips to invite him further and moaned deeply when their tongues entangled ravenously. He tasted of citrus, and Lily breathed in the scent of bergamot and mint while he explored her languidly. Lily attempted to mirror his motions until he finally pulled back.

He was panting heavily as he peered down into her face, raising a hand to gently brush her hair back.

"You smell like honey. It makes me want to ..." He shook his head, clearly unwilling to state his thoughts out loud.

"What? What do you want to do?"

Brendan stared deeply into her eyes, then lowered his head once more to whisper into her ear, setting off a riot of invigorating tingles. "It makes me want to lick every inch of your creamy skin to discover if you taste as sweet as you smell."

Lily gasped, raising her arms to curl around his neck and press closer to him. "Yes."

He growled, and within moments Lily felt his mouth moving down her neck. And farther down to the edge of her rail, to swipe his tongue over the swell of her breasts before she felt a warm hand tugging the fabric down.

Sensation raced in every direction, down to her very toes as she moaned. Overwhelmed, she almost fell back into the bed, but Brendan's arm around her waist kept her anchored to him. Their bodies were tightly pressed together from breastbone to navel as Lily tried to tug his banyan apart so she might see him bared.

"Lily," he muttered just before he pulled away and his mouth descended on her pebbled nipple. She bucked in surprise as heady delight flooded her senses, while his tongue flicked over the turgid tip. Her head fell back again, and she keened in passion, pressing up to allow him better access. "You do taste of honey."

The hand at her waist slipped down to cup her buttock, pulling her even closer as she tugged his banyan down his arms. Brendan slowly released her to shrug out of the garment, dropping it to the floor while Lily hungrily took in his bare chest.

He was sculpted like a Greek statue, all ridges and indentations that made her fingers itch to touch him. She settled her hands on his shoulders, before slowly tracing down his broad chest to comb through the dusting of curling hair that arrowed down to the linen trousers tied at his waist. Brushing her fingertips over the flat disc of his nipple, she watched in amazement as he flinched and his eyes fell half shut in response.

Continuing to trace his form, her hands moved downward as she leaned forward to lick at the bronzed disc. Brendan groaned, his hand sliding into her hair to cup her head. She continued to explore along his flat, muscled abdomen until he breathed sharply. "Stop!"

Lily leaned back, dropping her hands in alarm that she had done something wrong, as she gazed up into his face. Noticing her concern, he shook his head, gazing down at her with impassioned eyes. "It was too good. I need to ... maintain control tonight."

He pulled her back into a searing kiss before gently lowering her onto the bed. One of his hands reached down to straighten her legs, causing Lily to gasp in pleasure at his warm hand heating her skin through the thin silk of her rail. Brendan lowered himself over her, once more trailing kisses down to her exposed breasts, the sleeves of her rail trapped around her arms. He licked at painfully hard tips, tugging at the sleeves to lower her rail even farther to reveal her midriff. Lily was devastated with pure heat when his mouth trailed down her body toward her navel, instinctively gyrating her hips to ease the tension building between her legs as she gasped and moaned her descent into mindless sensation.

"Honey," growled Brendan, his tongue tracing a path while he quickly tugged her rail even farther down to reach her lower belly.

"There is honey in my soap." Her reply was reflexive,

because the feel of his mouth against her belly utterly distracted her. Then his head slipped lower as he finally pulled the rail off completely and threw it aside. "Ohhhhh!" Lily thrilled as his mouth reached the apex of her thighs and he swiped his hot tongue over her slit. Throbbing sensation streaked outward in powerful waves, making all thought vanish as she raised her hips, pleading for more.

Brendan's tongue swiped again, slipping between her slick folds to find the center of her pleasure. Lily threw her head back and wailed as her legs fell apart in silent appeal.

* * *

BRENDAN WAS UTTERLY INTOXICATED, lapping at the slick pearl between his bride's legs and captivated by her exuberant delight. He had never experienced such an immersion of sensation and emotion, the affinity that had been growing between them somehow capturing his full attention as he lost himself entirely in the act of lovemaking.

It had never been like this before. Because he had never liked the woman in his bed as much as he liked Lily. He wanted to bring her indescribable pleasure, so that she completely unraveled in his arms.

The unanticipated surprise was that as her passion mounted, so did his in direct response. As she bucked and gyrated in intense reaction, he found himself overtaken by the intensity of his own, ravenous to bring her to her peak.

In the matter of bed sport, Brendan was an experienced man, but currently he was an untamed beast seeking her finale with ruthless abandon until the sound of Lily's fervor suddenly climaxed with a surge of her rounded hips, a stiffening of her trembling young body, and a loud wail. Then, ever so slowly, she relaxed as she fell back to earth.

Brendan growled in victory as he scrambled back to his

feet, reaching for the tapes of his trousers. Lily was stretched out in boneless satiation, but she leisurely turned her head to follow his hands as he untied the garment and slipped it off. Her mouth fell open in amazement as his cock sprang free, but instead of shrinking back like a virginal young miss, her expression was one of great interest as she turned onto her side to observe him.

"Can I ... touch?"

Brendan inhaled heavily to fight back the invasion of ecstasy that flooded his body before nodding. Lily moved to the edge of the bed, reaching out a hesitant hand to wrap her delicate fingers around his hardened length. Brendan groaned, flexing his hips. When she ran her exploratory hand down before cupping his ballocks in her soft caress, he nearly spent.

Blazes!

He considered himself a man with skill and superb control in the bedroom, but Lily was destroying him with her innocent curiosity. She was wholly uninhibited in her passion, just as he had suspected she might be.

Her unrestrained interest in him was beguiling, thrilling, and seductive, leaving no words to describe how ... how ...

Catching her hand, he pulled it away lest he fail in his duty to consummate their marriage. Instead, as she fell back onto the bed, he braced a knee beside her and leaned in to capture her lips in another searing kiss, his naked skin making contact with hers. She was soft and delicate, but there was no denying that little Lily had feminine curves. From rounded breasts to flaring hips, she was all woman, and he was frantic to become one with her.

"Lily, you know this will hurt the first time?"

Her big brown eyes found his, glazed as his must be, and she nodded tremulously. "It could hurt a lot."

"I will try to make you as comfortable as possible," he

murmured in sympathy, catching her pink mouth with his. With one hand planted above her shoulder to hold him aloft, his other reached down and he guided himself to her slick entrance. Kissing her deeply, he penetrated her tight channel as her eyes flew open in surprise. Thrusting forward, he entered fully and then froze above her to give her time.

It was hell.

She had tensed in resistance but gradually relaxed the intimate muscles surrounding his length, and every tiny movement was an invitation to thrust and take his pleasure. He waited, clenching his jaw against the impulse until Lily's eyes drifted closed and her body relaxed—his signal that she was ready to continue.

He withdrew before gently surging forward once more and she gasped. It seemed to be a sound of pleasure, so he carefully continued the thrusting while every inch of his body screamed to unleash his passion and finish.

Kissing her honeyed lips, while she clenched around him, was agonizing joy. Brendan wet his lips, fighting for his patience, while his free hand found the slick pearl that was the key to her satisfaction and circled it until she was gasping and lifting her hips rhythmically against him, wild with wanting.

Brendan thrusted and stroked until Lily arched back into the bed and wailed as she reached a shuddering release, her intimate muscles pulsing around him as he stopped holding back and lunged to his own completion with a growl of triumph.

CHAPTER 13

"The art of war is of vital importance to the state. It is a matter of life and death, a road either to safety or to ruin. Hence it is a subject of inquiry which can on no account be neglected."
Sun Tzu, L'Art de la Guerre (The Art of War)

* * *

JULY 30, 1821

*B*rendan awoke with a start. The sound of racing footsteps could be heard from his room, confirming that he had not dreamt the loud crash that had jolted him from his sleep.

Lily was warm and very much asleep in the crook of his arm, and he gently rolled her over so as not to disturb her rest.

Slipping out of the bed, he pulled on his trousers, then arming himself with a heavy candlestick, he made his way through the dark of night to open the connecting door. It still felt out of place to be sleeping here, the former rooms of his uncle-father, but he had prevailed in anticipation of Lily's arrival.

Standing in his bedroom, he could vaguely make out that the door to the hall was standing open. Light suddenly flared in the room. His valet stood near the bed, having lit the oil lamp. They both winced and blinked rapidly, turning to inspect the water and shards, lying near the washstand, of what had once been a jug. Nearby, a chest of drawers hung open, its contents in disarray.

Brendan drew Lily's door shut behind him and spoke in a low voice. "Someone took advantage of my wedding night to search my room."

Peterson, a fastidious man in his fifties, frowned and rubbed his neck in disbelief. "It would appear so, milord."

Brendan heaved a sigh, gently kneading his temples in response to his headache springing back to life. "I must have forgotten to lock my door when I came up."

"I apologize, sir. I should have checked after you …" Peterson bobbed his head in the direction of Lily's door.

"We shall need to take more care, Peterson."

His valet nodded grimly.

Briggs's suspicions, that either a murderer or a traitor was in Brendan's home, had been confirmed. Danger lurked, and Brendan admitted his worst fear. Lily had quickly enchanted him, lightening the somber mood of Ridley House with fresh energy. Somehow, she was turning out to be the embodiment of the perfect woman for him, and if she were harmed because he failed to protect her, he would never forgive himself. Not after everything she had done for him.

It was time to take action. Immediate and decisive action to defend himself and his unexpected bride, who was quickly charming her way into his heart.

* * *

LILY GRADUALLY AWAKENED, stretching her limbs and grinning. Her plans to distract Brendan from Lady Slight had gone better than expected. She was certain they were well on their way to falling in love and making this marriage a genuine match.

She turned to embrace Brendan, surprised when she found she was in the bed alone.

He had left?

A slight spark of anxiety came to life in her belly as she sat up. It was still early morning, if the sunlight was anything to go by. Perhaps he had merely gone to his room to prepare for the day?

Slipping out of bed and landing on the floor with a soft thud, Lily donned her discarded night rail and hurried across the room. Knocking on the connecting door, she did not wait for an answer before flinging it open to find Brendan's dim room empty and tidy. Lily bit her lip. It was the first morning of their marriage together. After the success of their first evening together, she had expected a languid morning with him.

Perhaps he is eating breakfast?

Sighing, Lily returned to her room and rang for the maid. Hurrying her ablutions, she was soon dressed and her hair loosely styled. She was ready to descend and find her husband.

Flinging the door open, she stepped into the hall, almost running into a figure shrouded in shadows. Yelping in shock, she sprang back through her doorway.

"Do not be concerned, milady. I am here to protect you."

Lily's eyes adjusted to the gloom of the hall, and she could make out a burly man wearing a battered overcoat. He had a decidedly disheveled appearance, reminiscent of a grotesque leering from the desolate darkness to ward off evil spirits.

"Who are you?"

The man cleared his throat, hesitating a moment before responding. "You may call me John."

She narrowed her eyes. "John?"

"That is correct, milady."

Lily cocked her head as a memory was dusted off in the recesses of her mind. "One of the Johns who protected Lady Saunton last year?"

"Uh ... yes."

"You are not pretending to be a footman this time?"

"No, milady."

Lily clasped her hands, tapping her fingers on her hand as she tried to think. "Lord Filminster hired you to protect me?"

"Yes, 'e had Lord Saunton send for us this morning with the instruction to see to your safety."

"Us?"

"My colleague ... John ... is dow'stairs. We will be taking shifts."

"And you are to follow me around? My own home?"

"Yes."

"Why? Did something happen?"

The ... protector ... dropped his gaze to his worn boots. "I wouldna know, milady."

Lily clenched her jaw. Marching past ... John ... she made for the stairs, running down them in a manner that would have had Mama scolding, while John followed a few steps behind.

Reaching the main floor, she headed to the library, but there was no sign of her missing husband. Lily quickly checked the other rooms, except for the study, which was still closed, but she did pause to place her ear against the door. There were no sounds of life inside.

Each time she turned around, John was there, politely waiting. It was like having a shadow chasing her heels, except this shadow had a heavy tread and his breathing was audible.

Where in the damnation is my husband?

Turning to John, she finally admitted defeat. "Did Lord Filminster leave me a note to explain?"

"I wouldna know, milady."

Lily huffed in aggravation, no longer caring about the inappropriate display of emotion in front of a stranger. It was not even nine o'clock, and Brendan was gone, leaving only a rough chap as an explanation. The only positive she could conclude was that John was the personification of Brendan's desire for her to remain safe. Nevertheless, the bleakness of Ridley House was palpable without her husband there to dispel its dispirited fog.

* * *

BRENDAN alighted from his carriage to stand at the side of the teeming road. Pulling out his timepiece, he confirmed that the time was a few minutes past nine o'clock. He was to meet Halmesbury, Richard, and Briggs in his club at precisely nine, but traffic had held him up. London was awake and lively, with horses, carriages, and pedestrians heading in both directions on St. James's Street.

"Brendan?" Dulcet tones called out, and he whipped his head around to find Harriet peering at him from several feet away. The viscountess was about to climb the steps into her own carriage. Brendan restrained a grimace. He did not wish to engage in pleasantries with the widow while he had much more important issues to attend.

Lifting his beaver, he bowed politely. "Lady Slight."

The redhead was attractive in striped muslin and a jaunty

bonnet, as she raised a gloved hand to her mouth to giggle, but Brendan really wanted to dash off inside. "So formal."

He squashed his irritation as Harriet approached him. Glancing around, he noted that there were far too many people to witness their interaction. Had the fact that he was now married emboldened his former paramour to be seen conversing with him on a public street?

Slipping his timepiece back in his pocket, Brendan smiled politely in acknowledgment. Lady Slight came to a stop in front of him, and Brendan's general temperament and good breeding required he engage while every instinct was to walk away. This woman had no right to his time. She would have seen him tried and hanged rather than risk being married to him.

"Is it true that you wed the silly chit from my street?"

Well, this was a conundrum. How to remain polite while censuring the slight to his bride? "I married Miss Abbott yesterday, but I find that she has a lively mind. Not so silly, after all."

"My commiserations."

Brendan could not help it. He frowned. The truth was, he was growing to very much like his new circumstances, but he had no wish to discuss his sentiments with the woman who would not lift a finger to assist him. Now that she had revealed her character, and he had reassessed his own, he had no desire to speak with the widow. He needed to extricate himself and see to Lily's safety.

Harriet stepped closer. Too close. The cloying scent of her rosewater aggravated his senses, and all he could think was how simple honey smelled so much better than extravagant, gaudy flowers.

Raising her hand, Harriet stroked a slender finger down his lapel, causing him to step back in surprise. "Feel free to visit, Brendan. No need to be a stranger now that you are returning to society's good graces."

His brows drew together into a deep scowl at her insinuation. "I assure you that will not be happening."

Harriet drew her painted lips into a coy smile. "We shall see. The little debutante is bound to bore you, and now that you are a married man … it is all rather perfect for us to continue on."

Before he could respond, she sauntered back to her carriage. Brendan did not want to create a further scene by chasing her down the street or calling after her, so he was forced to tamp down his outrage and head into the club. He would need to be better prepared the next time he encountered the widow, but right now he had more pressing concerns.

Brendan made his way inside, quickly finding his party at a table in the corner set a little distance away from the other guests. As he approached, he noticed that men were pausing mid-conversation to watch his progress. Brendan resolutely ignored the curious stares. Arriving at the table, he pulled out a chair to flop down. The buzz of conversation slowly resumed, to Brendan's relief, despite his suspicion that he and Lily were now the subject under discussion.

"Thank you for meeting me."

Briggs nodded. Richard was fidgeting with his snow-white cravat, a sure sign he was agitated. Halmesbury was the most composed, leaning back in his chair with his arms folded over his broad chest and straining the sleeves of his navy coat.

"Is Lily in danger?" Richard's question erupted without warning, as he leaned forward on the table to glare at Brendan with glinting emerald eyes.

"Something happened last night that confirms Briggs's suspicions. I thought it best not to discuss it where we could be overheard by one of the servants. There is no specific threat against Lily, but I thank you for arranging the Johns to stand guard while we sort this out."

Richard pressed his lips together, exhaling heavily as he leaned back in his chair. "We should have done it before she joined your household. If anything happens to her, my wife will be ..." He waved his hand in the air, clearly finding no words to describe Lady Saunton's distress if Lily were harmed.

Briggs cleared his throat. "If I may, your lordship, what happened?"

Brendan raised a finger to rub at his temple, then rattled off what happened in the early hours. When he completed his narrative, the table fell silent.

Halmesbury rubbed his jaw, his gray eyes thoughtful.

Richard clenched his fists on the table's surface before raising a hand to summon a server. "I need a drink."

"It is just past nine." The duke arched an eyebrow.

"A small drink, but a drink nevertheless. This is all far too reminiscent of the troubles Sophia and I had last year, and I need to settle my nerves. When I leave here, I will need to inform my wife of what has happened."

"Your wife will have thoughts about you imbibing," the duke warned his cousin.

Richard sighed, waving the server away without placing an order. "I usually prefer keeping a clear head, but these past two weeks have been hell. However ... keeping a clear head is probably vital at the moment."

"Where do matters stand with the servants?" Brendan's question was addressed to the runner, who was obviously chewing on his news.

"I am still investigating Stanley and David, but thus far, Michaels is the only one who seems to have any motive. The baron has not been in Town in twenty years, so it is difficult to say what could have set this off. Outside of the servants, do we have anyone else to look into?"

"Maybe a handful of people who might visit Somerset or have homes there."

"What if this is not about something that happened recently, but something from the past? Briggs suspects Michaels because of what happened decades ago, but do we know about the baron's history in London? Are there any enemies he may have had?" The duke, like the others, was keeping his voice low so they would not be overheard.

Brendan cocked his head, thinking about whom the baron might have interacted with in the couple of days he was in London before he had been killed. "He might have visited the tailor for a final fitting because he had his coronation garments made in Somerset, but his valet could not say. And the baron would have spoken with the servants and the coachman, which Briggs has been looking into. Beyond that, he would converse with other lords at the coronation. The lords sat together at Westminster Abbey, did you not?"

"Like a gaggle of fops in our ridiculous trunk hose," replied Richard. "I was practically naked with that much leg exposed."

"So every lord in London is a suspect, then," Brendan said, throwing his hands up in the air.

The duke shook his head. "I think we could start with a list of men who sat in his row, and the row in front and behind. It would have been difficult to speak with others farther than that, and it stands to reason."

Brendan threw him a questioning look.

"He sat with barons. Some of them went to school or university with him. He would not have known the others because he never came to London, so the only lords he would know well were ones he knew from the past—from Oxford or Eton. Boys tend to band together according to their ranks, so perhaps that narrows the list down. Some barons will be too old or too young to know him."

"Agreed. We need more information. I suppose if I could get a list, I could visit them. Perhaps they might have heard or seen something the day of the coronation, but they won't allow Briggs through the front door. They will not turn me away."

Halmesbury nodded. "I can get you a list."

"I will help interview them. We can divide the list." Richard's offer was welcome news indeed. The prospect of tracking down a couple dozen barons daunted Brendan, but it would be better than waiting around for something to happen. The earl's help in tackling the mammoth task would speed it up immensely.

*   *   *

LILY HAD ASSUMED that her husband would return home at some point to inform her why she was now being followed through the house. Or send her a note to explain. But the entire day had passed without a word from him. She had dressed for dinner and made her way downstairs, but there was still no sign of Brendan's return.

Sitting in the grim library, while the second John stood guard at the door, Lily felt tense with repressed angst. She was not accustomed to having someone breathing over her shoulder in this manner. Visiting the necessary while a man hung about in the corridor had been humiliating, and she had to wonder why the first John had never needed to make use of it himself.

It was pointless fuming over the situation, but she found herself doing so at regular intervals. If the protection was needed, that was one thing. But the fact that Brendan had not explained why it was needed was galling.

His absence from their glum home made matters much worse. Lily had had a grand plan to ensure that they spent time together in the first few days of their marriage and fell in love. She had believed she had made great strides the evening before, that everything was going according to plan after the flirting and the ... lovemaking ... Lily blushed at the recollection, before gathering her wits back together. Currently, she did not know where he was and when he was returning. The only thing that had kept her sane all day was believing he would return for dinner.

Out in the entry hall, the great casement clock chimed, announcing the hour. Lily's shoulders drooped in disappointment. She was desperately lonely, having moved around the house all day. Reading a book had not distracted her. Visiting the kitchen to meet the cook and maids had only occupied the better part of an hour; all the while, the women had cast nervous glances at the hulking man standing by the door.

In the distance, she heard a door open and close, and then footsteps in the hall. Springing to her feet, she ran to the door, ignoring the second John to see if Brendan was finally home. As she reached the doorway, Michaels appeared out of the shadows.

"Dinner is ready, milady." The droll announcement hit Lily like a slap. It was just the butler. Brendan had not returned.

Lily nodded, then exited the room when Michaels stepped aside for her. Heading to the breakfast room, she felt her emotions slipping perilously close to despair.

What could Brendan be doing that was more important than dinner with her?

As she entered, the sound of rain began, reflecting her mood perfectly. Taking her seat at the table, she stared at the flowers arranged in a vase, the only bright color in the dreary room. Until now, she had believed that he was engaged in some sort of work. Perhaps visiting his solicitors or something of that nature. Now dinner was being served, which limited the number of places he could be. The people he could be visiting.

Stanley, one of the footmen Brendan had told her about, placed a plate on the table before stepping away. She supposed the footman was one of the reasons for the second John standing at the door of the breakfast room.

Lily raised a trembling hand to her brow, fighting back tears that burned her eyes. It would not do to break in front of the hired men, but ... was it possible that Brendan could be with Lady Slight?

CHAPTER 14

"Prohibit the taking of omens, and do away with superstitious doubts. Then, until death itself comes, no calamity need be feared."
Sun Tzu, L'Art de la Guerre (The Art of War)

* * *

JULY 31, 1821

*T*welve hours had passed, and Lily was back in the breakfast room. Alone.

Rain roared outside, the heavens still weeping as they had throughout the night.

It took a lot to depress her good spirits, but Lily had discovered that being ambushed with the two Johns, and not hearing from her husband since she had fallen asleep in his arms on their wedding night, along with the dreary weather, would do it. Sleep had been elusive, every rattling creak causing her eyes to fly open and her heart to jump despite knowing that second John stood guard nearby. His pacing only added to the ghostly atmosphere, his low footfalls occasionally startling her from a light doze when she managed to sleep at all. The sound of persistent rain had only added to the sense of isolation.

Their first evening together had been so perfect, a promise of all the good things to come.

Now her heart was aching. She enjoyed Brendan's company, and she had enjoyed their nocturnal activities. Her hope was that it would lead to more time together, but now she could not shake the suspicion that Brendan might have left her alone to see his paramour.

Perhaps their night that she experienced as magical had been merely boring to him. Perhaps she did not measure up against the wiles of a sophisticated widow who was skilled in the bedroom.

Perhaps she was a ninny and being overly dramatic.

It has been a day and a half since I last saw my new husband. Perhaps I am permitted to be a tad melodramatic.

Lily groaned, leaning her head against her hand. It was pounding something fierce. That first John was there to witness her distress no longer signified. It was exhausting to have someone watching every movement.

Last night she had gone to her room, closing the door on second John and doing her best not to be loud in her room in case he could overhear what she was doing. By the time she had awoken this morning, she no longer cared. She could not maintain a perfect front with first John nearby.

Reaching over the table, she pulled a stack of news sheets over to peruse while she sipped on her tea. Wesley had presented the fresh stack when he had shown her into the breakfast room, and Lily suspected it was because he pitied her isolation of the day before. It had been a thoughtful gesture, which had made her feel … seen.

She skimmed the news, reading about goings-on about

Town. There was still talk of the coronation and King George IV. Some political news was covered.

Moving the top sheet aside, she reached for another. This was more of a gossip rag that she rarely read. She started to put it aside when a line jumped out at her, almost causing her to drop her tea.

Shaking her head, Lily set the cup down on its saucer and pushed it away. Then she carefully reread the news sheet.

Just yesterday, Lord F. and Lady S. were seen conversing intimately on a public street. Has the notorious widow taken back up with him, despite his recent vows to Miss A.?

Her heart squeezed painfully. Lily released the page, dropping her head into her hands while tears welled despite her best efforts to hold them back. Brendan had assured her that their marriage would be a faithful one. What did 'intimately' mean? How was she to—

"Lily?"

She jumped in fright. Swallowing hard, she palmed her streaming eyes to wipe away the evidence of crying, and turned to find Brendan framed in the doorway. He appeared a little haggard, and she thought he might be wearing the same clothes as the day before because of the wrinkling of his cravat and coat. His hair and shoulders were damp, and his boots were a little worse for wear, with some mud splatter marring their polished surfaces.

"Brendan!"

"I must speak with you." He entered and closed the door, shutting first John out in the hall before crossing the room to take a seat on the other end of the table. Noticing that there was a covered plate, he yanked off his gloves and pulled it closer with a look of relief. Soon he was devouring the plate of eggs and ham like a starving man while Lily waited impatiently for him to say something. Anything. The urge to slap the fork out of his hand and demand an explanation was a physical force she had to fight against.

"Where have you been?" The rain eased at that precise moment, making her demand particularly shrill in the sudden reduction of sound. But Lily welcomed the anger coursing through her veins. It was far better than the crushing defeat from moments earlier.

Brendan was sipping at tea, his plate emptied of its contents. "I was questioning the other barons who attended the coronation."

Lily's brows flew up. That was certainly not the answer she had expected. "What?"

"I was running down the lords who sat near my uncle to find out what they had to say." Brendan yawned widely, throwing a hand over his mouth before shaking his head as if to rouse himself.

Silence descended while Brendan sipped on his tea.

"No lord received you in the early hours of the morning," Lily finally responded.

"Correct. I journeyed to Chiswick to see Lord Simmons at his estate before he left for his country seat, but when we started back to London, we were caught in the rain. Within an hour, we were stuck in the mud. When we finally got unstuck, the horses were exhausted and there were no fresh ones to be found that late in the evening, so we slept in the carriage until dawn. Not that I slept much with Stephen near." Stephen was one of the footmen who might have opened the door to the killer, or might have been the killer himself, so Brendan must have felt the need to keep an eye on him throughout the night. It was all so … threatening.

"Oh."

Brendan reached out a hand to cover her own, his fingers cool against her skin. "My deepest apologies. I would have preferred to spend the night with you."

Lily stared at his hand, not certain how to feel about all of it. When she looked up, she found Brendan smiling at her warmly, his brandy eyes molten with suggestion. "Oh!" Her anger dissipated to be replaced with shyness when she realized he was thinking about the last time they had been together.

He stroked his thumb over her knuckles, before reluctantly releasing her hand to lean back in his chair.

* * *

"Unfortunately, I do not think we will be sharing evenings for the foreseeable future."

Lily straightened up with a stony expression. "What does that mean?"

"It means ... I wish to spend time with you, but I have been thinking that perhaps you should stay with your parents for a little while."

"What?" Lily sprang to her feet, bristling with outrage. "Are you trying to get rid of me?"

Brendan shook his head. "Certainly not! This is about protecting you. Until we find the baron's killer, I do not believe Ridley House is safe. After all you have done, I cannot allow anything to happen to you."

Lily threw up her hands. "I refuse to leave. I can take care of myself!"

Brendan stood. Walking around the table, he pulled her into a tight embrace, enjoying the feel of her soft body against his and burying his face in her hair to breathe in the scent of honey. She stood stiffly against him, but he continued the embrace, unwilling to release her when he had been yearning to see her all night. Leaning down, he whispered into her ear, "If anything happened to you, I would be devastated, Lily Ridley."

She relaxed. After a moment, her arms stole around his waist and she embraced him in return. "Did something happen? I was … expecting to see you when I awoke, but then I could not find you anywhere and the Johns followed me about all day without explanation."

Brendan raised his head in surprise. "You did not receive my note?"

Lily craned her neck to stare up at him, her large brown eyes narrowed with suspicion. "There was no note! I searched for you throughout the house and saw no note in any of the rooms."

"I placed it on the pillow next to you. Perhaps it fell?"

Lily mewled in throaty exasperation. "I thought you had abandoned me! What did the note say?"

Brendan released her, stepping back to gesture at her vacated chair. Lily sat down, while Brendan returned to his where he picked up his tea and sipped. "I was asleep in your bed when I was awoken by a loud crash. Someone had been searching my room when they overturned the water jug in their haste. It confirmed that one of the servants must be involved. Keeping you safe from harm was my first thought, which was why I sent for the Johns, but after meeting with the runner, Halmesbury and Richard agreed I should try to find out more."

"So you were trying to protect me? Not …" Lily glanced at the news sheets she had been reading when he had entered earlier.

Brendan cocked his head, a little confused by what she had been about to say. "Yes, of course. What did you think?"

Lily twisted her lips, shrugging slightly. "Nothing … I was not sure what to think."

* * *

LILY DID NOT AGREE to depart Ridley House, but she agreed to think about it and to allow the Johns to guard her. She could not argue that a woman of her petite size would be unable to fend off a panicked attack from the unknown servant who had searched his room. Considering a man had been killed, they could hardly ignore the possibility of such an event. The discussion had caused disquiet for Lily, who assured herself that her athletic, healthy husband would be capable of fighting off a hypothetical attack if it were aimed at him. At least, she hoped that was the case. He certainly was on edge enough to stay alert.

Despite her reservations about parting so early in their marriage, when her plan to turn this into a love match was her most pressing goal, Brendan had made a good point. If she stayed at her parents' home while he sought a resolution to the investigation, she could move freely without the suspense of two Johns dogging her every step.

Leaving the breakfast room, with first John falling into step behind her, she noted the rain had stopped completely. The sudden silence in Ridley House was almost unearthly after the barrage of drumming rain.

Turning a corner, she encountered Michaels in the poorly lit hall, startling in surprise. Usually, one could hear the butler coming because he had a pronounced step that thudded on the wooden floors. She had not heard him approaching. Had he been hovering in the shadows?

Lily realized she was on edge, mistrustful of the servant after the news Brendan had imparted. Blazes! Perhaps she should go home so she would not jump like a scared little ninny every time she encountered one of the servants in her own home.

"Is the carriage ready?"

Michaels pursed his lips, appearing mildly offended by

the question. "Of course, milady. You requested it for ten o'clock so—"

In the entry hall, the casement clock began to toll the hour, cutting off the rest of his declaration, and Michaels arched an eyebrow as if to accentuate the chimes.

"May I have my pelisse and bonnet?"

Michaels gave a curt bow and disappeared down the murky hall to collect her things, leaving Lily to mull over her conversation with Brendan. Discovering that her husband had been running about Town in the interests of protecting her had taken the wind out of her sails. It was rather sweet that he cared so much. She had wanted to ask him about what she had read about him and Lady Slight, but it had not seemed like the right moment to broach the subject.

Or you are afraid of the answer.

She would address the matter when she saw him at dinner, she resolved. Visiting Sophia at her home would be a welcome respite. She had clarified with Brendan, and he had advised that first John must accompany her because the footman and coachman might pose a risk, but roaming Sophia's home without John shadowing her footsteps was not a risk. They concurred John could stay with the servants in the mews behind the Saunton townhouse until she was ready to return.

Brendan was to spend his day seeking more lords who might have conversed with the late baron, and Lily had made arrangements with Sophia, so it was with some relief that she left Ridley House to visit her cousin.

When she arrived at Balfour Terrace, the earl's London townhouse, Lily was overjoyed to find Miles in the drawing room with his mother. She barely stopped to greet Sophia, quickly scooping up her baby cousin from his mother's arms to coo into his cherubic little face. Miles gurgled, smiling widely as he raised a tiny hand to grab hold of a lock of her hair.

"Oh, Sophia! I want a little angel of my own!"

Sophia laughed. "Give it a moment. Perhaps let the menfolk solve this murder before introducing a child."

Lily sighed. Sitting down, she settled Miles on her knees to face her. Pulling faces, she was delighted as her little cousin's eyes sparkled and he chuckled out loud. "Brendan has informed me I am in danger."

"I know. Richard informed me he had arranged for the Johns to stand guard. Where is … one of them?" Sophia finished awkwardly.

"He is in the mews. We agreed that I only need protection while I am around our own servants. We discussed pensioning off Michaels and letting the footmen go, but it seemed unfair to punish so many for the acts of only one. And there is no point pensioning Michaels off if we do not get rid of all of them, because we do not know which one is the danger."

"So what happens now?"

"Brendan advised me to return home." Lily's shoulders sagged. "I wish to remain with him. Matters were progressing so nicely. I was certain we could fall in love, but now the focus has shifted to this. And I do not wish to contend with Mama. She will be a nuisance if she learns I am in danger. I will never hear the end of it!"

Sophia pulled a face in sympathy. "We are leaving for Saunton Park in a few days. If matters are not resolved by then, you could come with us. Perhaps come stay at Balfour Terrace until we leave."

Lily tickled little Miles, who squirmed in her lap, wiggling with glee. "It is not ideal, but perhaps I will do that. I would prefer spending the summer with you and Richard than having Mama criticizing my marriage."

"I think you are fortunate to have a mother, especially one like Aunty who cares so much, but I understand the need to lead your own life now that you are wed. The invitation remains open."

Lily spent the day with Sophia and Miles, happy to have a respite from her problems at Ridley House. It was only after she left much later that evening that she remembered she had not spoken with her cousin about the *on-dit* in the news sheets. However, what could Sophia recommend other than to ask her husband about it?

Lily's stomach tightened as she tried to plan how to broach the matter with Brendan. She supposed it might be because she did not want to hear an answer that would end her hopes for the future.

* * *

BRIGGS SHOOK HIS HEAD. "I can find no other suspects amongst the servants. Michaels is the only one who has any reason to harbor resentments toward your family."

Brendan cleared his throat. "However, it cannot be discounted that one of the servants has been paid by the killer to remain silent."

"Agreed. Given that we know that the study and your room have been searched, there are issues with believing that Michaels killed the baron out of some long-ago quest for revenge for what happened to his father. The accidental death of a gamekeeper more than thirty years ago would not explain why he would search your home."

"So, to sum it up, we know nothing of any use. The barons I visited could only tell me they shared some banal discourse before the ceremony began and once it was completed. The late baron did not attend any of the gatherings that came after, and Michaels states he returned home in time for dinner. He gave his valet the night off to visit family here in London, then ate his evening meal in the formal dining room. After dinner, he closed himself in the study and instructed the servants not to disturb him because he had correspondence to write. Sometime between ten o'clock and dawn he was bludgeoned over the head with a weapon of convenience—a sculpture that they took from the mantelpiece."

"He was killed much earlier than dawn, according to the coroner. By the time we arrived, he had been dead for several hours."

Brendan nodded. "We will assume, then, that he was killed sometime between ten o'clock and approximately midnight. Most of the male servants would have been in the servants' hall by midnight."

Briggs nodded. "Which means one of the servants could be lying about their whereabouts, and they had the opportunity to murder him …"

"Or Michaels, or one of the footmen, answered the door to let the killer in, who then paid or threatened them into silence …"

"And is searching for something in the house that perhaps connects the killer to the baron …"

"Or is searching for something entirely different," Brendan finished. "In other words, we do know nothing."

Briggs rubbed his neck, clearly embarrassed. "The problem lies in the fact that the baron has been at his country seat for two decades. There are no connections in London that I have been able to find. No acquaintances to look into. I questioned his solicitors, but they had nothing to reveal. The baron lived his entire life in Filminster. Perhaps the answer lies there."

"The baron hated to travel. Enough to shirk his duties at Westminster since inheriting the title so he could remain at home. Perhaps I should leave for Baydon Hall to find anything that might throw light on this? I could remove Lady Filminster from danger if I travel without any of the servants from this household."

Briggs stroked his mustache thoughtfully. "There might be merit to it. I could continue the investigation here, but I can recommend a runner that you might take with you to assist."

Brendan stood up, pacing the library as he deliberated this course of action. The truth was, he did not want Lily to leave his side. He enjoyed her company and their night together...

I would not complain about sharing more nights like that with my wife.

Lily was a revelation. She lifted his spirits with her exuberance, and had saved him from a chaotic and prolonged trial with her earnest sense of justice, and she brought all that energy to the bedroom. He was still marveling two days later about their night of shared passion. It had been disappointing to not make it home the night before.

"I will do it. Lady Filminster and I will leave for Baydon Hall as soon as I can make arrangements for transportation. Perhaps the duke can lend me a carriage and servants."

"Then I will contact the runner I have in mind and request his assistance in Filminster. I will bring him by in the morning."

After the runner left, Brendan checked the time, realizing the day was mostly over, despite the summer light shining through the aged windows of the library, and it was nearly dinnertime. Most of the arrangements would have to wait until morning, as Briggs had suggested.

Brendan was satisfied with the plan they had discussed. He could keep Lily safe by taking her to Filminster, and

Briggs would sort out the muddle with the servants in his absence. He would need to decide what he should take with him, so he sat down to make a list of tasks to prepare to depart with Lily the next day.

A knock on the library door interrupted his thoughts while he was straightening his papers on the table.

Michaels opened the door, making his announcement to the room in general with an air of boredom. "Lady Slight to see you, milord."

Brendan sprang up, horrified to see Harriet entering and astounded that Michaels had granted her entry without his authority. "What are you doing here?"

CHAPTER 15

"Now, when your weapons are dulled, your ardor damped, your strength exhausted and your treasure spent, other chieftains will spring up to take advantage of your extremity. Then no man, however wise, will be able to avert the consequences that must ensue."

Sun Tzu, L'Art de la Guerre (The Art of War)

* * *

Michaels had left in a hurry, shutting the door behind him. Brendan clenched his jaw in anger. Perhaps he would pension off his bastard of a butler, after all. It was high time he hired someone who respected him. Brendan had always treated servants well, and the butler's continued disdain was beyond the pale.

Breathing deeply, he fought for his composure. Finally, he repeated the question that had not been answered.

"Harriet, what are you doing here?"

The viscountess smiled coyly, her red curls bouncing as

she bobbed her head back in glee. "This is my first time visiting your home, Brendan."

She stepped close, and once again rosewater assaulted his senses, suffocating him with the cloying scent so that he could gag from the potency of it. "I came to the realization that you are a married man now, which means I can visit Ridley House and claim I was here to see that flibbertigibbet you married."

How had he ever found the jaded widow alluring? Her straining breasts were on display for any man to see, and she was a hairsbreadth from revealing a nipple. How had he never realized before seeing Lily in church that sincerity and effervescence were so much more appealing than this lurid display of sensuality?

"I do not wish to receive a visit!"

Harriet ignored him, arching an eyebrow to peer about the room with amused interest. "Your home is ... quaintly Gothic."

Brendan's blood boiled, but he clamped down his anger so he could remove the widow from his home as quickly as possible.

"Be that as it may, I am afraid I do not wish to receive a visit from you, so ..." He strode forward and flung open the door that Michaels had shut.

Harriet laughed, taking advantage of his proximity to move closer. Placing a hand on his lapel, she stroked the fabric provocatively. Brendan immediately moved away, but she followed him until he was cornered against the opened door. It had been an error to approach her with no plan on how to escort her from the room. He could hardly shove her away without the fear of hurting her, so how to untangle himself from the clutches of this succubus?

Damn Michaels for showing her in!

At this distance, he noticed the wine on her breath and

the flags of color across her cheekbones and realized the widow was soused. That was not going to help even a little bit.

"You do not prefer your silly debutante over me, do you?"

He shook his head in disbelief, then realized that it might appear to be a response to her question. "It is time for you to go."

"Because that would not make any sense. I am … fashionable … and attractive. Most men of the *ton* are honored to spend time with me. You would not discard me for a silly little mouse like Perry Balfour did last year, would you?"

Brendan shut his eyes in horror. Was Harriet having a sodding crisis of the soul? And was he not a thorough idiot for picking up with her after Perry had left Town to marry little Emma Davis? Perry had warned him to stay away from the widow, but Brendan had thought he could handle her.

"I beg of you. You must leave immediately!"

It would seem he was now going to pay for his error in judgment involving Lady Slight yet again. His affair with this particular widow was turning out to have been a very poor choice.

Somehow, he needed to get the viscountess out of his home before Lily returned. It would be the height of disrespect for his bride to find his former paramour in her new home, but how to remove the viscountess expediently without hurting her?

He did not know how to march a woman out, and his skills of diplomacy were failing him in such an unprecedented situation.

Brendan had never had an overlap with the women he was pursuing. He had always been a one-woman kind of man, so there had never been any jealous lovers or unseemly displays of emotion. His affairs had always ended naturally, both parties happy to move on. Brendan did not seek drama in his life, which was currently a hindrance because he had no relevant experience on how to part ways with Harriet.

I must get her out before Lily returns.

Carefully reaching out with both hands, he took hold of her by the arms and gently pushed her away so she was not standing so close to him. Harriet resisted, raising her arms to throw herself against him, her bountiful breasts pressing against his chest. It felt all wrong. He wanted his little chatterbox with her lithe body pressed against his, not this overblown trollop.

Brendan backed up farther against the door, but the widow threw him off balance with her lusty embrace. He attempted to push her off, but she was a leech, her limbs entangling with his as he did his best to remove her without hurting her.

* * *

"Good evening, Wesley. Do you happen to know where Lord Filminster is at the moment?"

Lily had decided to find Brendan forthwith to discuss the gossip in the news sheet that morning. She should have spoken to him earlier when she had the opportunity, because her anxiety over it had grown exponentially on the way home from Sophia.

Ordinarily, Lily preferred to tackle issues that were worrying her as quickly as possible. She hated having thoughts festering in her head, and there could be no more festering fear than the notion of her husband being unfaithful with the voluptuous widow. He had done nothing to deserve mistrust, so she must simply speak with him about her concerns.

"His lordship is ... in the ... library." Wesley's pleasant face was stiff, and he was clearly reluctant to impart Brendan's whereabouts. Lily's brows came together in query, but the footman merely turned a ruddy shade before darting off to put her bonnet and pelisse away.

Heading down the dim hall in the opposite direction the servant had taken, with first John following a few feet behind, Lily saw the library door was standing open and made to walk through it. She stopped in shock, staring at the sight of Lady Slight locked in a passionate embrace with Lily's husband in the doorway. Her head began to swim, which made her realize she had stopped breathing. Inhaling a reedy breath, her eyes flickered to Brendan who appeared appalled.

Appalled he has been caught?

"Lady Slight! What an unexpected ... Has anyone offered you any tea? I must apologize for not being here to receive ... I do hope that Lord Filminster has been ..." From a great distance, Lily heard herself speaking, and she wished she could slap herself into silence.

Shut up, Lily!

She had never hated her propensity to babble more than she did in that moment. Her nerves were speaking for her when she really wanted to scream at the widow to unhand her husband. It was pure drama, a scene from a Drury Lane production, complete with the three of them and first John standing in the wings. And, suddenly, Lily did not have the energy to deal with it.

She just wanted to hide in one of the many gloomy rooms of Ridley House to cry. All her worst fears had been realized, and her hopes of finding love with Brendan Ridley were for naught.

"I shall leave you to your visit, then."

Spinning away, Lily ran down the hall, passing first John as she hurried to the little drawing room where she and Brendan had shared their first kiss. The day she had believed their marriage stood a chance. The wonderful, perfect day when she had fallen in love with her new husband.

"Lily!" Brendan's strangled voice called after her, but she did not hesitate. Running inside, she slammed the door behind her and fumbled to lock it with her trembling hands. First John was not a welcome visitor right now.

Hurling herself onto a settee, Lily curled into a ball and wept in the empty room. She had thought that—after what she had done for him, and the way he had looked at her on their wedding day—they could build something real. That she had progressed on her campaign to compel Brendan to fall in love with her.

How had she ever thought she could compete with all that luscious womanhood on display? Most men of the peerage would give their eyeteeth for a place in Lady Slight's bed, and stupid little Lily had thought she could convince a sophisticated man like Brendan to fall in love with her by being honest and cheerful, and changing her wardrobe.

What a farce!

* * *

"Oh, dear! Your wife seems a trifle upset."

Harriet giggled, leaning her face into his neck and snuggling into him. Brendan growled in fury, reminding himself to be gentle as he firmly shoved the widow off him. A cloud of rosewater and wine had him gagging as he gently walked the woman back into the library, her blue eyes wide in surprise. This time Brendan was not brooking any argument. He was going to make his stance clear, rid his home of her, and then find Lily to straighten this travesty out.

To think that minutes earlier he had been planning to take Lily away from Ridley House and the lurking danger within, to give her the attention she deserved as his bride, only to have the vexing viscountess create havoc.

Pressing her down into a chair, Brendan walked around to take a seat, ensuring that the library table was between them lest Harriet develop any new notions about leaping onto him as she had done before.

"Lady Slight, you are not welcome in my home."

Harriet's face flushed, and she narrowed her eyes in piercing hatred. Brendan considered his options. If he were cruel or scolded her mercilessly, the viscountess would have endless opportunities to seek revenge by belittling Lily, or spreading gossip to other members of the *ton*. Worse, she could attempt mischief like this again if he pushed her too far, which would hurt his wife again.

If his mother were here, she would advise him to be kind. She would point out that each person carries their own burden. That life could be crushing, and one cannot know the trials a person has endured. And when it was possible, one should attempt to lighten their load and disengage without fighting.

Damnation! He would really rather berate her and throw her out of his home in a rage after such ignominious behavior, but ... *I do not know the burdens that Harriet might carry. Or what vengeance she might seek against Lily!*

"I enjoyed our time together." Brendan struggled to find cajoling words to persuade her to leave his home and never return. "We enjoyed our time together. But this was always to be a temporary arrangement. You have no wish for permanent ties, and I ... find that I do. Because of circumstances beyond our control, Lady Filminster is my wife, and I am not a man to dally with multiple women."

"You no longer want me?"

Brendan raised a hand to the pulse beating in his temple

and applied pressure while he tried to think how to convince Harriet to walk away.

And never return!

"It does not signify. You are a beautiful woman, and you are quite aware I pursued a place in your bed ferociously for several months, but that chapter is over. I believe, if you think on it for a moment, that you grew weary of me. You made excuses not to see me in recent times, made arrangements which kept us apart."

Inspiration hit while he was talking, and Brendan realized the best strategy would be to persuade Harriet that their parting of ways was, in fact, her idea. He permitted a regretful expression to settle upon his features to complete his argument. "I think, perhaps, I knew you would end things with me soon, and it seemed wise to move on rather than have to experience the pain of being sent away."

He watched her closely, in breathless suspense, as he waited for her response. He had come to realize since spending time with Lily that Harriet was essentially a selfish woman who only thought of her own wants and needs. Appealing to her basic nature might convince her to lose all interest in him if he could just—

"That is true."

He almost straightened in relief, but carefully maintained the expression of regret. Slowly he lowered his eyes to stare at the table, to provide the appearance of melancholy, even allowing his shoulders to sag just a fraction, as if devastated at her declaration.

"I thought it might be. When you forgot our appointment that night of the coronation ..." He shook his head as if overcome, hoping his performance was natural but not daring to look up at her in case he broke the illusion he was attempting to cast. The illusion of an enamored man, attempting to protect himself from pain.

"I decided it was time to see to my duty before you …" He waited with bated breath to see if she would respond to his cue.

"Brendan, I am afraid that our time has come to an end. Your circumstances have become too complicated for a woman in my situation, so I think it would be best if we no longer meet."

He exhaled in a puff, dropping his head as if hearing the worst news. When he sorted out this muddle with Lily, he would confess to her how he had addressed the widow's peeves, but right now he stood on the precipice of a resolution and it was imperative he remove this troublesome distraction. There were actual life and death matters to contend with.

"I … understand. And I thank you for our time together." *I shall always remember our time fondly.* He could not bring himself to say the words, which would have been untrue and an assault on his integrity, regardless of how perfectly they would conclude their scene together.

A rustle of skirts informed him that Harriet had risen, but he dared not glance up in case his deception was revealed upon his face. The widow walked around, placing a hand on his shoulder and squeezing gently in commiseration. "Do not despair, Brendan. I shall always remember our time fondly."

He nearly burst into incredulous laughter when Harriet echoed his thought from seconds earlier. Instead, he bobbed his head in acknowledgment, keeping his eyes fixed on the grain of the mahogany table. "Thank you."

With that, Harriet walked away. Finally able to look up, he watched her, noting she was unsteady on her feet. He could only hope she was not too soused to recollect that she had ended things with him.

He waited in the library, playing out his tragic air until he was certain she had left. It would ruin everything if he sprang to his feet too soon, determined to find his bride and explain this invasion of their home.

* * *

LILY HAD BEEN WEEPING in the dismal drawing room, while outside the bright sunlight of a summer afternoon mocked her. She was going to have her trunks packed as soon as she could stop the storm of tears—

"Milady?"

She screeched in fright, jumping up to swipe her eyes dry before slowly turning around the room to find the source of the voice. As she swiveled toward the fireplace, she was utterly astonished to find Wesley standing by an open, previously concealed door with a tea tray.

There was so much to comprehend.

First, there was a door next to the fireplace she had never noticed before. It was covered in oak paneling and wallpaper to blend in with the rest of the wall. Under normal circumstances, she would be fascinated to discover what was ostensibly a secret entrance, the kind that wealthy homeowners had a penchant for, but with other issues on her mind, she concluded she would inspect it later.

If there is a later.

Wesley stood with a pained expression on his face, raising the tray as if to remind her he was there. Lily shifted her gaze back to him. The footmen hired in noble residences were part of the presentation of the household's wealth and status, an extension of the grand houses they served in. The footmen of Ridley House were no different, Wesley and the others being tall, lean men who were distinguished even in the dated style of livery that they wore.

He had a pleasant countenance, as did the other footmen, with a spattering of freckles across his cheeks and nose which spoke to the reddish tint of his brown hair. The servants had the customary white stockings and shining buckled shoes that any household livery included, but the style of the navy breeches and coat were faded and of a bygone era.

"I do not wish to be impertinent, milady, but … I thought perhaps you would like some tea?"

Lily blinked in surprise. Given all that had happened in the past few minutes, this mundane conversation was completely unexpected. She recollected Wesley had seemed uncomfortable earlier, reluctant even, when he had directed where to find her husband. Now he had taken pains to find her to offer her tea? It was unbearably sweet, and Lily realized she had no wish to continue with the strain she had been experiencing this past week or so.

She thought about how she had been friends with many of the servants in her parents' home. How their footman, Thomas, had once caught an intruder when Sophia had convinced him to lay a trap for a man seeking to abduct her. How Nancy had been her constant companion since Sophia had married. Suddenly, Lily just wanted to experience an ordinary interlude with another person.

No murders, no enforced courtships, no hasty weddings, no reluctant or unfaithful husbands, no fear. Just a normal conversation between two normal people.

"Only if you join me," she replied, gesturing to the tray.

"Oh no, milady! It is not permitted."

"Wesley, I … order you to sit down and have a cup of tea with me."

Wesley stared at her, his eyes wide as he thought about it. "Very well, milady. If that is what you wish."

"It is."

He nodded, moving forward to place the tea tray on the table by the settee. Then he looked about before walking over to collect a tumbler from the drinks cabinet. Returning, he sat across from her, perched awkwardly on the edge of the armchair as if he were ready to spring to his feet.

Lily straightened up on the settee, lowering her feet to the floor, and leaned forward. Placing the strainer over the cup on the tray, she poured her tea and then raised the teapot toward the footman. Wesley placed the tumbler down. "I hope it is acceptable for me to use this? I only brought the one cup."

She could not care two pennies about what happened to her faithless husband's crystal tumbler after what she had witnessed in the library. "It is suitable."

Moving the strainer to the glass, she poured his tea for him. The orange-brown tint made her mouth water in anticipation, and Lily felt a genuine moment of peace. These past weeks had been hell, and it felt so wonderfully commonplace to enjoy a cup of tea.

Sitting back, she sipped on the hot liquid, and the tension slowly melted away. Soon she would have to confront Brendan with the remnants of their marriage, and make decisions about how to repair her shattered dreams, but that moment was not now.

Wesley raised his glass and sipped uncomfortably. Lily supposed it was fortunate he wore the gloves of his livery because the glass must have heated considerably from its contents.

"How long have you worked at Ridley House, Wesley?"

The footman lowered his glass and cleared his throat. "A few years, milady."

"So you never met the baron before the coronation, I suppose."

"No, milady. But I did not meet his lordship even then. I was away for several days because my brother got married in

Yorkshire. Mr. Michaels generously allowed me the time off, and I returned the morning the baron was found."

Lily vaguely recollected that Brendan had mentioned this when he had informed her of the situation on the afternoon of their wedding. "I never met the late baron either. His death certainly has created a pickle for those of us left behind."

Wesley appeared unsure of what to say. "Yes, milady." He raised his glass to sip on his tea again, and Lily suspected it was to avoid further conversation.

She sipped on her own tea, flinching slightly and spilling some drops when a distinctive knock sounded on the door she had locked.

"Lily, we must speak."

Sighing, Lily put her cup down while shooting Wesley a glance of apology. The footman seemed relieved to rise. Bowing, he walked away, tumbler in hand, to exit through the concealed door, which he quietly pulled shut behind him.

She crossed the room. Drawing in a deep breath, she turned the key and stepped aside.

Brendan must have heard the click of the lock because the handle turned, and her rogue of a husband entered.

* * *

BRENDAN WAS RATHER proud of how he had handled Harriet, but he had no inkling how to explain what had happened to Lily who was sitting on the settee with her arms folded and her expression mutinous in the last rays of the day.

He could hardly blame her after what she thought she had witnessed in the library.

"I did not invite Lady Slight into our home."

"That did not seem to be a problem."

He shook his head. "It was definitely a problem. I had no

desire to see her, and I was attempting to make her leave when she threw herself into my arms moments before you happened upon us. The door was open, and I knew you were returning for dinner, so it would be incomprehensible to believe I thought I could hide her presence."

Lily's face gradually eased as she considered his defense. She lowered her arms, her hands gripping the edge of the settee. Turning to stare out the window, she finally responded. "Be that as it may, it does not explain the gossip in the news sheets."

Brendan frowned, trying to follow the sudden shift in conversation. "What gossip?"

"You and Lady Slight were mentioned. How you were seen conversing intimately on the street!"

He rubbed a hand against the side of his cheek, growling in irritation. "That is what started this. Harri—Lady Slight approached me in the street yesterday before I met with Halmesbury, Richard, and Briggs. She intimated she would be willing to continue our arrangement. My reply was an emphatic no, which she apparently took exception to because she had evidently been drinking and stewing on why I would prefer to spend time with my wife rather than her."

Lily jumped to her feet. "There is no need to coddle me, Brendan Ridley! I am not a child. I am a grown woman and I can handle the truth!"

Brendan threw up his hands in confusion, shaking his head while he tried to make sense of what he was being accused of. "What truth?"

"That you were forced to marry me! That if the baron had not been killed, you would even now be in *Harriet's* bed! That you never chose me! So do not pretend that you would rather spend time with me than that ... that ... that trollop!"

Brendan dropped into a chair and stared sightlessly at the ceiling. Apparently Lily believed him about what happened, a trait he appreciated in her as part of her general impulse to be honest and sincere. But how to respond to her envy of his previous attentions, he was uncertain. His feelings were developing for Lily, and his fondness for her was growing in leaps and bounds. But he was not ready for a discussion regarding how their relationship had come to be. They needed to spend time together and foster the affinity that was growing between them. To allow their connection to develop naturally. Discussing it now, so early in their marriage and with so many challenges facing them, was premature.

Shaking his head, he rose and came around to take hold of Lily's hands in his own. "I am here with you now. The past is inconsequential to our present. I have spent every waking moment since you agreed to marry me, ensuring your safety. Taking steps to end this danger and take care of you."

"So you do not deny you would be with Harriet tonight if I was not here?"

Brendan wished to curse. Lily was a wonderful, generous person, but the widow had made her jealous and now they were arguing when he had been looking forward to having dinner with his new wife before taking her to bed. "I cannot say where I would be. I can only state that I am here with you now, and that I have arranged that the viscountess will never return to Ridley House again."

"And how many times has she been here?" demanded Lily, her face stiff with angry outrage. He hated seeing her this way. His Lily was soft and sweet. She chattered about life and her thoughts, and he liked her. He did not like this hard woman staring at him with rage in her eyes.

"Never! I have never invited her to my home. You are the only woman I have ever brought into my home, or allowed entrance to my bedroom!"

Lily glared at him, chewing on her lip. "Pshaw!"

Brendan wanted to tell her what she needed to hear, but he wanted to be honest, too. He was not clear what his feelings for Lily were exactly, only that she had made him feel hope. Hope that they could build a strong future together, hope that their affinity would continue to grow, and hope that he could one day experience a genuine meeting of the minds with this woman.

But until he had achieved clarity of his feelings, he did not want to say things he was not sure of. He and Lily had been honest with each other since the morning of their wedding, and he did not want to throw out words without sorting it all out. That would take time—the words could not be forced. They had only just been wed three days ago, confound it!

Stalking back to the settee, she flopped down to stare at her slippers peeking out from below the hem of her emerald dress. She was splendid in the jewel tones she had been wearing recently. But that was neither here nor there while they were quarreling.

Brendan sat back down and waited for her to speak.

"I wish ... you had chosen me," she finally admitted in a small voice, her voice thick. "All my life, I just wanted someone like you to notice me. To choose to wed me. To ..." She pressed her lips together, before finally continuing, "I cannot even walk the halls of my home without one of the Johns, and now that ... trollop ... has invaded ..."

Lily's eyes welled with tears, and he ached for the sweet girl who was shouldering so much because of him. Brendan could not deny that Lily was in the right, and he had no defense for the risks she had taken on his behalf. He owed her everything, which confused his thoughts more.

Do I have genuine regard for Lily, or am I merely grateful?

Certainly it would take more than a single conversation and a few hours in her company to uncover the truth of it? If he could, he would open his mouth and assure her they were forming a genuine match, but he needed … clarity. Room to breathe.

"I am sorry for everything you have had to deal with."

Lily's face hardened once more, and Brendan realized he had said the wrong thing. Perhaps she wanted different words from him, but he did not have them to give yet.

"Sophia has invited me to Saunton Park, so I do not have to live with my parents. She said I could stay with them at Balfour Terrace until they leave London, so I believe … I shall accept her offer."

Brendan felt a surge of disappointment. But after everything he had put Lily through, he was hardly in a position to debate what she chose to do in response to the danger she was in. He had asked so much of her; it was only fair to acquiesce to her wishes.

"That would be wise."

A flash of something crossed Lily's face. She seemed unhappy that he had conceded, and Brendan was at a loss for what to say. Once her safety was secured, they would finally have the time to mend their rapport.

CHAPTER 16

"The general who advances without coveting fame and retreats without fear of disgrace, whose only thought is to protect his country and to do good service to his sovereign, is the jewel of the kingdom."
Sun Tzu, L'Art de la Guerre (The Art of War)

* * *

AUGUST 1, 1821

*M*ichaels directed the maids to pack Lily's trunks with a sour expression on his lined face. What a relief it would be to get away from Ridley House, so she no longer had to look over her shoulder, wondering if Michaels or one of the footmen were going to attack her out of its many shadows.

After providing instructions, she left the servants to it and descended to eat her breakfast, with first John at her heels like a heavy-breathing shadow. She and Brendan had parted ways the night before after agreeing she would move her things to Sophia's home, and Lily had sent a note to her cousin before having her dinner brought to her bedroom on a tray. Brendan had remained downstairs when she had retired, and if he had come upstairs, it was after she had fallen asleep in the early hours of the morning, with the sound of second John shifting about out in the hall.

It had been a miserable night, with Lily berating herself for foolishly falling in love with a man who had been forced into a marriage with her. She should have protected her heart while she waged her campaign to win his regard.

Entering the breakfast room, she noted with disappointment that Brendan was nowhere to be seen. She wished she could see him before she left. They had not discussed when they might reunite, but she supposed that it would have to wait until this murder investigation was resolved once and for all.

I am not admitting defeat.

She was merely retreating in order to plan her future without the threat of impending danger or wicked widows invading her home.

Reassuring herself did little to fend off the disappointment she had been feeling since finding the ravishing Lady Slight draped over her equally handsome husband. She could not shake the thought that she could never hope to compete. Brendan was sartorial elegance, and Lady Slight was a practiced seductress. The notion that little Lily Billy could hope to be a contender for his affections was laughable. He might be attempting to keep his word and remain faithful to their marriage of friendship, but that would never alter the fact that Lily's intervention had interrupted what Brendan had wanted his life to be.

He had never chosen her. No one had ever chosen her. And now that she was married, she would never have the opportunity to know the privilege of being the center of a man's attention. Lily had always believed that things would work out for the best, her optimism something that had set her apart from others. But even she could not think of a way to straighten out this muddle with any sort of confidence.

Sitting down at her usual seat, she uncovered her meal and picked up her fork. Perhaps a respite at Saunton Park would restore her spirits and provide inspiration on how to proceed. It would certainly not be amiss to escape the foreboding pall of Ridley House.

* * *

BRENDAN HAD WANTED to join Lily in her bed the night before. He had stayed downstairs to control the urge because he doubted he would be well received. The memory of their one night together still haunted his thoughts, taunting him with what could be. He wanted to spend time with her, grow to know her better, and make love to his wife.

Which was why he was now walking down a quiet Mayfair street. If he had breakfasted with her, he knew it was only a matter of time before he broke down and begged her to stay at his side.

Brendan had never realized how lonely he had become since his mother had died thirteen years earlier. They had been close, his mother and Annabel and he. Richard had become a close friend at Eton and helped assuage the loss of his parent, but then the baron had sent him to Cambridge and separated him from his closest friend. Until, on the day he had come of age, his uncle had banished him from Baydon Hall and estranged him from his sister.

Since then, Brendan had lived in London, with his friends

for company. He had been surrounded by people but had come home to no one. When he and Annabel had come back together, when she had married Halmesbury, it had been a relief to finally reconnect and know he had family again. Observing the closeness of his sister and her husband, along with the arrival of their son, Jasper, Brendan had been reminded what it was to be part of a tight family unit.

The night of his wedding, when he had held Lily in his arms and listened to her snoring gently in her sleep, he had experienced a moment of pure bliss. This was what it would be like for them, he had thought. They could be partners. He could trust the woman in his arms, because she had the heart of a lion beating in her small chest and would follow her conscience.

The summer light should have uplifted his spirits. The lush green trees in the square whispered in the morning light, and he had never seen the sky bluer than it was above him. Birds chirping in the branches overhead were idyllic, but Brendan just felt terrible.

Stopping by the large iron gates that led into the fenced-off square, he stared at the riot of colorful flowers within, but he saw nothing. His new wife was leaving, and he did not know when he would see her again. After what he had put her through, he had no right to any expectations of her.

Will she be gone when I return home?

The very idea of that was a weight pulling him back into the tedious ennui he had finally escaped when he had wed Lily on Sunday morning.

* * *

LILY WAS WAITING in the little drawing room down the hall, while first John stood guard at the door.

Soon she would be leaving. But she refused to think about

it, resolutely reading through the news sheets that had been brought in. Turning the page, a print dropped out and slowly drifted through the air to fall on the floor. Putting the sheets aside, Lily leaned down to grasp it just as Wesley entered with a tea tray.

"Wesley! You read my mind."

The footman's face creased into a smile. "I wanted to serve you tea before you left, milady. I …" He stopped, and Lily concluded he had been trying to say his goodbyes but must have decided it was too forward to speak of the future.

She grinned. "You brew excellent tea. When the new housekeeper begins work at the end of the week, you shall have to ensure she knows how to do it correctly for when I return."

"Thank you, milady."

He moved forward to place the tray on the table near her. Lily sat back in the settee, holding the print she had retrieved from the floor. Glancing down at it, she chuckled out loud. It was a caricature of the lords wearing their striped trunk hose for the coronation. The illustrator had drawn a gaggle of spindly legs, with the bulbous breeches ballooning around their hips.

Wesley stopped in confusion, evidently not sure if she had lost her mind.

"It is the coronation attire," she offered, holding the print up for him to see. "My family was highly amused when my father came downstairs dressed like this on the day of the coronation. Lord Saunton maintains it was an elaborate prank by the King to make them all look like fools."

Wesley tilted his head to view the image, suppressing a smile of his own. "It was difficult not to react when I saw the baron."

Inside her chest, Lily's heart stopped mid-beat, and her

lungs lost the capacity to expand, but she carefully prevented any flicker of change on her face.

When I saw the baron?

She chuckled once more, an attempt to cover her reaction as she glanced toward the door to see if John was still there.

"Quite ridiculous!" Lily rose to her feet, preparing to dart toward the door while she watched Wesley from the corner of her eye. The footman stood frozen, staring at the illustration in her hand, time slowing down as Lily realized he knew he had made a mistake.

Stepping in the direction of the door, she saw Wesley darting forward to intercept her.

"JO—"

It was too late. He had grabbed her around the waist, pulling her against his body as his free arm wrapped around her throat and he lifted her off her feet. Wesley was strong. Lily could feel the steel in his muscles as he held her against him.

First John had spun at her shout of alarm, rushing into the small drawing room.

"STOP!"

Wesley's command cracked like a musket, firing through the gloom, and first John stopped dead in his tracks. "I will snap her neck like a twig if you come any closer."

Lily struggled, raising her hands to claw at the muscled arm that was throttling her.

"Can't ... breathe!" she wheezed, her lungs burning in protest as she kicked her legs back and forth. The footman eased his hold just a fraction, allowing her the much-needed air her body was crying for. He watched first John from over her shoulder, as he slowly lowered her back to her feet, but he was careful to maintain the stranglehold around her throat, leaning slightly down and forward.

As her feet made contact with the floor, she looked over at first John, who was primed to rush forward but could not.

"Back up! Out the door!" Wesley's voice was hard, and he would brook no argument. Whatever John could see on her assailant's face, he obviously took seriously because he shifted back out of the room into the hall.

Lily swallowed hard against the band around her throat.

This is what Brendan had warned her of. Wesley had been backed into a corner, and in his panic, he had now taken her hostage. She might not survive this, and she wished … she wished she had spent last night with Brendan. She wished she had told him that her wedding day with him had been the best day of her entire life. She wished she had told him she loved him and wanted to spend her life with him. That it might have been a strange series of events that had led them to be wed, but he was everything she had ever dreamed about, even if he did not reciprocate.

And she wished to live so she could experience the highs and lows of love firsthand.

* * *

BRENDAN HAD STOOD at the iron gates to the square for some time. Finally, he straightened up and made a decision. He could not allow Lily to leave without him. This was not what he desired, and it was time for him to become decisive and tell his wife what he wanted.

He supposed he should be tracking down more of the lords from his list, but his wife needed to come first. Resolutely, he set off for Ridley House, determined to take Lily to Baydon Hall. They needed to focus on their future. He would sort out this argument with her, and he would order his own trunks to be packed as he had originally proposed during his meeting with Briggs before Harriet had arrived to overturn his plans.

When he reached home, Michaels opened the door to let him in.

"Where is Lady Filminster?"

"I believe she is in the small drawing room, milord."

Brendan nodded, striding to the hall leading off the foyer. He was going to find his wife and repair their growing rapport.

Entering the corridor, he paused when he saw that Lily's guard was positioned at the door of the drawing room, holding his hands aloft as if trying to appease someone inside.

"I assure you I will not enter!"

Something was amiss. He ran forward, nearly skidding into the guard as he stopped by the door to view the interior. Brendan's blood ran cold at the sight of Wesley clutching her with a thick arm wrapped around her throat. Lily was panting in agitation as if she had been running, her eyes wide with fear. Her gaze found his, and her large brown eyes stared directly into his as if peering into the depths of his soul, imploring him to help her.

"Do not enter, milord! I will kill her if you enter!" the footman cried out, his voice firm despite the frenzy written on his features.

Brendan stepped back and raised his hands in the conciliatory gesture that John had been displaying moments earlier. "Do not panic, Wesley. We can reach an agreement."

Out in the hall, Brendan heard the heavy tread of Michaels approaching. The footsteps stopped, indicating the butler must have surmised that there was a problem.

"What is the meaning of this, Wesley? Has something happened?"

"Her ladyship noticed a slip. She knows I was involved

with the baron's murder, so I am afraid she will have to be my leverage to escape."

Brendan's pulse raced in fear at seeing Lily in peril, but he noticed that the panic in Wesley's face had reduced slightly after he had backed out of the room.

Faith! He should have sent Lily away the morning he had found his room ransacked. If anything happened to her now, he would have only himself to blame. And he would lose the woman that ... that ... that he loved, damn it all to hell! He loved his new wife. He had fallen irrevocably in love with her the night of their wedding, and he could not allow her to be harmed. Not one tiny, delectable inch. It would break his very heart in two if something happened to her because of him!

Rubbing a hand through his hair, he attempted to relax. The only thing he could think to do was to talk. To negotiate with the footman for Lily's release.

"Did you kill the baron?"

Wesley's face scrunched with anger. "Of course not!"

"But you know who did?"

A mutinous bob of the head was the only reply.

"Is it someone in this household?"

Wesley frowned at him, shaking his head as if dealing with an imbecile. "Why would a servant want the baron dead?"

"Did someone outside of this household pay you to remain silent?"

There was a pause, followed by another bob.

"Why are you still here, then?"

"I was promised additional coin if I could find a letter that the baron had written. They needed someone inside the household to search for it."

Brendan nodded, trying to think of a plan. "I will pay you double."

"I am not a fool!" cried Wesley. "My only option is to leave and take the baroness with me so you cannot apprehend me."

Shaking his head, Brendan lowered his voice, attempting to keep his voice even and cajoling, even while he struggled for composure. The idea of Lily being taken away made him want to toss his head back and howl. "If you take the baroness with you, we will be feverish in our pursuit. Perhaps ... I could pay you what I have and you can tie us up so you can make your escape?"

Brendan winced. That was a terrible plan. If they submitted to being captured, then Wesley could do anything he chose. What if the man was lying, and he was merely a lunatic who murdered people?

Lily must have had a similar thought. Despite the horror of what she was experiencing, she wobbled against Wesley's arm in response to this suggestion, her eyes so huge in her pale face. She was so tiny, engulfed in the footman's grip, increasing Brendan's desperation to help her. "No! You will not risk your safety for me, do you hear, Brendan Ridley? If Wesley feels he must take me, then you will allow it so you remain unharmed!"

Wesley glanced down at his captive, clearly startled by what she had said, but it did not surprise Brendan to hear his valiant bride demand such a thing of him. However, he could not conceive of letting the footman leave with his wife. If something happened to Lily, Wesley might as well bludgeon Brendan to death on the way out of Ridley House because he would never recover from letting the woman he loved be killed because of his own stupidity.

"Take me instead!"

Lily cried out, "No!"

Wesley scowled. "Are you funning me? I should take a grown man, instead of this tiny girl as my hostage?"

The reprobate had a point. Brendan wondered if Michaels might summon the runner to assist, because he was out of ideas other than to keep the footman conversing so he did not steal Lily away. Desperate men did desperate things, and Lily's life hung in the balance.

"I will pay you everything I have in the house, and you can lock us into a room, but I beg of you … do not harm the baroness!"

As if thinking of the butler had summoned him, Brendan saw that behind Wesley the concealed door was slowly opening. Michaels peered carefully around the corner.

Brendan's thoughts scrambled. What was Michaels planning to do? The butler was several inches shorter than Wesley and a good twenty years older than the strapping young man. Nevertheless, Brendan's only option was to keep the footman distracted.

"Who killed the baron?"

Dead silence followed, all parties frozen at the question.

"That … is my secret. The killer will have to pay me. I will demand passage from England, and they will arrange it to hide their identity." Wesley's voice was hesitant when he finally responded. He was not certain he would receive help, Brendan realized. There was an opportunity to negotiate and strike a deal.

In the background, where Brendan resolutely refused to look in the event he alerted Wesley to Michaels's proximity, the butler stepped out from behind the door.

"I do not care about the baron's murder as much as I care about my wife. I will pay you to release her and allow you to leave without hindrance, Wesley. On my word."

That was the moment when Brendan noticed Michaels was raising a rifle to his shoulder. Brendan wanted to shout out for him to stop, that Lily could be hit, but before he could react, the butler cocked the hammer and then pulled the trigger.

It was as if time stood still, the musketball firing from the barrel with a loud bang and belting of smoke, and Wesley crumpled to the floor, dragging Lily down under him.

"Lily!" Brendan ran into the room, dropping to his knees to pull the large footman off his wife.

CHAPTER 17

"100 soldiers who are in a desperate situation lose the feeling of fear. If there is no refuge, they will stand firm. If they are in a hostile country, they will show a stubborn front. If there is no help for this, they will fight hard."

Sun Tzu, L'Art de la Guerre (The Art of War)

* * *

*L*ily was curled beneath Wesley in a mild state of shock. She had heard a blast, but she did not know what it had been. The footman appeared to be insensate above her. She struggled, trying to push him off her.

Seconds later, the dead weight was lifted, and she inhaled with relief, flopping onto her back.

"Lily, are you hurt?"

It was Brendan. He was leaning over her and frantically exploring her body with warm hands that reminded her of their night of passion.

"My throat feels bruised and my knees are rather banged

up. And I think I strained my wrist when I landed on it. I have quite forgotten how to breathe, and I have never been so petrified in my life, but I am thrilled that ..." She raised her hands before dropping them once more, not knowing what she was thrilled about, or what had just happened. *Not a great time to babble, Lily Billy!*

"What happened?" she continued. Brendan gathered her up in a hard embrace, which felt heavenly after the strain of being subdued by the demonic Wesley whom she had believed to be kind.

"And what are you doing here?" she ended.

Brendan shook his head against her neck, continuing their embrace for what seemed an eternity before raising his head.

"What the hell, Michaels?"

The butler's response was stated in his usual dry tone. "I was protecting the baroness."

"With a firearm? What if you had missed?"

Lily heard Michaels tut behind her, but she was ecstatic to be in Brendan's arms so she did not look about.

"I know that runner of yours must have informed you that my father was the gamekeeper, so I hardly need to state that I know my way around a rifle. Not to mention, her lady-ship is a good foot shorter than this beast."

There was a soft thud behind her. Had the butler kicked something?

Rifle! Michaels shot Wesley?

Her husband's face returned to rest against her neck. "Thank you."

"It is my pleasure, milord. Shall I send someone to summon Briggs?"

"Yes." Brendan was wrapped so tight around her she could scarcely breathe, but unlike when Wesley had held her captive, Lily was happy to allow it. Her hand stole around

NINA JARRETT

Brendan's waist. She realized he was pressing kisses into her hair just as he cupped her chin, his warm lips finding hers. Lily sighed in happiness, kissing him back and feeling weightless as Brendan lifted her in his arms to stride from the small drawing room.

"John, find a sheet to cover the body until the coroner arrives and meet us in the drawing room at the top of the stairs."

Ridley House was running out of rooms for them to use, Lily mused in a haze as she snuggled into her husband's broad chest.

Brendan carried her down the hall, up the stairs, and into the bigger drawing room on the next floor. Striding over to the windows which faced the street, he sank into the faded navy settee and held her close, not saying a word as he lowered his cheek to the crown of her head.

Lily did not mind, not even a little bit. She found herself in a befuddled state after everything … whatever … had happened downstairs, and she was blissfully giddy to be held in his arms. Perhaps she was just giddy after the assault by Wesley, not to mention the difficulty breathing when the footman had choked her. Nevertheless, she was blissful at being reunited with Brendan when she had believed she might never feel his embrace again. She refused to allow her thoughts to wander to what had just happened, just soaking in the joy of being alive after the terror of staring death in the face.

They sat in silence for a while until Lily's pulse returned to normal and her chest eased while she slowly gathered some of her wits together to make sense of what had just happened. "Michaels shot Wesley?"

"He did."

"Is he … dead?"

Brendan said nothing, bobbing his head in assent. Lily

216

quelled the burst of revulsion, nauseated at the thought that she had been buried beneath a dead man. The lassitude she had been feeling since hitting the floor was beginning to wear off. "That is … horrifying."

"God, I have never been so terrified in my life. I thought I was going to lose you."

Lily kept her ear pressed to his chest, enjoying the steadiness of his heartbeat. "Would that have been a bad thing?"

Brendan squeezed her tighter. "A very bad thing, Lily Ridley."

"Why—"

Michaels cleared his throat from near the door. "I have sent for Briggs, and I have arranged to notify her ladyship's family of what has happened. Should I bring a drink for Lady Filminster? For the shock."

Brendan did not move at all, maintaining his embrace while responding. "Nay, Lady Filminster does not imbibe."

"Perhaps some sweetened tea, then? Or coffee, perhaps?"

Lily shifted. "Coffee? I have never tried coffee before. Is it any good? It is certainly expensive! I saw the household accounts at my parents' home, and I could not believe what Papa pays for his. He is usually so frugal about expenditure."

Brendan chuckled, raising his head. "Coffee, then. But, Michaels, lots of milk and sugar."

Michaels's heavy tread announced his departure.

"I would not recommend developing a fondness for coffee. You are lively enough without its effects."

Lily nodded, then squirmed. "I think I would like to sit up now," she announced.

Brendan carefully swung her off his lap, settling her on the settee next to him. Lily tugged at her dress, straightening her clothing out while trying to think what she wanted to say. Brendan did not say a word, just clasping her hand between them.

Michaels arrived back with the tray of coffee before she had settled her thoughts. Brendan poured her a cup and added the milk and sugar he had requested.

Lily blinked as he stirred the cup. "So much sugar?"

"To help you focus after your shock. And coffee is very bitter." He proffered the beverage to her.

Leaning forward, she took it up, taking a sip. "How strange it tastes!"

"It would be better to drink tea. Coffee can have some strange effects on one's energy."

Lily nodded. She did not want to babble any more than she already did, if that was what he was alluding to.

"Why did you come ba—"

"Lily!"

She looked over to see her brother striding in. He must have been exerting himself, because his flushed face was covered in a sheen of sweat, his hair mussed and his cravat askew. "Aidan? How did you get here so quickly?"

"Ran here … as soon as we heard the news … Left our parents … to take the carriage … Terrifying … to hear you had been attacked. I …" Her brother raked his hands through his damp hair before crossing the room to drop on a knee by her side. Taking her hands up in his, and shaking his head as he sought words, he exhaled sharply. "This is my fault! If I had taken care of you that night, instead of abandoning you to carouse with my friends …"

Lily frowned, pulling him closer and lifting her arms to hug him. "It is not, Aidan. I am well. Gracious! You must have run like the wind to arrive here so quickly."

"I should never have left you alone."

"But you did, and now I am married. Life goes on."

Aidan groaned. "Until it does not."

"I am safe. See, you are speaking with me at this very moment. The entire matter is settled."

Aidan pulled away. Her brother was so tall that even lowered to one knee, they were practically eye level. From this close, she could see his pupils were dilated. "Is it over? Was the footman the one who committed the murder?"

Brendan cleared his throat. "No, I am afraid not. He claims he was paid to conceal the identity of the killer. At least we know now that it was nobody in the household."

Aidan jumped to his feet. "How do we know it is true?"

Her husband must have felt uncomfortable with her brother towering over them. He rose up, walking into the cleared space in the middle of the room. The drawing room had plenty of the large, wooden furnishings of the rest of Ridley House, carefully placed around the perimeter of the room. They were surrounded by the exceptional strapwork of very fine pieces, even if their home was as gloomy as a cave. But Lily had heard that the King preferred to arrange his furniture in a different manner. Perhaps when they renovated Ridley House, they would rearrange the furniture into the informal groupings of the royal household.

Brendan's voice called her back to the more pressing subject at hand. "I suppose we shall search his things to find evidence of the payoff."

Aidan's nostrils flared. "If it is true, then there is still a killer out there. Someone who might harm my sister!"

"We will keep our guards to patrol the house—"

"What?"

Brendan glanced over at Lily, who had straightened in dismay. She did not want to be followed around the house now that they knew Wesley had been the one on their staff working in collaboration with the true perpetrator.

"They do not need to shadow you. Simply take care of our home until we know we are safe. In addition to that, we will have a new housekeeper and maids at the end of the week, so Ridley House will be properly staffed, along with a new lady's maid. It will be far more difficult for any attempt at intrusion once there is a full staff on duty."

Lily turned her gaze to her brother, who appeared mollified by Brendan's assertions.

"See that you do, Filminster. My sister is irreplaceable."

* * *

BRENDAN WISHED he could speak with Lily, and communicate to her all the thoughts simmering in his head, but after allaying Abbott's fears, more family arrived.

First Lord and Lady Moreland, the latter sweeping in the room with a frantic expression and wailing in distress when she caught sight of her daughter. Soon Lily had been enveloped in her embrace, appearing to be crushed by the taller woman.

Then Lord Moreland had shaken his head, dragging Lily into another hug. In her father's arms, Lily was the most diminutive Brendan had ever seen her. Just when he thought he might be able to speak with the Abbott family to assuage their panic, Richard and his wife were announced.

That was the moment when Brendan realized that his family connections had grown significantly in the past week. Richard and he were vaguely related through the duke because of Annabel, the earl and duke being cousins. They had not really thought of each other as family, the tie being rather distant. Now he was married to someone the earl considered to be under his protection, a mild throbbing of his jaw reminding Brendan just how protective Richard could be about his wife's cousin and closest friend.

Then, too, he now had a new brother-in-law, who was currently watching him with a tense expression. Given the younger man's fears for his sister's safety, Brendan suspected he would be seeing Abbott regularly.

Then there were Lord and Lady Moreland, who after they had checked on Lily, turned their attention on him. Lord Moreland gestured him over.

"This is quite a pickle, son. I am just glad no one innocent was harmed. Is this matter settled now?"

"Not fully. We still need to confirm that the footman was acting with someone, and try to uncover their identity. But our household itself is now safe, I believe."

"Wesley confessed to his involvement?" Richard demanded.

"He did. The killer paid him, according to what he told us."

"If he was paid, why was he still here? Do you think he was waiting to quit in order to not raise suspicion?"

"That, and he had been promised additional blunt if he could find a letter that the baron had written."

"A letter?"

"I was going to task Briggs and Michaels with searching the house to see if they could locate it. It might reveal the identity of the murderer."

Richard exhaled hard, shaking his head. "That would be a wonderful thing, if we could find it. This situation this morning with Lily could have turned lethal. Sophia would be devastated if ..."

The earl turned his gaze across the room where Lily and the countess were seated together, Lady Saunton's arm around Brendan's wife as they both sat in relieved silence together.

"There are no words to describe how devastated I would be right now if something had happened to Lily."

When Brendan turned back, he found Richard contemplating him thoughtfully, his emerald eyes glimmering. "There is something special about these Abbott girls. Have you informed your wife that you are in love with her?"

Brendan felt a blush rising up his neck. "Not yet."

Lord Moreland, whom Brendan had quite forgotten, clapped a hand on his back. "That is excellent news. Life is far more rewarding when you love your wife, not so Saunton?"

The duke and Annabel arrived, his sister rushing in with no thought to her dignity to lay eyes on him. Running across the room, she pulled him into a hard hug, trembling with emotion and wiping the tears from her eyes as she scolded him. He did not know for what, but he recognized her fear and acquiesced to her admonishments before she pulled him into another hug. Halmesbury clapped him on the back, swallowing hard as if he could not find the words to express himself, so he just shook his head before clapping him on the back once more.

Then Briggs appeared in the doorway, and Brendan left the gathering to inform the runner of what had happened. Richard and the duke joined them, and they all agreed to meet in the library. Peering back into the drawing room, Brendan assured himself that Lily was surrounded by family before descending the stairs.

It was when he entered the library where the others were waiting, turning to shut the door behind him, that he noticed Abbott had followed him down.

"I need to help," was the only explanation Lily's brother offered.

"What of Lord Moreland?"

"My father wishes to be with Lily. He asked me to apprise him of the specifics."

Brendan nodded, stepping aside to allow him entry.

CHAPTER 18

"For it is precisely when a force has fallen in danger that it is able to strike a blow for victory."
Sun Tzu, L'Art de la Guerre (The Art of War)

* * *

"Where did you get the rifle?" Briggs was taking notes in his book, a stubby pencil in his hand.

Michaels huffed in disdain. "From the study. There is a collection of flintlock rifles displayed on the wall, which I believe you have seen."

Briggs continued taking his notes, ignoring the butler's rebuke.

"Those rifles are decades old. How did you know they would be serviceable?"

This time Michaels's irritation was not veiled. "I am responsible for maintaining them. As you are aware, my father was a gamekeeper at Baydon Hall."

"But how did you happen to have fresh gunpowder at hand? It would not have been advisable to attempt what you did with gunpowder that had been stored for three decades?"

Michaels's expression was stony. "I ordered a small batch of fresh gunpowder through the household accounts when the late baron was killed."

"Why?"

"Because I concluded that one of my servants must have assisted the killer or must be the killer. I felt it was my duty to take steps to protect the household."

"Did you suspect Wesley?"

Michaels straightened in his chair, turning a frosty glare on the runner. "As a matter of fact, I did. I surmised you were too busy investigating me after over three decades of loyal service to the Ridley family to notice that his story about arriving back from Yorkshire on the morning after the coronation did not wholly line up with the mail coach schedules. I thought it possible that he reached London the same night as the murder, so I ..." The butler gestured at the room in general, as if presenting the morning's events as evidence of his conclusions.

Brendan grimaced. "I apologize you must be questioned thus, Michaels. We are in your debt for the swift action that you took."

Michaels breathed deeply, then gave a brief nod of acknowledgment. "I grew up with Master Josiah. The idea that I could harm the man ..."

He shook his head, and Brendan suddenly understood the cantankerous servant who had served him for nearly seven years. Michaels might be thorny, but he was loyal to Brendan's family. He still referred to the late baron as Master Josiah, obviously remembering him as a boy at Baydon Hall all those many years ago, before he was assigned to maintain the London townhouse.

"I am sorry for the loss you must have suffered when Lord Filminster was killed. And I am sorry that you were put in a position where you had to take a man's life today. You are a valued member of this household, and we shall discuss recompense for your courageous service and foresight in preparing the firearms in case of an emergency."

A flash of emotion crossed the older man's face, and he bobbed his head. Brendan could only be grateful that he had not attempted to pension the man off based on an overreaction to the events which had been transpiring. If the butler had not acted so swiftly, even now Lily could be missing or injured. Or worse.

Briggs interrupted the silence. "I apologize, Mr. Michaels, if my questions seem intrusive. I am hoping to collect all the facts before the coroner arrives so that I may facilitate a fast inquiry by his office. I believe this household has experienced enough troubles in recent weeks, and that your actions were in the right. You deserve recognition for taking action to protect the young wife of a peer."

Michaels relaxed his defensive stance. "I appreciate that, Mr. Briggs. I have no wish to prolong this matter."

"I shall definitely put in a good word and ask the Home Secretary to have this matter closed as quickly as possible. There are certainly sufficient witnesses to what transpired with Wesley to settle it." The duke spoke from across the library, where he had been listening from the window facing the street.

Brendan reflected it would be a wonderful thing to close this chapter. Two dead men in their home in about as many weeks was a lot. Right now, he wished he could shoo every last visitor out and return to Lily's side. He had so much he wanted to say to her.

"I suppose that leaves us with the question of finding the

letter that might reveal the true killer's identity." Richard spoke out of the dim stacks.

Brendan shook his head. "We should not raise our hopes regarding that. Given that Wesley had been searching the house for about two weeks now to no avail, we may never find it. If it even exists."

When Briggs was done, Brendan allowed everyone to leave, indicating to Michaels to stay behind. They stood at the window, Brendan with hands clasped behind his back as he watched a carriage passing on the street outside.

"I am very grateful for what you did for my wife. For me. I would be more than willing to provide you with a generous pension, Michaels."

The butler stiffened. "Do you want rid of me, milord?"

"Of course not. I thought perhaps you might enjoy retirement. I could provide you with a cottage in Somerset, if you wished."

Michaels scowled. "I am not ready to stumble into my old age. Ridley House is finally coming back to life, and I would very much like to oversee its new era."

Brendan thought for a moment. "Very well. I will have your wages increased, and have a formal arrangement set in place with my solicitors for the cottage and pension when you feel the time is right."

"Thank you, milord." Bowing, the butler departed.

IT HAD DISAPPOINTED Lily to look up and find Brendan was gone. She still felt a bit woolly in the head since Wesley had collapsed on her—for just a second when she had felt his weight bearing down on her, she thought he had decided to kill her, and her life had flashed before her eyes. Or rather, the life she had hoped she might have.

Chattering with her family, Sophia's arm about her waist, Lily slowly oriented back to normal, but her mind was on the thoughts that had raced through her head. Regardless of Brendan's feelings for her, she wanted to inform him what was in her own heart. To live every moment of every day free of regrets.

When the men returned, everyone agreed to meet for dinner. Halmesbury offered to host it at their home, which Lily was grateful for. The duke's townhouse was more prepared for a large family dinner than Ridley House, notwithstanding that two men had now been killed on the premises.

Brendan and Lily escorted everyone down to the entry hall, waving goodbye as their carriages collected them in turn. Finally, they were left standing alone with Michaels.

Brendan grabbed his wife by the hand, coaxing her to the stairs. "Come with me."

She hurried behind him as he climbed, noticing how mindful he was to adjust his stride for her much shorter legs. Soon they were striding down the hall to her bedroom, Lily almost jogging beside him to keep up, but he did not slow down then. Reaching her door, he twisted the handle to fling the door open.

Inside, a maid shrieked with fright, almost dropping the oil lamp she was filling. Thankfully, she caught it up and put it back down on the short chest next to the bed.

Lily suppressed her impatience at yet another interruption. She wanted to be alone with Brendan in the worst way, but hanging about downstairs was a rather morbid prospect, given the circumstances.

"Could you leave us, Beth?" Despite his polite warmth, Brendan sounded a tad stilted to her ears. Clearly, he was as impatient to be alone with her as she was to be with him.

"Yes, milord." Beth gathered her things and quickly

crossed the room to pass them into the hall. Hesitating as she reached them, the buxom maid halted. Beth was the one who had been helping Lily until her new lady's maid took up her post.

"It is true, milord? About Mr. Michaels shooting Wesley?"

"I am afraid it is. It has been a dark day."

The maid nodded. "I am glad that her ladyship is unharmed."

"Thank you, Beth. We both appreciate that."

Lily nodded in fervent agreement. She was thrilled to be unharmed, even if she still felt some distress over Wesley's fate. Had his previous kindness been feigned, or had he been a decent man who succumbed to temptation? They would never know, she supposed.

Finally, Brendan closed the door, still clasping her hand in his. Escorting her across the room, his hands came up to brace against her waist and he lifted her effortlessly to sit on her bed. Even as she sat perched on the edge of her incredibly tall mattress, he still towered above her as he took her hand up once more to gaze down at her. In the afternoon light, his eyes glimmered, and the flecks of gold buried in their brown depths fascinated her once again. They truly were the rich amber-brown of a fine brandy poured into a crystal-cut glass. Brendan appeared to be as fascinated in return, staring deep into her soul.

"I choose you."

"I love you."

They had both spoken at the same time. Now they both stared at each other in startled awe.

"You love me?" Brendan finally broke their impasse.

"You choose me?" Lily breathed in wonderment.

Again, they found themselves in a deadlock, both having shot their questions out at the same moment.

Brendan opened his mouth at the same time as Lily again, but this time he reached out a finger to gently press it against her lips. "Allow me first."

Lily gazed at him, brimming with joy, but shut her mouth in agreement.

"I choose you, Lily Ridley."

Lily was elated to hear such glorious words on the tongue of her beloved, her heart picking up speed.

"I choose your effervescent chatter."

"Some would say I talk too much."

"But I would say you talk the perfect amount."

She blushed, the heat rising until her ears burned. But Brendan was not finished.

"I choose your courage in doing what you believe is right, despite the trouble it causes you."

"I could not watch you be arrested for something you were innocent of."

"Nevertheless, it was honorable beyond words. But I am not done ... I choose your beautiful face and your glorious, chocolate brown hair."

Lily reached up a hand to tuck a lock of her hair behind her ear. "Chocolate brown?"

Brendan lifted a finger to coil the lock she had tucked away before his glimmering eyes returned to hers. "The richest, most decadent chocolate that money can buy."

"Oh," she breathed, spellbound by the liquid heat of his gaze as she remembered their night of passion.

"I choose your incandescent eyes." He unraveled the hair from his finger, and gently ran it down her cheek.

She caught her lower lip between her teeth, melting in her desire to feel his mouth on hers.

"And I choose the boundless energy with which you attack life."

He leaned in to kiss her, but Lily put up a hand to stay him. "What about my diddeys?"

Brendan stopped, his brows coming together in confusion.

Lily looked down at her bosom. "They are not as full as Lady Slight's?"

He chuckled, dropping his eyes to glance at them. Lifting a hand, he cupped her, and Lily sighed at feeling him through her bodice and stays while wishing she was unclothed so she could feel him properly.

"I will allow that Lady Slight has very full breasts, but yours are the perfect size to fill my hand. I have come to the realization that I need no other breasts than yours. See?"

Gooseflesh broke out across the surface of her skin as Lily took in the sight of Brendan's hand plumping her round breast, sensation streaking to accumulate between her thighs.

"I was hopelessly beguiled when I saw these breasts at our wedding ceremony. It was such an utter relief to find out that you were a grown woman beneath those lacy debutante dresses."

"Mama made me wear them. I knew they were unsuitable for me."

Brendan chuckled again, his gaze coming up to meet hers at the same time she raised her head. "I love you, Lily Ridley."

This time, when he lowered his head, Lily said nothing. Instead, she reached up, moaning with elation when his lips met hers, her arms curving around his neck. He pressed close with great ardor, but he did not attempt to part her lips to explore her mouth as he had done before. Lily was almost disappointed until she felt his fingers working the buttons along her back, her nerves thrilling in response as he undid her gown.

Brendan's lips retreated from hers, nuzzling against her

jaw while he slipped her gown off her shoulders. His mouth explored her neck as he raised his hands back up to undo the tapes of her stays, deftly removing them faster than she could do herself. Then his hands rose to cup her breasts, and she keened in pleasure at the touch of his warm fingers through the fabric.

It is even better than I remembered!

Too quickly, his hands abandoned her cleavage to take hold of her waist. He lifted her to place her on her feet beside the bed, before stripping the gown from her quivering body. His large hands returned to her waist to lift her back onto the bed. Stepping back, he swiftly divested his coat, then unbuttoned his waistcoat to toss them both aside. Unfurling his cravat, it too was dropped to the floor. Then he grabbed at his shirt, pulling it from his breeches and over his head until he was bared down to his hips.

Lily bit her lip, reaching out to graze her fingers across his broad chest and trace the musculature beneath the crisp, curling hair adorning his lean body. He reached up to grab her hand, his other coming to cup the back of her head. Leaning in for another kiss, he licked at her lips, until she parted her mouth to let him in and their tongues tangled together.

She breathed in the scent of citrus and mint, parting her legs as he lowered her to the bed and his weight came over her.

"I love you, you wild, uninhibited creature!" He whispered his words against her cheek, sensation shooting out at the flutter of his breath, before his mouth returned to hers.

Hungry hands swept over her body, cascading heat in every direction until Lily was squirming against him in mindless excitement. The heat from his body warmed her skin through the thin linen between them, and she strained to feel more of him. "Take it off," she slipped her head away to cry out.

Brendan captured her lips once more, sipping deeply. But she felt one of his hands on her calf, and then he was lifting the hem in compliance with her demands. His hot fingers swept up her leg until the garment was bunched at her hips, and, before she could comprehend what was happening, he pulled away to drop to his knees on the floor.

Startled, she raised herself on her elbows to peer down at him as his hands braced around her hips and pushed the shift up to reveal her to his gaze. Lily gasped, attempting to close her legs, but he moved swiftly to hold her thighs apart.

"You are beautiful, Lily. Ravishing!"

Brendan leaned in to press a kiss against her inner thigh while she wriggled in mortification that her nether regions were on display in broad daylight! Well … in the dusky interior of their dark home, which badly needed to be renovated to let in more light, at least.

His hot mouth moved up her thigh, holding her legs apart as his chin scraped against her tender skin. She yelped at the roughness, which stirred her senses and made her feel delirious with unbridled desire.

"Oh," she cried out, collapsing back onto the coverlet and flinching when she felt the wet lick over the offended area. "Oh, great heavens," she cried even louder, her hips jolting up. "Brendan, I love you!"

She felt his mouth pull into a smirk. "Just wait, you will love me more in a moment." He moved to the crease of her thigh to press his lips against her sensitive skin, causing her to squirm and arch her feet in rapture, before moving his mouth to lap at her crease.

Lily howled, praying that there were no servants on their floor to overhear as she unraveled into mindless insensibility. His tongue languidly contemplated the folds of her quim while Lily writhed in something akin to agony, desperate to reach the pinnacle that Brendan had taken her to only days before. When he finally made contact with the nub at the apex, stimulating her to mindless raptures, she could no longer hold back as wave after wave of pure sensitivity lifted her to the peak and she threw her head back to scream her climax.

Brendan continued to lap until she relaxed her tortured body back onto the bed, satiated.

"I love being married," she exclaimed.

Rising, Brendan's eyes ran down her form in a drawn-out surveillance. "As do I," he purred, appearing rather smug as his fingers worked the buttons of his breeches loose.

Despite how wrung out she felt, sprawled out on the bed without an ounce of modesty because of her boneless state, Lily watched as he lowered his breeches, and giggled in delight when he revealed his erection.

"It is so strange, how it grows! And how pleasing it is to be the cause of it!"

Brendan turned to sit on the edge of the bed, awkwardly removing his riding boots and stockings so he could take the breeches off. "Here I was, so proud of my performance, but then I remove my clothing in the wrong sequence because of my haste to ..."

"To?"

He turned his gaze to her, his eyes shining in the gloom. "Take you."

It was a simple statement, but Lily's desire came rushing back. Between her legs, her core thrummed back into tingling excitement, and she found herself panting again. Suddenly aware of her own garment still bunched around her waist, she made quick work of tossing it aside.

Brendan stood, shoving the breeches off to pool at his feet, before stepping forward and placing a knee between her thighs. "You are an enchanting woman, wife. I have not had you out of my thoughts since you entered the church on Sunday."

Lily licked her lips, which had gone dry at the growl of his admission. "Truly?"

"Every damn minute. I admired you greatly before that day. Then you walked into church and I saw you as a woman for the first time. It took little more than that to fall for you. I needed a second to catch my breath after all that has happened, but since that night I have wanted to be back here, to feel you wrapped around me as I ..." He shook his head as if overcome, before lowering himself down. Lily gasped at the feel of his naked skin against her own, gyrating her hips to press his hard length against her mound.

"I have been thinking of it, too," she admitted breathlessly as he swiped his tongue against her earlobe. "But this is better now that I know you are choosing me."

"I choose you, Lily. I choose every entrancing inch of you," he whispered against her throat.

Lily felt his length nudge against her, and her legs clung to him in invitation. As he entered her slowly, it was overwhelming. This time there was no pain, so she could just focus on the pleasure of his invasion. Throwing her head back, she mewled in throaty abandon and lifted her hips against him as he seated fully within her throbbing channel. Instinct drove her to pump against him, the bundle of nerves at her center rubbing against his pelvic bone as she sought her release once more.

"God, Lily!" Brendan thrust, groaning as she continued to move her hips against his. At first his strokes were measured, but soon he lapsed into a frantic pace, until Lily hit the point of no return, keening as she found her peak once more. As if it was a cue for him, too, Brendan growled loudly, spending deep inside her as her toes curled in deep appreciation of the man she loved.

"I choose you, Lily! I choose you every single moment of every single day."

He dropped to his elbows, leaning over her with an expression of complete surrender, and Lily realized her campaign was finally victorious. General Tzu would be proud of her. Their marriage was a true love match.

CHAPTER 19

"Therefore in chariot fighting, when ten or more chariots have been taken, those should be rewarded who took the first. Our own flags should be substituted for those of the enemy, and the chariots mingled and used in conjunction with ours. The captured soldiers should be kindly treated and kept."
Sun Tzu, L'Art de la Guerre (The Art of War)

* * *

AUGUST 2, 1821

*L*ord Aidan Abbott paced the library, his hands flying around in agitation. "There is still a killer out there, Filminster. And if this man believes there is a letter connecting him to his crime, he might take it into his head that you or Lily know something. That means my sister is still in danger."

"Or woman."

"What?"

"We do not know it is a man who committed the murder. It could be a woman."

"Why would a woman kill the baron?"

"Why would a man kill the baron?"

"Bloody hell! I have quite forgotten my point."

"You were stating that Lily and I are still under threat, especially if the killer believes we might find this mysterious letter."

Abbott stalked over to slump into an armchair. Brendan waited patiently, understanding that Lily's older brother was anxious. They stared at each other for several moments until a disturbance out in the hall had them both shifting their gaze to the open door.

"Lord Trafford, his lordship instructed me he was not to be disturbed. He is in a meeting!" The ire in Michaels's voice was evident even from this distance.

"Unhand me immediately, you ... you serf!" Trafford's ire sounded feigned to Brendan's ear.

"Lord Trafford!" Despite Michaels's usual reserved and recalcitrant manner, the last was more of a shriek than a rebuke.

His friend Trafford had a propensity for being easily bored as the heir to a healthy earl, and frequently acted in a buffoonish manner to, according to him, liven things up. Brendan was afraid that his butler was going to lose his head.

"Just a jest, Michaels. You know what a rapscallion I am."

Michaels responded, but from this distance, it was a mere mumble.

"You see? Admit it. I am your favorite."

More mumbling ensued. Seconds later, the butler came into view, his reserved air reinstated. "Lord Trafford to see you." Turning on his heel, Michaels walked away.

Trafford came striding in and looked about with deliberation, surveying Abbott before his gaze swung round to meet

Brendan's. "What is this I hear? A man was killed in your home yesterday? You did not think to summon me?"

Brendan was not sure if Trafford's indignant question was serious or in jest, so he swallowed the chuckle that threatened. "Summon you?"

Trafford tended to change his style from season to season, depending on his mood. It was the antidote to boredom, he claimed. Last year, he had engaged in terrible poetry, attired in the style of Lord Byron.

This year, he was trying out some sort of foppish fashion. He wore polished buckled shoes, slim-fitting trousers, and a purple jacquard coat over a waistcoat embroidered in gold. It was quite startling in contrast to his thatch of blond curls, and cropped brown hair on the sides and back.

Brendan recognized it was all part of the show.

Trafford sniffed before crossing over to the library table. Tugging his fluttering cuffs and flicking a piece of lint off his lapel, he took a seat. Stretching his legs out and folding his arms, Trafford turned his brown eyes back on Brendan. "Am I not your friend? Should I not be informed when you are in mortal peril?"

This time, Brendan did not hold the laugh back. "Are you taking umbrage regarding the peril, or are you more outraged that something of intrigue took place and you were left out of it?"

Trafford looked him over with a withering expression. "The intrigue, of course."

Abbott had been watching with his mouth agape, but he straightened up with a scowl. "Who is this ... this fool, Filminster?"

Trafford's face crumpled into mirth.

"Allow me to introduce Lord Julius Trafford, heir to the Earl of Stirling. And first-rate clown."

Trafford pulled a face, contemplating the description.

"Clown? Like the performer, Grimaldi? I am not fond of the garments, but I admire the slur. Well done, little Ridley."

Abbott sprang to his feet. "My sister was almost killed, you ridiculous fop!"

"Now you know who I am. Who are you?"

Brendan intervened before Abbott took it into his head to strike the other man. "This is Lord Aidan Abbott, heir to Viscount Moreland. My wife's brother."

"Ah! Another token title like my own. Dear Papa holds a barony, I suppose? Or is it an Irish viscountcy?"

Abbott was inspecting Trafford with narrowed eyes. "You were at the wedding breakfast."

"I was. Which is why Filminster should have sent for me."

"A desperate criminal manhandled my sister. Your amusement was not foremost in our minds."

Trafford cocked his head to think before finally responding. "I concede your point."

"Dammit! Concede this—" Abbott stormed forward and Brendan had to jump in his way.

"Trafford is attempting to get a rise out of you. He acts out when he finds himself excessively idle, but he is not the fool he appears to be."

Trafford beamed, even as Brendan calmed his brother-in-law. "Why, Filminster. I do believe you like me."

Brendan coaxed Abbott back to his seat, both irritated and entertained by his friend's troublemaking. As aggravating as Trafford could be, there was a certain humorous charm to the man. Accompanied by a fierce loyalty to his friends, Trafford enjoyed a vast number of supporters despite his diabolical vagaries.

"Only in small doses, Julius."

Trafford pouted, as if overcome by sentimentality, holding a hand over his heart. "So how can I help?"

Brendan returned to his own seat, contemplating the two

heirs who could not be any different. "I have nothing to tell you, gentlemen. Ridley House is being searched, but beyond that, we have no clues to who paid the footman off. All we can do is wait for something new to come to light."

"The murderer must be part of the peerage," Trafford offered.

Abbott frowned. "Why do you say that?"

Trafford rolled his eyes. When he finally responded, he spoke slowly, as if explaining something to a child. "The baron never visited London, and the only event he attended was the coronation itself. And he sat with lords. So it can only be one of them or their connections who committed the crime."

Brendan's brows shot up. "How would you know that?"

Trafford pulled a face at him, his contempt for the question obvious. "I asked around. What do you think I have been doing since the murder? Trimming my nails?"

Brendan snorted. "More like having your valet bleach your hair with lemon juice."

Trafford straightened in his seat, his face falling as his hand shot up to finger his blond hair. "It is not ..." He shook his head without finishing. Brendan felt a twist of guilt, realizing that he had touched on a nerve.

Trafford continued, "As you are aware, I have a wide circle of acquaintances. I asked around to confirm the late baron did not attend any social events within the few days he was in London."

Abbott snorted. "You cannot know that. There could have been a small gathering at someone's home. A dinner, perhaps."

Trafford shook his head in disbelief, shooting an accusatory glance at Brendan without responding.

Brendan sighed. "Trafford means he checked with above and below stairs alike. He does not discriminate when it comes to seeking information. I should state that he is very thorough in gathering information about members of the *ton*."

"Why?" Abbott was sincerely astonished at Brendan's explanation. "Why would he be an expert in such a thing?"

Trafford burst out laughing. "What a little-breeches you have on your hands, Filminster. Is your brother-in-law truly so unsophisticated?"

Brendan soughed heavily. "Women, Abbott. Trafford is highly skilled in gathering information about women of the *ton*. I should have thought to request his help in learning about my ... father's ... movements." He hoped Abbott and Trafford did not notice his hesitation, or ascribed it to the pressure he had been under.

Trafford smirked. "Just so."

Abbott shook his head, as if to reshuffle his thoughts. Brendan could not blame him. Trafford had that effect on people. It was hard to imagine what it would take to ultimately tame the impudent showman, but in the meantime, Brendan would gladly accept his help. Trafford could be useful when one needed loyal friends, like how he had gone to a great deal of trouble to help Perry Balfour the year before.

"So, what do we do now?"

"I discussed it at length with Saunton and Halmesbury. There is not much to be done, I am afraid. We remain vigilant and continue our search for information." Brendan wished he had a better answer, but it was the only one he had.

* * *

IT WAS A GLORIOUS SUMMER DAY, made even more glorious because her husband was accompanying her to Hatchards.

The bookshop was one of her favorite places in all the world, and now she could share it with one of her favorite people in all the world.

"I think we should order a number of novels for the library. Most of the books in there are fusty old texts about agriculture. We should have some Byron, Wordsworth, and Keats. I also wish to order Frankenstein, along with Ann Radcliffe and Jane Austen."

Brendan nodded, perusing some books on the front stacks and pulling out several. Lily picked one off the top to see what had caught his attention.

"Coleridge's *Lyrical Ballads*! It did not cross my mind, but I love it!"

She and Brendan had discussed modernizing Ridley House. He was amenable to her taking charge and agreed to stocking up their library. Soon their new housekeeper would arrive, and Richard had recommended that they speak with his brother, Mr. Thompson, about their home.

Barclay Thompson was a renowned architect who had attended their wedding, and his firm had worked on numerous townhouses for the wealthy of London. Lily was excited to meet with him and his assistant in the near future when he returned to Town. It would be a wondrous thing if they could set things in motion before leaving for Baydon Hall in Somerset.

Soon, they were placing their order at the counter. Lily had never placed such a large order before, and her hands trembled with her excitement to bring Ridley House to its full potential. Wiping away any traces of the past would be an excellent strategy for dispelling the shadow of death that currently haunted its sinister halls.

"Have you read much?" Lily inquired. Her husband appeared to be astute about which books to buy, despite the sorry state of their own library.

"I have, but I mostly took advantage of the libraries of others. Annabel and the duke have an excellent selection, and I had access to Trafford's and several other friends'."

Brendan opened the door and stood aside to allow her to exit onto the street. She turned back to question him. "Who is your favorite?"

"Well, well. It is the scandalous Lily Ridley, if my eyes do not deceive."

Lily spun about to find Lady Slight accompanied by a friend. She looked luscious in a striped, blue dress, her breasts lifted prominently. Lily backed up to avoid getting banged in the face by them. Lady Slight's companion, a blonde with a low-cut gown and cold blue eyes, giggled at the coy remark. Lily supposed her friend found the widow's greeting to be devilishly amusing.

For a moment, Lily was unsure how to respond, but then she decided she could not apologize for her recent adventures. She must attack ... with words.

"Oh, do you mean the scandalous night I spent with Lord Filminster while his father was being bludgeoned to death?" Reaching out, Lily grabbed Brendan by the arm. He cooperated, stepping through the door and shutting it behind him, before tucking her hand into the crook of his arm.

"Or do you mean when I stepped forward to speak to the coroner in order to clear Lord Filminster's name of those dreadful accusations of murder?"

Both Lady Slight and her friend had drawn back with expressions of wide-eyed horror.

"Or perhaps you mean our hasty marriage to protect my reputation?" She gave them a chance to answer, but no words were forthcoming.

"Perhaps you mean when our footman attempted to abduct me and my husband bravely offered to take my place? Before our butler shot the man dead, of course." Lily tapped a finger to her lip as if thinking. "But, no, I think you must mean all of it."

Settling the matter, Lily dropped her hand to gesture widely. "If I think about it, I must confess that I am. I am scandalous. Scandalously happy, that is!"

Lady Slight's jaw was hanging open. Apparently, the widow had not expected to be assaulted with the brunt of Lily's chatter, nor her innate candor. Lily was not known for her subtle manners.

Beside her, Brendan raised a hand to cover his mouth, his eyes sparkling as he struggled to not burst out laughing. Lily fought to keep a straight face, fighting back the urge to burst into gales of glee as she watched Lady Slight and her friend struggling to contain their shock.

Turning to her husband, she lifted a hand to cup his neck. Tugging down, she leaned up on the tips of her toes. Brendan dropped his hand from his mouth and leaned down to capture her lips with his, more than willing to go along with her performance. He deepened the kiss, wrapping his arm around her waist to pull her closer, and Lily quite lost her breath as her breasts crushed against his hard chest.

From behind her, Lady Slight gasped at the public display. It was not fashionable to like one's husband, nor to be seen enjoying his company, but Lily could not care a fig for what other people might think. She was deliriously joyful, and the entire world could get hanged if they wished to complain. Her dreams had come true, and she would not apologize for it.

Dropping back on her heels, she drew a tremulous breath to calm her quickened pulse before turning back to the widow. "Whomever it was that my husband was with before me, I am ever so grateful that they set him free ... so that I could catch him."

Lily tilted her chin in challenge, daring the viscountess to say something, but Lady Slight could only open and close her mouth like a fish struggling for air. It was then, for a moment, that Lily felt a pang. The widow must be a very unhappy person deep down. Her life was empty. She had married a geriatric lord who had died shortly after they wed. She had no children, and she dabbled with men, changing paramours more frequently than Lily ordered a new pair of stays. These were not the actions of a content person. General Tzu would advise kindness to the fallen foe.

Letting Brendan go, Lily stepped forward to reach out and touch Lady Slight on the back of the hand, which flinched as if burned.

"I wish you the boundless joy of truly connecting with another person. Of opening your heart to another, and finding that you care more about them than your own self. I wish you a strong young husband and healthy children. And I wish you a long and full life filled with laughter, Lady Slight."

With that, she turned back to take Brendan by the arm, and they walked away toward their carriage. Brendan lowered his hand over hers and smiled down at her with blazing eyes. Leaning in, he whispered in her ear, "I choose you, Lily Ridley. Every kind, fiery, honorable inch of you."

Lily smiled back at him. "And I choose you, Brendan Ridley."

EPILOGUE

"Knowledge of the disposition of the enemy can only be obtained from other men."
Sun Tzu, L'Art de la Guerre (The Art of War)

* * *

*A*fter their afternoon shopping for books, Brendan watched Lily as she climbed the steps to change for dinner. Reflecting on how much his life had changed, he started toward the library when Michaels cleared his throat behind him.

Pausing, he spun on his heel. "What is it?"

The butler hesitated, blowing a breath. "The study is ready, milord."

"The study?" Brendan's mind was blank, trying to understand the butler's point.

"We have … managed to … clean the floors, and a new rug has been placed. I took the liberty of moving the furniture and rearranging the *objets d'art* to …" Words apparently failed. Despite the butler's uncharacteristic awkwardness,

Brendan surmised Michaels was attempting to inform him that all traces of the murder had been removed, including the offending sculpture.

A hand came up to knead his temple. Catching himself in the motion, Brendan realized that his tension had returned.

"I see." Brendan had not entered the room since he had found the body. He supposed it might be time to reclaim his place of work. "After you."

The butler gave a curt nod, then led the way to the study door. Opening it, he stepped aside to allow Brendan entry, who walked inside while Michaels remained in the hall.

The study had been lit, the oil lamps casting their flickering light in the dim room. Drapes had been tied back. His mahogany desk, which had faced east, now stood on the other side facing west. The rug had been replaced, a brighter spot of color in a room that was in need of remodeling.

Looking about, Brendan confirmed that the objects on the mantel over the fireplace had been rearranged, along with the contents of the shelves between the windows on the far wall.

"It was an excellent idea to rearrange the furnishings. I do not think walking in to find everything … To find it how it was that night would be macabre, to say the least."

Michaels nodded. "It was a sad day for Ridley House, milord. I have no wish to think of it each time I enter the room."

"Are you … holding up? It must be difficult to take a man's life."

Michaels pressed his lips together, gazing out the window for several seconds before replying. "It would have been inconceivable to allow Lady Filminster to be harmed. Her ladyship is a vibrant mistress to forge the next chapter of the Filminster title. I find myself quite looking forward to … the progression of the Ridley family."

Brendan's lips twisted into a smile. The oblique reference to Lily's procreation was a subject that he, too, anticipated fondly.

Michaels left him, shutting the door, and Brendan walked over to the desk. His desk. He ran a hand over the polished surface, admiring the carved edges and elegant legs. It was good to be back. Dropping into the chair, he stretched his legs and contemplated the room.

Michaels had done excellent work refreshing it until it could be renovated. The Aubusson rug on the floor, in deep red and rich blue, already hinted at the improvements to be made by replacing the faded wallpaper.

Leaning back, he ran his hand over the decorative carving on the side of the desk facing him. He had always enjoyed writing in his journal, but since the late baron's arrival in London, he had not had the opportunity to do so. His fingers found the clasp, the one he had discovered years ago when he had taken up residence in London. His mother had once shown him a similar drawer in a matching desk at Baydon Hall, so he had known to search for it.

The secret drawer sprung open, and he reached for his leather-bound journal. He caught sight of a loose page just as his hand made contact with it. Frowning, Brendan pulled the page and quill pen out, along with his journal, and placed them on the desk.

He stared, transfixed, as he slowly comprehended that the late baron had, indeed, written a letter.

The page was covered in the scrawl of his uncle-father. It appeared his visitor had surprised the old man, who had hurriedly swept the letter he was writing, along with the quill, into the drawer to shut his secrets away. The ink must have spattered from the tip because there were spots of ink obscuring some of the written words, as if they had been censored by the dripping pen.

Before him lay the possible answer to the baron's death. Brendan was almost reluctant to lift the letter and read it. A feeling of dread crept into his chest, while he stared without seeing and thought about the fact that this awful venture was not yet resolved.

He flinched in surprise when a knock sounded, shifting his gaze to the door. It swung open to reveal Lily, refreshed for dinner.

She must have noticed something amiss, because she entered quickly and crossed the room toward him. "What is it?"

Brendan shook his head. "I think I found the letter."

Lily gasped, rushing forward to stand at his side. "What? How?"

"There is a secret drawer where I keep my journal. When I opened it ... I found this." Brendan held up the letter with a trembling hand. He had believed the letter to be a figment of imagination. Certainly, despite Briggs and Michaels searching Ridley House from top to bottom, he had never truly believed in the possibility that they would find it.

"What does it say?"

Brendan hesitated, his chest tight with worry. "I have not read it."

She gazed down at him, then swung her arm around him for a tight embrace. "It will start everything up again."

He nodded.

"But eventually this story will end, and we will have our entire lives ahead of us."

Brendan nodded. "We shall see what the baron has to say, then."

Raising the letter, he decided to read it out loud while Lily kept her arm draped over his shoulders.

"It is addressed to the Home Secretary. Some of the words are obscured by the ink that soaked into the paper."

. . .

SIR ROBERT PEEL

London, July 19, 1821

Sir,

It has come - - my attention that the true heir to Lord - -
- - - - - - has not been acknowledged.

I was speaking with his lordship before the coronation,
and he informed me of his recent bout of ill health. He spoke
fondly of his youngest brother, informing - - of his strength,
intelligence, and wit at great length. There was no mention
of his lordship's middle brother, Peter, who you may be
aware died near twenty years - - -.

Peter and I attended Oxford together, - - - his death was
tragic - - - unexp- - - - -. I have thought of him often over the
years, which is why I feel the need to pass this information -
- - - - -u.

Before departing England, Peter married a wom- - of
Catholic descent. She convert- - - - - - - - - were married - - -
- - Church of England, before leaving our shores. I maintained correspondence with him until his death. He had
written just months before his death to inform me of the
birth of his son.

I cannot say for certain where the boy and his mother are
- - - - - all these years, but he would be the true heir and I
implore you to look into th- - matter. - - - - - - - - - is the
true heir to the title of - - - - - and his father's legacy cannot
be ignored.

I understand the trials of being a second son, and I cann-
- allow this matter to stand. Whether - - - - terrible injustice
is a mistake due to ignorance of the child Peter sired, or a
deliberate obfuscation of the facts, I must speak on my
friend's behalf. His son is the true heir and must be found
immediately. I will locate our shared correspondence when I

return to Somerset and have them forwarded to - - - - - - - -
- - -

J. Ridley, Baron of Filminster

Lily stood with her mouth agape as Brendan finished reading the letter. "This truly must be the reason the baron was killed! Do you think the false heir was the one who killed your uncle?"

Brendan did not answer, rather stupefied by what he had read. Inheriting a title could mean a transfer of wealth and power beyond comprehension. It certainly would explain why someone might have visited the baron that night, and could very well be the impetus for a fit of murderous passion wherein a man grabbed a convenient weapon to silence the threat to his future inheritance.

"We do not know enough."

Lily threw up her hands. "What are you saying? We have everything we need right here."

"But we do not know the identity of the lord he spoke with. Are you aware how many titled families might have a minimum of three brothers, and the second brother is named Peter?"

"But we know that the second brother died about twenty years ago. He married a Catholic, which might mean a woman from the Continent, and he left England before his death. That must narrow down the number of potential families by ... um ... well ... quite a bit?"

Brendan reached up to cover her hand on his shoulder. "You are correct. This is a lot to absorb. The baron's death seems so trivial in light of this letter. It was a matter of chance. I suppose I shall meet with Briggs and the others to discuss where this takes the investigation."

Lily sighed, resting her chin on the crown of his head. "The baron's murder was a tragic event which led us to each other. It is dreadful to ponder the reason why you and I are now married, but I cannot bring myself to regret that we are wed."

Brendan felt his lips quirking into a smile despite the unpleasant interruption of their nuptial bliss. Reaching over, he pulled Lily into his lap to plant a kiss on her soft mouth. "Despite how it came to be, I regard myself as very fortunate to have married such a unique and intriguing woman."

"Intriguing?" Lily breathed against him.

"Absolutely captivating. Endlessly amusing. Ravishing beyond words." Lily's arms came up to curl around his neck. "Thank you. For being here. For helping me overcome this ordeal. For keeping me out of prison."

"You are very welcome."

Lily deepened their kiss and Brendan quickly forgot the letter, his chest easing as he pulled her close.

Their passion quickly mounted, and Brendan ran his hands over her lithe form, thinking how much he would like to scoop her up in his arms and take her to—

A knock on the door had them pulling back in surprise, their breathing labored as Brendan brushed his thumb over her lips, plumped from his kisses.

"Dinner is served, milord." Michaels stood in the doorway, resolutely staring at the far wall with exemplary dignity considering he had just interrupted them in a bout of newlywed lust.

"Thank you, Michaels."

The butler departed hurriedly, shutting the door. Lily looked at Brendan with sparkling brown eyes before bursting into a fit of giggles. Brendan chuckled, pulling her back into his arms for a quick embrace before setting her on her feet.

"Time to eat, my love."

AFTERWORD

Napoleon was considered a brilliant military strategist, so it was no surprise when I discovered that *The Art of War* had been translated into French. In *To Redeem an Earl*, you might recall Sophia's advice to Lily to improve her French so that she might study and apply Sun Tzu's strategies to the marriage mart of London.

Sophia was well familiar with the general's rules of battle, but Lily is still a novice in her story. She applies them energetically, but not always with finesse, which leads to some awkward situations.

By the Regency, there were just over three hundred coroners serving all of England. They were always educated men of property, and it helped if they had money and political connections to get appointed or elected.

One imagines a certain amount of cherry-picking of cases by the coroner for the assigned area, considering the workloads. And there would be a variety of reasons a man would seek the office in the first place, which leads us to Grimes and his political aspirations. Fortunately, Lily was there to thwart the ambitious coroner's campaign to raise his status by landing a peer in prison.

Now that Lily and Brendan have secured their household, Aidan Abbott is going to feel the pinch of culpability when danger continues to stalk Ridley House. Making it his mission to find the killer, a certain Miss Smythe is going to find herself in his arms at exactly the wrong moment, provoking a high society scandal.

When Aidan is forced to marry into the family he is investigating to protect his sister, is there any chance for these newlyweds to find a path to happiness? Or will Aidan's secrets ruin their love before it starts? Find out in *Moonlight Encounter*, the next chapter of Inconvenient Scandals!

ABOUT THE AUTHOR

Nina started writing her own stories in elementary school but got distracted when she finished school and moved on to non-profit work with recovering drug addicts. There she worked with people from every walk of life from privileged neighborhoods to the shanty towns of urban and rural South Africa.

One day she met a real life romantic hero. She instantly married her fellow bibliophile and moved to the USA where she enjoyed a career as a sales coaching executive at an Inc 500 company. She lives with her husband on the Florida Gulf Coast.

Nina believes in kindness and the indomitable power of the human spirit. She is fascinated by the amazing, funny people she has met across the world who dared to change their lives. She likes to tell mischievous tales of life-changing decisions and character transformations while drinking excellent coffee and avoiding cookies.

Follow Nina Jarrett on your favorite platform at:

linktr.ee/ninajarrett

DOWNLOAD TWO FREE BOOKS!

FREE GIFTS FOR SUBSCRIBERS:
Two captivating prequel novellas by Nina Jarrett full of
unrequited feelings and steamy romance.

**A writer for fighting for his muse. A captain returned
from war, searching for his wife.
Two delightful novellas about the power of true love.**

* * *

London, 1818. Dinah Honeyfield can't wait any longer. In
love with her family's long-term houseguest, she's
determined to get him to reveal his affections before her rich
industrialist father marries her off.
Lord John Pettigrew gave up his birthright to follow his
dreams. And with nothing to offer a potential wife, the
aspiring author despairs he'll never be able to win the hand
of the one who's been his muse.

Can they rewrite their future and plot a path to forever?

* * *

Mrs. Lydia Lewis has given up on broken promises.
Marrying her soulmate only to be attacked during his
heartbreaking absence, she finds refuge as an incognito ducal
housekeeper.
Captain Jacob Lewis is angry and hurt. Returning from
military service to discover his spouse has vanished into thin
air, he begins an almost hopeless search to bring her home.
Can this star-crossed pair reclaim newlywed bliss?

* * *

Interview With the Duke and *The Captain's Wife* are the
delightful prequels to the Inconvenient Brides Regency
romance series. If you like worthy heroes, fast-paced plots,
and enduring connections, then you'll adore Nina Jarrett's
charming collection.

Subscribe for instant access to these twin tales of passion:
NinaJarrett.com/free

ALSO BY NINA JARRETT

INCONVENIENT BRIDES

INCONVENIENT SCANDALS

The Duke and Duchess of Halmesbury will return, along with the
Balfour family, in an all-new suspense romance series.

* * *

BOOK 1: THE DUKE WINS A BRIDE

**Her betrothed cheated on her. The duke offers to save her. Can a
marriage of convenience turn into true love?**

In this spicy historical romance, a sheltered baron's daughter and a
celebrated duke agree on a marriage of convenience, but he has a
secret that may ruin it all.

She is desperate to escape...

When Miss Annabel Ridley learns her betrothed has been unfaithful, she knows she must cancel the wedding. The problem is no one else seems to agree with her, least of all her father. With her wedding day approaching, she must find a way to escape her doomed marriage. She seeks out the Duke of Halmesbury to request he intercede with her rakish betrothed to break it off before the wedding day.

He is ready to try again...

Widower Philip Markham has decided it is time to search for a new wife. He hopes to find a bold bride to avoid the mistakes of his past. Fate seems to be favoring him when he finds a captivating young woman in his study begging for his help to disengage from a despised figure from his past. He astonishes her with a proposal of his own—a marriage of convenience to suit them both. If she accepts, he resolves to never reveal the truth of his past lest it ruin their chances of possibly finding love.

Can be read as a standalone book or as part of the Inconvenient Brides series of Regency romance books.

* * *

BOOK 2: TO REDEEM AN EARL

A cynical debutante and a scandalous earl find themselves entangled in an undeniable attraction. Will they open their hearts to love or will his past destroy their future together?

She has vowed she will never marry...

Miss Sophia Hayward knows all about men and their immoral behavior. She has watched her father and older brother behave like reckless fools her entire life. All she wants is to avoid marriage to a lord until she reaches her majority because she has plans which do not include a husband. Until she meets the one peer who will not take a hint.

He must have her...

Lord Richard Balfour has engaged in many disgraceful activities with the women of his past. He had no regrets until he encounters a cheeky debutante who makes him want to be a better man. Only problem is, he has a lot of bad behavior to make amends for if he is ever going to persuade Sophia to take him seriously. Will he learn to be a better man before his mistakes catch up with him and ruin their chance at true love?

Can be read as a standalone book or as part of the Inconvenient Brides series of Regency romance books.

* * *

MY FAIR BLUESTOCKING: BOOK 3

A young woman who cares little about high society or its fashions. A spoilt lord who cares too much. Will they give in to their unexpected attraction to reveal a deep and enduring passion?

She thinks he is arrogant and vain ...

The Davis family has ascended to the gentry due to their unusual connection to the Earl of Saunton. Now the earl wants Emma Davis and her sister to come to London for the Season. Emma relishes refusing, but her sister is excited to meet eligible gentlemen. Now she can't tell the earl's arrogant brother to go to hell when he shows up with the invitation. She will cooperate for her beloved sibling, but she is not allowing the handsome Perry to sway her mind ... or her heart.

He thinks she is disheveled, but intriguing ...

Peregrine Balfour cannot believe the errands his brother is making him do. Fetching a country mouse. Preparing her for polite society. Dancing lessons. He should be stealing into the beds of welcoming widows, not delivering finishing lessons to an unstylish shrew. Pity he can't help noticing the ravishing young woman that is being revealed by his tuition until the only schooling he wants to deliver is in the language of love.

Will these two conflicting personalities find a way to reconcile their unexpected attraction before Perry makes a grave mistake?

Can be read as a standalone book or as part of the Inconvenient Brides series of Regency romance books.

* * *

BOOK 4: SLEEPLESS IN SAUNTON

An insomniac debutante and a widowed architect befriend each other. Will little Tatiana finally get the new mother she longs for before this country house party ends?

In this steamy historical romance, a sleepless young woman yearns for love while a successful widower pines for his beloved wife. Hot summer nights at a lavish country house might be the perfect environment for new love to bloom.

She cannot sleep ...

Jane Davis went to London with her sister for a Season full of hope and excitement. Now her sister is married and Jane wanders the halls alone in the middle of the night. Disappointed with the gentlemen she has met, she misses her family and is desperate for a full night's sleep. Until she meets a sweet young girl who asks if Jane will be her new mother.

He misses his wife ...

It has been two years since Barclay Thompson's beloved wife passed away. Now the Earl of Saunton has claimed him as a brother and, for the sake of his young daughter, Barclay has acknowledged their relationship. But loneliness keeps him up at night until he encounters a young woman who might make his dead heart beat again. Honor demands he walk away rather than ruin the young lady's reputation. Associating with a by-blow like him will bar her from good society, no matter how badly his little girl wants him to make a match.

Can these three lonely souls take a chance on love and reconnect with the world together?

Can be read as a standalone book or as part of the Inconvenient Brides series of Regency romance books.

* * *

BOOK 5: CAROLINE SAVES THE BLACKSMITH

A fallen woman. A tortured blacksmith. When the holidays force them together, can they mend their broken hearts?

She has a dark past that she must keep a secret. He has a dark past he wishes to forget. The magic of the festive season might be the key to unlocking a fiery new passion.

She will not repeat her past mistakes ...

Caroline Brown once made an unforgivable mistake with a handsome earl, betraying a beloved friend in the process. Now she is rebuilding her life as the new owner of a dressmaker's shop in the busy town of Chatternwell. She is determined to guard her heart from all men, including the darkly handsome blacksmith, until the local doctor requests her help on the night before Christmas.

He can't stop thinking about her ...

William Jackson has avoided relationships since his battle wounds healed, but the new proprietress on his street is increasingly in his thoughts, which is why he is avoiding her at all costs. But an unexpected injury while his mother is away lays him up on Christmas Eve and now the chit is mothering him in the most irritating and delightful manner.

Can the magic of the holiday season help two broken souls overcome their dark pasts to form a blissful union?

Can be read as a standalone book or as part of the Inconvenient Brides series of Regency romance books.

* * *

BOOK 7: MOONLIGHT ENCOUNTER

A lord determined to protect his little sister. A young lady who is in the wrong place at the wrong time. When scandal forces them to wed, can they find a way to work together?

In this steamy historical romance, the heir to a viscountcy is determined to protect his sister, accidentally ruining a young woman while searching her father's home. Now he will need to choose between his crusade and the growing love between them.

He feels guilty for failing his family ...

Lord Aidan Abbott neglected his duties as a chaperone when his parents left his little sister in his charge. Because of him, Lily was forced to wed under a cloud of scandal. Now Aidan must solve a murder to keep his sister and her new husband out of danger.

She is caught unawares ...

A charming but arrogant lord interrupts Miss Gwendolyn Smythe while she is taking air on the terrace. Unfortunately, they are discovered together, so she is forced to marry a man she has never met before to quell the scandal. Now Gwen is determined to make the best of their new marriage, with or without his cooperation.

While Aidan continues to secretly investigate Gwendolyn's family, he realizes that the fiery redhead now holds his heart in her hands. How can he reveal what he has been doing without shattering their only chance at love?

Moonlight Encounter is the delightful second book in the Inconvenient Scandals series of steamy Regency suspense romance books. If you like worthy heroes, strong heroines, fast-paced plots, and enduring connections, then you'll adore Nina Jarrett's charming novel.

Can be read as a standalone book or as part of the Inconvenient Brides series of Regency romance books.

* * *

BOOK 8: LORD TRAFFORD'S FOLLY

A bored heir engages in a dangerous pursuit. A young woman is pulled into the ensuing chaos. Will this unlikely pair forge a fiery new passion while they run for their lives?

A steamy historical suspense romance, about an idle lord who agrees to help his friends with their quest to solve a murder. Now he must fend for himself while protecting the young lady he has endangered with his choices. Can he keep her safe from harm from both the enemy pursuing them, and his urge to kiss those sarcastic lips?

He thought it would be a lark ...

When Lord Julius Trafford, the indolent heir to an earl, agrees to help his friends in a quest to solve a murder, it was simply because he was bored. Now he is in hot water, and he has dragged his father's delectable ward into danger with him. Together, they are forced on the run, and Lord Trafford must engage his wits before it's too late.

She is furious with him ...

Miss Audrey Gideon always believed Lord Trafford was a fool, but now that he has brought danger into their lives, she is convinced he is a brainless numbskull. Except, as they make their escape from London in search of safety, Julius begins to demonstrate his true potential and Audrey wonders if there is more to the foppish heir than meets the eye.

Can this unlikely pair rise to the challenge and discover true love along the way?

Lord Trafford's Folly is the delightful third book in the Inconvenient Scandals series of steamy Regency suspense romance books. If you like worthy heroes, strong heroines, fast-paced plots, and enduring connections, then you'll adore Nina Jarrett's charming novel.

Can be read as a standalone book or as part of the Inconvenient Brides series of Regency romance books.

Made in the USA
Middletown, DE
12 September 2024